BADLANDS

Center Point
Large Print

**This Large Print Book carries the
Seal of Approval of N.A.V.H.**

BADLANDS

BENNETT FOSTER

CENTER POINT PUBLISHING
THORNDIKE, MAINE

This Center Point Large Print edition
is published in the year 2003 by arrangement with
Golden West Literary Agency.

The text of this Large Print edition is unabridged. In other
aspects, this book may vary from the original edition. Printed in
Thailand. Set in 16-point Times New Roman type by
Bill Coskrey and Gary Socquet.

ISBN 1-58547-341-3

Library of Congress Cataloging-in-Publication Data

Foster, Bennett.
    Badlands / Bennett Foster.--Center Point large print ed.
        p. cm.
    ISBN 1-58547-341-3 (lib. bdg. : alk. paper)
      1. Large type books. I. Title.

PS3511.O6812B33 2003
813'.54--dc21

2003048879

For
FRANK JONES of the 44

CAST OF CHARACTERS

CHANCE PAGAN ran the J Pen . . . until the law ran him out.

WAYNE ELDER owned the Spear but didn't have much say.

BILL FAHRION, foreman for the Spear, wasn't quite heavy enough for the job.

SILVERTIP UPTON, outlaw, bossed the Basin and had a peculiar set of friends.

TOM MELODY, sheriff, promised Chance they wouldn't hang him . . . too quick.

CLIFF NOWLEN, rival ranch owner, was sure happy to see Chance.

BEN GODMAN, cowpuncher for Spear, never backed down a step in his life.

TULLY PILLOW was all for picking up a few steers he didn't own.

LOIS ELDER, ranch owner's daughter, wasn't so sure she still loved Chance after three long years.

SAM PASMORE, brutal gun hand, was quick to grab what he wanted.

ARLIE PILLOW hated her father.

CARL TERRIL came from Texas . . . and proved it in a fight.

SUEL JAMES and **BABE WILMOT** carried out the Basin's orders.

1

THE SNOW, wind-whipped from the level of the flats, beat against Chance Pagan's legs, clung like frost to his sheepskin, and stung against the hard brown of his cheeks. Farmer, the big six-year-old bay gelding, fought steadily along the road, where the wind sought to obliterate the wheel ruts. Now and again the horse snorted, clearing his nostrils, and now and again Chance raised a gloved hand and wiped the whiteness from his collar and cheek. Wind and snow and cold, and Chance Pagan grinned at them. This was home. This was his country and he was back in it. He would not, at that moment, have traded one icy breath of air for all the dulcet warmth of Arizona, for all the quiet calm of New Mexico. Home! And he was back, back were he belonged, after three years of wandering.

Farmer, big enough for a plow horse and quick and fast enough for a rope horse, jerked up his head, and Chance Pagan, also lifting his head, saw through the sweeping snow the cluster of buildings that was the Spear headquarters. A quarter of a mile and he would be in; a quarter of a mile and old Wayne Elder would be pumping his arm and saying, "So you got my letter, did you?" A quarter of a mile and Lois Elder would be smiling shyly, would be . . . Chance wondered if Lois would do more than smile. He wondered if . . . Three years is a long time, but Lois had kissed him when he left; had kissed him and held the old warm gold of his father's signet ring against his cheek. He would have to get Lois a new ring, a diamond. He had the money in the bank and . . . The quarter of a mile was done.

With the yard gate behind him, Farmer made for the barn and, entering the door in the lee of that structure, stopped. Chance swung down from his horse and with cold numbed fingers fell to stripping saddle and bridle from the big bay. No need to wait for welcome here, he knew. This was almost as much home to him as the old Pagan place, the old J Pen, south against the rim of Calico Mesa.

With Farmer cared for, Chance put his gear in the room at the end of the barn and sallied out into the wind again. Fifty yards brought him to the back door of the big house and as he reached it the door opened. A wizened yellow face showed through the opening.

"Hello, Lee," greeted Chance.

The yellow face split into a grin. Lee Su, who had cooked for the Elders for twenty years, crackled his answer. "H'llo, Chlance. You come back? We got cinnamon rolls for dinna'."

"You devil!" Chance slapped Lee on a thin shoulder. "You must of known I was coming. Where's the boss?"

"In front room," answered Lee. "Boss sick."

Chance moved on across the kitchen, the odor of hot strong coffee and of cinnamon rolls, fresh from the oven, assailing him. The kitchen opened into a big room, half living-room, half dining-room, and at the entrance, Chance stopped. A man sat across the room from him, and beside the man stood a girl.

"I got your letter, Wayne," said Chance. "I've come back."

From Lois Elder there came a little, half-articulate sound. With two swift steps the girl moved from where she stood; then, hesitating a moment, approached more slowly. The man turned his head with an effort, and for the first time Chance noticed that the man was crippled. The smile left Chance's face and concern was written in his blue eyes.

"Chance!" the girl exclaimed.

"You came back," said the man in the chair, his voice weak. "You came back, Chance."

"Of course I came back." Chance crossed the room toward the chair. As he advanced, the girl stepped back, drawing away from him. Chance did not note the movement. His whole concern was with the man in the chair.

"What's happened, Wayne?" he demanded. "What's wrong with you?"

"Rheumatism!" Elder's voice was stronger. "I'm a blasted cripple. I . . ."

"Dad has to get out of this weather," Lois interrupted. "I'm taking him to Hot Springs today. We were just waiting for Ben to come in with the team and hitch the buckboard."

Chance noticed the bags piled beside the door. "Rheumatism!" he echoed. "You're leaving?"

"Right after dinner," Lois answered firmly.

"But you wrote me . . ." Chance began, turning to Wayne Elder.

"You didn't answer my letter," said Elder. "I didn't know if you'd got it."

"No," Chance said slowly, "I didn't write. I just quit my job when I could, and came a-running. I didn't know you were laid up, Wayne. I'd have been here sooner."

Elder's voice was gruff. "Wanted you to come an' run the Spear while I was gone," he said.

"I'm here," answered Chance. "I can look after things, Wayne. I can't tell you how cut-up I am. I never thought from what you wrote that you were laid up. I never knew . . ."

There was asperity in Lois' voice. "You weren't here to know," she accused.

"But I'm back now," stated Chance. "I can take hold for you."

Wayne Elder spoke hesitantly. "You didn't answer my letter, Chance. I didn't know if you'd gotten it. I had to do something. I . . ."

Chance anticipated the old man's words. "You got somebody else to take over," he completed. "Why, that's all right, Wayne. I was coming back anyhow. You just hastened me a little."

Elder grunted his relief. Lee Su came through the kitchen door, china and silver rattling in his hands. "Dinna' ready," announced Lee.

"Help me get up, Chance," commanded Elder. "This dang' rheumatism . . ."

Chance put his hand under Elder's arm and the old man grunted with the effort of gaining his feet. Once he was standing he waved Chance away and hobbled toward the table. Chance, dropping back, looked at the girl. Lois Elder shook her head and nodded meaningly at the hobbling figure. Her cheeks flushed, red showing beneath the olive, and her dark eyes held concern.

"After dinner, Chance," she whispered.

When Elder was seated and Lois had taken her place, Chance sat down. There were a thousand things he wanted to ask, a thousand things he wished to know, but he did not voice his thoughts. Elder took the conversation in hand, quizzing Chance as to the happenings of the last three years.

"You been south," said Elder. "Went right to Texas from here when you left. You been pretty good to write, Chance, but you didn't tell us much. What you been doing?"

Chance Pagan grinned. "Learning my trade," he answered. "I popped cattle in the brush for three or four Texas outfits. I skinned a mule team for a mine outfit in Mexico, and I learned about browse range over in Arizona. I been around some, Wayne."

Elder grunted. "You been around," he agreed. "You might give us a little more of the details. Wasn't you workin' for a stage company one time, and didn't you get mixed up in some shootin'?"

"A little trouble," Chance answered. "Not much."

The questions continued. Little by little Wayne Elder pried information from his visitor. Lois sat by, eating her food, saying nothing.

"You growed up," Elder said suddenly. "I'm glad of it, Chance. You see much change in Lois?"

Chance did see a decided change. He favored the girl with a long slow look and under it she blushed hotly. "She's prettier," Chance answered. "She's grown up, if that's what you mean."

"That's what I mean," agreed Elder. He put down knife and fork and changed the subject suddenly.

"I'm sorry I didn't know you were coming Chance," he said. "I've put Bill Fahrion in charge here while I'm gone. If you'd written I'd have waited, but I didn't know . . ."

"Why, that's all right, Wayne," Chance said again. "Fahrion's a good man. He's honest and he knows the business. He's always been your foreman and there wasn't a reason not to put him in."

Elder nodded. "Had to have somebody," he agreed. "Fahrion's a good man, like you say. Mebbe he ain't quite heavy enough for the job, but he can't do the Spear much damage in the time I'll be gone. I'm glad it's all right with you."

"It sure is," Chance assured. "I'll go on up to the old place and stay there. I need to look after it, anyhow."

"Well," Elder pushed against the side of the table, sliding back his chair, "I got to go to my room. No, never mind. I'll make it," as Chance came to his feet. "That dang' Ben Godman ought to have the team in and hitched by now. We got to make the evenin' train from Cassidy."

Painfully reaching his feet the old man hobbled across the floor. Chance remained standing and Lois Elder, too, was on her feet. At the door Elder paused.

"You an' Lois can talk, I reckon," he said. "Let me know when Ben comes. Fahrion will be with him." He went on into the other room.

Left by Elder, Chance Pagan looked at Lois Elder. He

had left a girl, immature and beautiful. He had come back to find a woman grown, still beautiful, with the promise of girlhood now fulfilled.

"Well?" said Chance. As he spoke he moved a step, putting out his hand. The girl moved back from his advance and Chance stopped.

"What's the matter, Lois?" he asked.

"I . . . I don't know, Chance." The answer was hesitant. "You've been away a long time, and I . . ."

"I wrote to you," Chance urged.

"I know. But that isn't the same as your being here. Somehow seeing you and . . ."

"And you're upset about Wayne." The smile returned to Chance's face, lighting his eyes and curving his firm lips. "I sabe, Lois. Just how bad is Wayne?"

"He must go to a milder climate." The girl's voice showed her relief. "He isn't too badly off but the doctors say that Hot Springs is the place for him. We're going there. He will come back when the weather gets better, but he can't spend any more winters here."

Chance nodded. "I'm glad it's no worse," he said. "I didn't know . . ."

"You weren't here." Once more the girl accused him.

"No," agreed Chance, accepting the accusation. "I wasn't here and I should have been. Has that made the difference, Lois?"

Lois shook her head. "I don't think so," she replied. "It's just that I . . . You've been gone so long, Chance, and . . . See? I'm still wearing your ring."

One slender hand went to her bosom and a thin gold chain was withdrawn. A heavy signet ring glinted at the end of the chain.

"I . . . I still love you, Chance," Lois said hesitantly. "It's just that I . . . you're strange."

Chance nodded his understanding. "I sabe," he said again, slowly. "I won't crowd you, honey. But I have been gone a long time and I'm in love with you, girl."

At the words Lois Elder moved a step closer. Her arms half raised, and her face, flushed and beautiful, lifted toward Chance. Chance advanced to meet her and then stopped short. Boots thumped on the porch floor. The door creaked threateningly. Lois dropped her arms and Chance stepped back. The door opened and a round fur-capped head was thrust inside.

"Team's ready, boss," announced Ben Godman. "All hitched . . . Well, by grab! Chance Pagan! I wondered whose horse that was in the barn!"

Godman's round body followed his head, revealing the face of an immature cherub and the body of a miniature Santa Claus. Following Godman into the room came a square-built, solid man, grizzled haired and with heavy gray eyebrows above steady gray eyes. This was Bill Fahrion, foreman of the Spear.

"I came back, Ben," said Chance, advancing and taking the hand that Godman held out. "How are you? How are you, Bill?" In turn he shook hands with Fahrion.

"We're all right but the boss has got the misery," said Godman. "We're takin' him to the train, leastwise I am. By grab, I'm glad to see you back!"

Wayne Elder hobbled into the room. "It's time you come with that team," he snapped. "If I got to go I don't want to miss the train. Lois, you get your things on. Bill, you come here a minute."

Fahrion walked over to his boss and Godman, standing close beside Chance, spoke again. "Bill's goin' to run things while the old man's gone. You look mighty good, Chance. You growed up."

"Some," Chance agreed absently.

Lois returned wearing a hat and furs. Lee Su, wrapped to the ears and with a big canvas bag in his hand, issued from the kitchen.

"Are you going too, Lee?" Chance asked.

"I go," assured Lee. "You eat poor cookin' now, Chance."

". . . An' that's all, Bill," completed Wayne Elder. "Now we'll load up an' pull out. I hate to leave just when you come, Chance, but . . ."

"Don't you think of it," interrupted Chance, picking up two of the bags. "You get that rheumatism boiled out of you, Wayne, an' I'll be here when you get back."

The luggage was carried out to the waiting buckboard. Lee Su was ensconced in the back, and Ben Godman climbed up and took the reins. Wayne Elder was bestowed, snug and warm between his daughter and the driver. Good-byes were called and Godman, clucking to the team, swung the buckboard away from the house and out through the gate. When it was lost to view amidst the snow flurries, Chance Pagan turned to Bill Fahrion.

"Well," he said slowly, "they're gone. I wish . . ."

"They're gone," agreed Fahrion heavily. And then, after a moment, "And what was it you wished?"

"That I had come back sooner," replied Chance.

Fahrion said no word to that but turned and stalked toward the house. After a moment Chance followed him.

Fahrion had stopped inside the room and when Chance entered and closed the door the two men looked at each other for a long moment.

"You wish that you'd come back so that you could have run the Spear," blurted Fahrion suddenly. "Is that it?"

Chance shook his head. "No," he answered. "I wish that I'd been back here to take care of Wayne. I didn't know he was sick and he's been mighty good to me since my dad died."

"But you weren't back an' you won't run the Spear." Fahrion disregarded Chance's statement. "I'm runnin' the Spear."

"Did I say different?" Chance sensed the antagonism in the man and his own swift temper rose to meet it. He had always liked Fahrion, had always been on friendly terms with the man, but here he met jealousy and, perhaps, a little fear.

"You can't say different!" Fahrion bit the words off.

"I take it," Chance began to drawl, a dangerous sign in him since his childhood, "that I ain't welcome here?"

Fahrion shrugged. "You can ride the grubline as long as you want," he observed, letting a little contempt creep into his tone. "The Spear never turned a man away, but we ain't short-handed."

"And you ain't been asked for a job!" Chance flared. "I stay no place I'm not welcome."

"That's good," Fahrion assured. "That's the way to get along."

"Who is at the J Pen?" Chance was holding his anger in check.

"We're usin' it for a line camp." Fahrion returned to normal with the statement. "John Comstock is there. Why?"

"Because I'm headed for my ranch," snapped Chance. "You can pull your rider out of it."

A sardonic smile lifted the corner of Bill Fahrion's mouth. "That," he stated, "would be about your speed. You weren't here when old Wayne needed you an' now you'll throw his rider out of your cabin. You're quite a help, Pagan."

Instantly Chance would have liked to recall his words. Pride would not let him back down. "You can pull him out," he repeated. "I'll be in as soon as I can get a load of grub from Cassidy. That'll be tomorrow or the day after. And I'll tell you, Fahrion: I'll ride the roughs and I'll keep Spear cattle out of 'em. I'll watch the line and I'll watch *you!*"

Bill Fahrion grinned again. "You do that," he directed. "You do that, Pagan. I don't trust a man that won't stick an' help a friend. I've got no use for a man that won't stick an' help a man who's been a father to him. You watch me all you want; it'll make it easier for me to watch you."

Fahrion stood while his words sank in, while Chance Pagan got the full impact of them. He watched while the knuckles of Chance's hands became white as he clenched his fists and then Bill Fahrion drove home his final point. "That hurts you, Pagan, because it's true," he stated flatly, and turning, he stalked across the room and through the kitchen door.

2

FOR A MINUTE, perhaps for two minutes after Bill Fahrion left him, Chance Pagan stood alone, fighting down his wrath. Then snatching his coat and hat from a chair he flung on his sheepskin and jerked his hat down over his angry eyes. All his pride was outraged, the more so because Fahrion's last words had sunk in deeply. He would not stay at the Spear, he would not submit to insult, as he considered it, and so with anger boiling within him, Chance stalked out of the house and through the blowing snow to the barn.

Farmer had come forty miles but was good for as many more; would have to be good for twenty more at least. Chance flung his saddle up on the big bay, tightened the latigo, bridled, and leading the horse from the barn went into the saddle.

He rode north from the Spear and now the wind that struck him was bitter cold and the snow stung his cheeks. He had not minded the cold when he rode to the ranch, and riding from it he failed to note the weather. Recollection and anticipation had warmed him, riding in; rage fired his veins riding away. Farmer paid strict attention to the filling ruts and the business of covering ground, and Chance, except for setting the horse upon the track, paid no attention at all.

In three hours, with the early evening of March darkening the already dark sky, the horse and man reached the little cluster of buildings, dwellings, stores, saloons, and shops that made up Cassidy. Lights were twinkling as Chance rode up to the door of the livery barn and stopped.

A hostler admitted him, grunted at the condition of the bay horse, and promised feed and a grooming for Farmer. Leaving the livery, Chance went down the street. There was a hotel in Cassidy; there were two restaurants and five saloons. Debating between the saloons and the hotel, Chance chose the latter. He would get a room, a place to sleep, then he would move out. In Cassidy he could find men that he knew, men who appreciated him and his worth, men who would realize that he had come back to help when his help was needed and who would honor him for it. Chance would find those men and bask in their friendship and commendation. He did not consciously think of these things but, like a hurt child, sought them none the less.

At the hotel Ed Strangler, the proprietor, thin and jaundiced, gave Chance a laconic welcome and assigned him a room. Chance put a silver dollar on the counter for Strangler to pick up, and taking the key that was given him, went down the corridor to the door of Number Four. Once in the room Chance did not pause even to light the lamp. There was nothing to keep him in the hotel, and indeed, Chance did not know why he had gone to the room. He did pull off his chaps and spurs and dump them on the floor, then closing the door he returned to the little lobby, hung his key on the rack, and addressed Strangler.

"Who is in town?"

Ed Strangler shrugged his thin shoulders. "Nobody much," he answered. "Ben Godman's here for tonight. He come in to put Elder and the girl on the train. There's one or two more in, but I doubt if you would know 'em. Outside of that, there's just the usual bunch."

Chance grunted, turned on his heel, and strode to the door. First a drink to warm him, then supper. That was Chance's program. After that he did not know.

The Longhorn Saloon was two doors from the hotel. The Spear men had always patronized the Longhorn, and by habit Chance turned in. Ben Godman was at the bar, rolling an empty glass between his fingers. Further down the bar there were two men that Chance did not know, talking with a third that he recognized as Cliff Nowlen; and in the center Tom Melody, the sheriff, leaned his gaunt length half across the dark wood and spoke to Con Rady, the owner of the saloon. Every man in the room looked up as Chance entered. Ben Godman set down his glass, surprise showing on his round face. Melody straightened up and advanced toward Chance, and Nowlen turned from the men with him. Godman was the first to speak.

"What brought you in, Chance? Want to see the folks? I already put 'em on the train."

"My horse brought me in," Chance answered shortly. "Set out a drink, Rady."

"Ain't you speakin' to yore friends, Chance?" Tom Melody was advancing, his hand extended. "I ain't seen you for some time. Ben said that you was back, that you'd gone out to the Spear."

Chance could not refuse the hand and had no desire to do so. He had known Tom Melody all his life. The old man, lathe-thin and weathered like the splinter of a pine stump, had been present when Chance Pagan was born. The two shook hands and Melody's kindly brown eyes scanned the younger man. "Well," commented Melody, "you look more like old Jack Pagan every day, Chance. I'm glad to see you back in the country."

"It's fine somebody's glad," Chance answered shortly, self-pity taking possession of him. "I ain't been so welcome elsewhere."

Melody lifted his eyebrows slightly but made no comment, and Chance, turning, gestured to Con Rady. "Set Tom out a glass," he ordered. "You'll take a drink with me, Tom?"

"A small one," said Melody. "I've had my before-supper drink."

Rady put out a glass for the officer and stood holding another in his thick fingers, glancing from Chance to Ben Godman. Plainly the saloon keeper expected Chance to buy Godman a drink.

Chance interpreted that look. "I buy nothing for a Spear man," he announced, lifting the bar bottle. "Say when, Tom."

Liquor spilled into Melody's glass and the old man watched it. Trouble here, Tom Melody saw. He had anticipated trouble all his life and beaten it. What was this grief?

"When!" he said, humorous complaint in his voice. "I

said a little drink!"

Ben Godman, round face red and ears crimson, was staring hard at Chance. The little, rotund man who for thirty of his fifty years had punched cows for the Spear, had never backed down a step in his life and he was too old to start.

"What's got into yore craw?" blurted Godman. "You was friendly enough this noon. The Spear grub was good enough for you to eat then, wasn't it?"

"It ain't good enough now," snapped Chance. "I'm done with the Spear."

"Then to hell with you!" Godman rasped. "I never thought I'd see the day when Jack Pagan's kid acted like a spoilt baby! Sore because you come back an' found Elder had turned the place over to another man to run, are you? Fahrion's twice the cowman that you'll ever be, an' he stuck! He was there when the old man needed him. He didn't go galavantin' off . . ."

"Ben!" Melody's smooth drawl held a warning. Ben Godman closed his mouth, his sentence half-finished. Chance, his face dark with the blood beneath his skin, stood poised beside the bar.

"Finish it," Chance commanded. "Finish it, Godman, and be set to back what you say!"

"You an' me was about to take a drink, Chance," interposed Melody, smoothly. "Con, you set Ben out a drink on me."

"I'm drinkin' with nobody!" snapped Godman and, turning, stalked out of the door.

Chance watched him go. For a moment after the little man's departure he stood fixed, then turning he faced

Melody. "Is that what everybody's thinkin'?" he demanded hotly. "Do they think around here that I held out on Elder when he needed me an' that I've come back now hopin' to run the Spear?"

Melody picked up his glass. "Let's you an' me sit down at the table, Chance," he suggested.

"No!" Chance snapped. "I want to know. Is that what they're thinkin'?"

"I think," drawled Melody, "that yo're actin' like a kid that's had his toes stepped on. You ain't actin' like Jack Pagan's son. Now come on an' sit down."

Chance obeyed the command in the old man's voice. Carrying his filled glass he turned from the bar and went to the little cloth-topped table. Following him, Tom Melody seated himself and leaned forward toward Chance.

"Somethin'," said Tom persuasively, "has riled you, Chance. Want to spill it?"

Chance gulped his whiskey. The liquor stung his throat and for a moment he did not answer. Then, just as he had done ever since he was old enough to talk, he blurted out his troubles to old Tom Melody.

"I got a letter from Wayne tellin' me to come back here, that he needed me," Chance told him, aggrievement in his voice. "I didn't write an answer; I just pulled out and came a-running. When I got here I went straight to the Spear. There was Wayne, all crippled up with rheumatism and ready to go to Hot Springs. He had expected to hear from me and when he didn't, he put Fahrion in charge of the place."

Melody nodded understandingly and after a

moment's pause Chance went on. "That was all right. Fahrion's a good cowman." This statement came grudgingly. "I told Wayne that it was all right, that I'd just go up to my place and stay, and that everything was O. K. It was, too. It was all right with me. I'd do anything Wayne said. You know that, Tom."

Again Melody nodded and Chance continued. "Wayne and Lois left and I went back to the house. Fahrion jumped all over me. Told me that I was jealous of him, that I'd expected to come back and run the Spear. Why, I had no such idea. All I knew was that Wayne had said he needed me. I didn't know what for. You believe me, Tom?"

"Sure I believe you, kid."

"Well, Fahrion told me that I wasn't wanted around the Spear, hinted that I was ridin' grubline. I never rode grubline in my life! Why, damn him! I'm twice the cowman he'll ever be an' . . ."

"And what did you do?" interposed Melody, checking the tirade.

"I told him I was going to the J Pen," answered Chance. "Told him to get his man out of there, that I'd hold it down. He can get him out, too. He can . . ."

"I thought you liked Wayne," interrupted Melody.

"I'd go to hell for Wayne Elder an' you know it!"

"But you can't take a little rough talk for him, can you?" Melody drawled. "Chance, yo're just like yore daddy. You get mad quick an' easy. The trouble with you now is that yo're sore at yoreself for goin' off half-cocked. Ain't that it?"

Melody's brown eyes held Chance's blue ones in a

steady look. After a moment Chance lowered his head. "I reckon that's it," he said softly.

"Then why don't you square yoreself?" demanded Melody. "Why don't you talk to Fahrion, tell him to keep his man on at the Pen? Why don't you . . ."

"No!" Chance Pagan's head came up and his voice raised. "I'm goin' to the Pen. I'm goin' to stay in this country an' run my own place. In the mornin' I get grub and an outfit and I'll pull out."

"Yo're just like Jack," repeated Tom Melody. "Yo're proud as Lucifer an' you won't back down. You come on to supper with me, Chance. I want to talk to you."

"I'll go to supper," Chance answered, "but there's no need to talk."

Melody unfolded his length from his chair. "I'm afraid not," he sighed.

At the end of the bar Cliff Nowlen spoke swiftly to the men with him. Chance had talked loudly, so loudly that his declaration concerning his intentions had been plainly heard. "Let's go to the hotel," suggested Nowlen, and moved forward, the others following him.

Chance was on his feet when Nowlen reached the table, and the ranchman stopped. "Hello, Chance," he said, holding out his hand.

"Hello, Cliff," Chance answered, taking the hand. Chance had never particularly liked Nowlen, had never particularly disliked him either. Nowlen ran his NOW cattle on the east side of the Big Muddy, his range separated from the Spear and the J Pen by the river. Riders called the NOW the "Sudden" ranch, for the brand, burned big along the side, meant "at once, immediately," and the cowmen are apt at nicknames.

"I'm mighty glad to see you back," Nowlen kept up a friendly pressure with his hand. "You going to stay with us?"

"For the balance of the year."

"That's good." With a final squeeze Nowlen released Chance's hand. "I found two J Pen yearlings across the river a couple of weeks ago. They looked a little thin so I threw 'em with the nursery bunch in the stack yard."

This was a friendly gesture in any man's country and Chance rose to it. "That's white of you," he said.

"Just neighborly," depreciated Nowlen. "Come over to the Sudden, Chance. You'll be welcome. Come over an' stay with us if you get lonesome at the place. We'll be lookin' for you."

"I sure will," Chance agreed, warming to the friendliness.

"We'll be lookin' for you," Nowlen said again and, smiling, went on toward the door.

"Let's go eat," grunted Melody, touching Chance's arm. "Come on."

"One more drink," insisted Chance. Reluctantly Melody nodded.

Outside the door of the Longhorn, with his companions flanking him, Nowlen spoke. "Pagan's sore at the Spear," he said.

The slight, humpbacked man beside him grunted affirmatively and the other tall fellow said, "He acted sore."

"And a damn' good thing," grunted Nowlen. "Art, you hit for the ranch. You tell Suel to get out with one

28

of the boys and cross the river and pick up two J Pen yearlin's and put 'em in our stack yard."

Art Ragland, the tall man, grunted and grinned. "I wondered about that," he remarked.

"Never mind the wondering," snapped Nowlen. "You have Suel do it."

"All right."

"What does it get you?" Tully Pillow, the hump-backed man at Nowlen's left, grunted. "Calves eat hay and you've got none too much."

"But I'm goin' to have more," vowed Nowlen. "You talked to me about a bunch of steers once, didn't you, Tully?"

"I said that maybe the boys could bring in a few steers," admitted the hunchback dryly.

"They can get 'em," said Nowlen. "I'll have the J Pen vega to cut hay from this summer. I'll have the J Pen range if I want it. You wait and see! Pagan's sore at the Spear. He'll throw with me. You been wanting a steer market, Tully. You've got one."

"Mebbe." Tully Pillow was skeptical.

"No 'maybe' about it."

Three steps in silence and then Pillow spoke again. "Well," he said, "I reckon we can go ahead, Cliff. If young Pagan don't throw with you, there's ways to make him. The boys will pick up some steers, come this spring an' summer."

"An' some of 'em will be Spear steers," said Ragland from Nowlen's other side.

Pillow nodded, a short jerk of his head, and the men walked on. As they reached the door of the hotel the humpbacked man spoke again.

"He'll be wantin' to take a bunch of truck up to his place," said Pillow, referring to Chance. "I've got a freight outfit leavin' here tomorrow for the store. I reckon it would be a friendly move to haul it for him."

"You do that," agreed Nowlen. "Tully, this is a break! We been afraid to get any cattle because we didn't have the winter feed for 'em, but with two sections of vega to cut hay from we can . . ."

"Make a little money," finished Pillow. "I been tired of layin' off this Calico Hole country anyhow. It's time the outfits here contributed a little."

Nowlen pushed open the door and the men went into the hotel.

3

ON THE MORNING after his advent in Cassidy, Chance Pagan got up with a brown taste in his mouth, a headache, and a realization that he had made a fool of himself. He had, through his own hard-headedness, placed himself in an untenable position and he had to stay there. Tom Melody had talked to Chance across the supper table, had drawled a slow philosophy of living and getting along, and had gently pointed out to Chance the error of his ways. Melody knew how to do just that and Chance left the old sheriff with a lot of ideas in his mind and his head still full of mulishness and false pride. He had been forced to agree with Melody's logic, but he hadn't backed down an inch.

Leaving Melody he had visited several saloons, intent on finding Bed Godman and bending his own stiff neck in an apology, but Godman had not been in evidence, while whisky was. Chance had taken more than one drink, had talked after the third or fourth, airing his grievance against the Spear, and now, stamping his feet into his cold boots, he realized that he was a fool and had talked too much. He couldn't back down now.

After using the communal comb and the wash basin in the hotel, Chance left his key at the desk and went out into the morning. The wind had died and the air was crisp and cold. Snow crunched under Chance's boots as he walked to the restaurant.

Coffee, flapjacks, three eggs and plenty of bacon made him feel better, and leaving the eating house he went across the street to Sol Apfel's store. There were things to buy and to haul out to the J Pen if Chance was to make good his brag. Chance had sold his outfit in the south when he received Wayne Elder's letter, and except for his saddle and gear, his horse, and the clothes he stood in, he had nothing.

Apfel's store was open and Chance went in to stand beside the big-bellied stove that roared in the center of the room. There Sol joined him.

Sol Apfel's belly, in proportion, was as big as the belly of the stove, and his face above the black beard glowed as red as the stove pipe. He greeted Chance heartily.

"I hear," said Sol, "they say you are goin' to the Pen. Maybe you will need some grub, yes? No?"

"Yes," answered Chance, "I'll need a wad of it, Sol,

and some blankets and fixings too."

"Well," Sol shrugged, "you got the money. I saw Squire Hurt last night an' he says you got money in the bank."

That caution was so typical, so like the little merchant, that Chance laughed. "You get a piece of wrapping paper, Sol," he directed. "I'll give you an order but I sure don't know how I'll get it to the ranch. Maybe I can get the livery to haul it up for me."

Sol Apfel departed and came back with a square of wrapping paper which he laid on the counter. "Go ahead," he directed, his pencil poised.

Chance gave his order: Flour, baking powder, coffee, salt pork, sugar. The necessities of life were named one by one and scribbled down. Apfel made suggestions, some of which were taken, others rejected. It was while Chance was looking at blankets that Cliff Nowlen entered the store accompanied by Tully Pillow and came back to where Chance and the merchant stood.

"I tried to find you again last night," greeted Nowlen. "This is Tully Pillow, Chance. He runs a little store up in the Basin on top of Calico. He's haulin' some stuff up today and he said he'd haul anything you wanted him to."

Chance shook hands with Pillow, feeling as he let the humpback's hand go, as though he had been holding a dead fish. "It's mighty kind of you," he stated. "I was wondering how I'd get my stuff up there."

"I'll have the wagon stop for it," Pillow announced, his voice colorless. "Be along in half an hour."

Chance frowned in thought for a moment. "Maybe,"

he said, "I'd better stay in town tonight. You'll hardly make it to the J Pen this evening and . . ."

"I'll be there about dark," interposed Pillow. "I'm usin' three teams and I figure to go almost home."

Chance grunted. Even with six horses, the Basin atop Calico Mesa was a long haul from Cassidy for one day. "Well . . ." he said doubtfully.

"It'll be there," announced Pillow confidently.

"I'm sure obliged," Chance said again.

Pillow grunted and turned away, and Nowlen, stepping close to Chance, spoke low-voiced. "You can count on his getting there," said Nowlen. "He's got the best horses in the country."

The NOW owner paused a moment and then, as though struck with a thought, spoke again: "How are you fixed for horses?"

"I've got one good one," Chance answered.

Nowlen nodded. "You'll need more than one if you ride much country," he stated. "There's hay at the J Pen, ain't there?"

"There always has been," answered Chance. "Why?"

"I've got three or four bronks that need riding," said Nowlen. "You always were a master hand with a horse, Chance. If you'd ride out the bronks for me I'd be obliged."

Chance nodded decisively. "I'll sure take 'em and be grateful," he said. "You're being mighty nice to me, Cliff. First the yearlings and then loaning me a mount."

"I'm just glad to see you back," Nowlen grinned. "Suppose you go out to the ranch with me when you get done here, stay for dinner, and pull on over to your place this afternoon? You could drift the horses over then."

"I'll go you," said Chance, and turned again to Apfel.

Nowlen waited while Chance finished with his order and the two men stood near the front of the store until Apfel and his scurrying clerk had the goods piled beside the door. Chance wrote a counter check for the amount of his purchases, went over to the bank to cash the check, and brought the money back. At the bank he spoke to Squire Hurt, the banker, found that he had a comfortable account, and felt reassured. He hadn't enough money to buy cattle, that was sure, but he really did not need to buy cattle. During the past four years Wayne Elder had been branding twenty head of calves, ten heifers, and ten steers to Chance Pagan's J Pen iron, these serving as payment for the hay that the Spear cut from the J Pen vega. Chance had forty or fifty cows and calves on the Spear range and perhaps forty steers. He was already in the cow business.

When the goods were paid for, almost before Apfel had counted the purchase money, a heavy freight wagon drawn by three teams of strapping big Clydesdales halted in front of the store. Pillow climbed down from the seat and came in, signifying that he was ready, and Chance, with the assistance of Nowlen, Apfel, and the clerk, carried out the pile of supplies. With the wagon loaded, Pillow climbed up beside the robe-covered figure that had not stirred from the seat, clucked to his team, and the wagon creaked away. Chance and Nowlen, bidding Apfel good-bye, went down to the livery barn.

The two rode out from Cassidy side by side, Farmer apparently as fresh as though he had not covered sixty miles the day before.

"That's a good horse," commented Nowlen, eyeing the big bay. "He can stand a lot of riding?"

"Plenty," Chance answered, "but I'll lay him off when I get the horses you're lending me. I had a couple of hundred pounds of grain put on the load, Cliff, and your bronks won't suffer any."

"I know that," grinned Nowlen. "I'm giving you some salty horses, Chance. You'll have a rough string."

"I need a rough string," answered Chance.

The two men talked as they rode along south, Nowlen retailing happenings in the Calico Hole during the three years Chance was away, and making interested inquiries as to what Chance had been doing. Chance warmed under Nowlen's friendliness and before he realized it, was telling the ranchman of the happenings at the Spear.

When he finished Nowlen nodded. "I don't blame you a bit," he said. "Fahrion's jealous. He knows that if you'd come a day or two sooner he'd be sitting outside sucking his thumb. That's why he popped off. I think you're just right, Chance."

This was the first approbation Chance had received and he rose to it. "I couldn't do anything else," he stated. "I couldn't let Fahrion run over me. I think you're right, Cliff. He's got his wind in his craw."

The two passed Pillow's wagon three miles out of Cassidy. The Clydesdales were covering country, walking right along, and Pillow lifted an arm to the riders as they went by. After passing the wagon the two swung east, crossed the Big Muddy River where it spread into a shallow ford, their horses crunching through the thin ice, and just at noon reached the cluster of cabins, barns, and corrals that made up the Sudden headquarters. Dinner was ready when they rode in.

In company with Suel James, the NOW foreman, and two other riders, they ate dinner. While cigarettes were being rolled after the meal, Nowlen and his foreman went into the office and when they came out again Nowlen walked over to Chance.

"Like to see your yearlin's?" he asked.

Chance got up from his seat on a bench and putting on his hat went out with Nowlen; and Suel James, calling one of the riders, started for the corral.

"They'll run in the broom-tails I'm loaning you," informed Nowlen. "The yearlin's are down in the stack yard."

The two men skirted the barn and arriving at the stack yard saw a J Pen heifer and steer beside the fence. The animals seemed to be in good condition. They were at the fence, not at the rack, a fact that Chance noted casually.

"They look good," he said.

"They've picked up since we brought 'em in," commented Nowlen. "You might as well leave 'em here, Chance. You won't want to be bothered driving them with the horses and we'll be turning all this stuff out in a week or two, anyhow. We'll throw 'em across the river when we work the country in the spring."

That was a relief to Chance. He did not want to be

troubled driving the yearlings when he had a string of horses on his hands, and Nowlen's offer was thoughtful. Consequently he thanked the NOW owner and accepted.

"Here comes Suel with the bronks," said Nowlen waving away Chance's thanks. "Let's look 'em over."

Going to the corral the two stood by until James and his rider had finished penning a little bunch of horses. Nowlen closed the gate and joined Chance at the fence. James came walking over and all together they stood watching the animals quiet down.

"You better take one or two broke horses," said James, "then if you want a couple or three bronks we can accommodate you. That bay horse and the black are summer horses, and the buckskin looks like he'll make a good one."

James' suggestion was good and Chance took it up. The bay and the black horses James had mentioned, a buckskin and a sorrel were left in the corral and the others turned loose. Thanking Nowlen, Chance signified his intention of pulling out immediately.

"I want to get to the place," he said. "I'll want to build a fire and get cleaned up before my groceries come in. I reckon I'll just ride that black and give Farmer a rest."

"The black bucks," Suel warned. "I'll rope him out for you while you get your saddle."

Chance went off toward the barn and James, rope in hand, went through the gate. When Chance returned carrying his saddle, Suel had the black roped and snubbed up short.

The black, not ridden since the fall work closed,

fought the saddle but was subdued. James tied up a hind leg and Chance screwed his saddle down tight. Then, with the pen free of other horses, he mounted and James released the rope.

The black ducked his head and went to work. He bucked through the dirt and the muddy water in the corral, liberally splattering his rider and the three onlookers, tried to rub Chance off against the fence, and finally finding that he could do himself no good, ceased and stood, sullenly waiting for what came next. James opened the gate, Chance rode through, got his coat from Nowlen who held it up to him, and thanking the ranchman again Chance collected his horses and left. He had twelve miles to go to the J Pen. As he rode down the slope from the barn he lifted his arm and Suel James and Nowlen returned the salute.

"You said showy horses," reminded James, turning to Nowlen. "I did the best I could."

Nowlen nodded. "They're all right, Suel," he commended. "Everybody knows that black and the bay. Babe had them in his string when he repped for us last year. The buckskin is out of our Bluff stud, and I bought the sorrel from Elder myself. Everybody on the Spear knows him. There won't be any mistaking those four."

James looked curiously at his boss. "You're bein' mighty good to Pagan, Cliff," he said. "Must be a reason."

"One of the best," assured Nowlen. "I'm glad to loan him horses. You know, Suel, the three of us are about of a size, aren't we?"

James nodded.

"And," continued Nowlen, "if one of us was, oh say a half mile away, the only way a man could tell us apart would be by the horse we rode."

"And everybody knows that black and bay, and the sorrel and the buckskin are easy picked," grunted James. "I'd know that sorrel in a thousand."

"Keep him in mind," warned Nowlen. "You might have to remember him in public."

A slow grin spread over James' thin face. "I thought that somethin' was up when Art brought the word about the yearlin's," he said. "We were out early this mornin' pickin' 'em up. Art went to the Basin and I brought 'em over. Notice how the little devils hang by the gate? They want to get home. I picked them up out of the J Pen stack yard."

Nowlen scowled. "You took a chance," he rebuked.

James shook his head. "There's nobody at the J Pen," he said. "Comstock has pulled out. I heard that Pagan and Fahrion had a jangle and Pagan told Fahrion to pull his man out of the Pen."

"He did," Nowlen answered. "Well, let's go to the house. I want a cup of coffee and I want to tell you a few things, Suel."

Chance Pagan jingled his little bunch of horses along toward the Big Muddy. He had twelve miles to make to the J Pen and he was anxious to get there. The black horse behaved himself and Farmer, taking the lead, swung right along. Horses and man crossed the river at the Sudden crossing, struck southwest, and shortly came upon the tight three-wire fence with which the

Spear protected the vega land. Wayne Elder had ordered that fence, and seeing it Chance felt a twinge of conscience which he resolutely put aside. He would hold down the J Pen for the Spear, would do it with no cost to Elder. When warm weather came and Elder returned, he could get things all straightened out and everything would be all right. In the meantime he wouldn't back down a step.

The J Pen was deserted when Chance rode in. He put the horses in the corral, intending to keep them there until he could look over the fence in the trap. If the NOW bronks got out they would go straight home and Farmer would go with them. Chance had no desire to be left afoot. The NOW was twelve miles away and the Spear was seventeen. Either distance was a long walk.

Having unsaddled the black horse and thrown down hay for all his mounts, Chance put his saddle in the shed and went to the house. The J Pen was cold and lifeless. Chance pulled up on the latch string and walked in.

Only one of the cabin's two rooms had been in use. There was wood in the box, cooking utensils hung on the wall, and there were dishes on a shelf. These things belonged to the J Pen. Walking over to the table Chance saw a note scrawled on a piece of wrapping paper. He read it:

"Chance. You're a damned fool. John."

Chance grinned. John Comstock was a youngster of about his own age. He and Chance were close friends, had been together through all the usual scrapes of youth, had fought side by side and had battled each other more than once to a draw. Comstock was a

40

bigger man than Chance but Chance was the quicker. Chance Pagan would take more from John Comstock than any other man except Wayne Elder. He wished, standing there holding that note, that he had not been so hasty. It would have been nice to have John to fuss with and talk to in the evenings. With a shrug he put the note aside. He had been hasty and there wasn't any help for it now. He would have to see John and explain.

For some time Chance busied himself about the house. He built a fire and swept; he relaced the rope lacing of the bunk, tightening the cords. He did any number of small things, killing time, and suddenly he found that he was very much alone.

With dusk he lit a kerosene-filled lantern, and shortly after that, when his stomach was beginning to feel very empty, he heard the creak of wheels and harness. Throwing open the door he stood, lantern in hand, looking out into the yard. Pillow's big Clydesdales were stopping before the door and Pillow's hoarse voice came from the wagon.

"Said we'd make it, didn't I?"

Chance went on out with the lantern. Pillow climbed down from the seat and, stiffly as though almost frozen in place, Pillow's companion moved. They reached the ground together and Chance, lifting the lantern high, saw with a start that the person with Pillow was a girl.

For an instant Chance saw her face in the light of the lantern, a thin face, pinched and white with cold. Pillow came around the wagon end and spoke gruffly. "Go on in to the fire, Arlie."

"I didn't know . . ." began Chance.

"Daughter," grunted Pillow. "I'll give you a hand with your stuff, but I can't carry much."

The two fell to work, unloading the things Chance had bought in Cassidy. Each trip that Chance made into the house he saw the girl close beside the stove. On the second trip he stopped and spoke to her.

"You open the oven and put your feet in it. Take off those wraps and get warm."

When he came in again, carrying his bedding, the girl had obeyed. She sat beside the stove, her feet in the opened oven, her wrappings laid aside, and her thin calico dress held tightly about her knees. Chance looked at her sharply. The girl was small, so small that she seemed almost elfin, and her blue eyes, big and frightened, followed Chance's movements as he dumped the bedding on the bunk.

When the last armful had been brought in, Pillow spoke to the girl. "Come on, Arlie. Get your coat on."

Chance, beside the door, interposed. "You'd better stay here the night, Mr. Pillow," he said. "I'll cook up some supper and take care of your teams, and you'll be warm. Your girl looks like she was about frozen."

Pillow shook his head. "Got to go on," he stated.

It was Chance's turn to shake his head. "Not tonight," he announced cheerfully. "I reckon I'm the one that put you out and I ought to make up for it. Your horses have been standing until they're stiff and it's a long, hard pull to the Basin."

Pillow thought that over, then he shrugged. "Mebbe yo're right," he agreed. "The teams are stiff and it's a

42

piece up to the Basin, like you say. We'll camp with you."

Nodding his approval Chance went to the door. "I'll stable the team," he offered.

Pillow, moving after Chance, spoke to Arlie. "Start supper," he ordered curtly, and followed Chance out of the house.

When the teams had been unhitched and put in the barn, and when Chance had thrown down hay for them, the men went back into the house. Arlie Pillow had been busy during their absence. Coffee was beginning to simmer on the stove. The girl had opened cans of food and had two frying pans busy. She slid a pan of drop-biscuits into the hot oven as the men came in.

Pillow stripped off his coat, tossed it on a chair, and sat down to pull off his overshoes. Chance hung coat and hat beside the door and carried the wash basin to the stove. Pouring hot water into the basin from the tea-kettle, he tempered the hot water with cold from a bucket, and spoke to Pillow.

"There you are," he said, gesturing to the pan that he had put upon the wash bench. "Help yourself. It looks like your girl has supper ready."

Pillow used the pan and threw the water out the door. Chance in turn made his toilet, and when he had done, supper was on the table. Pillow seated himself. Chance moved to a chair and then noted that the girl was standing. "Sit down," he invited.

Pillow looked up. "My house the women don't eat with the men," he snapped.

"But this is my house," reminded Chance, grinning

amiably. "Sit down, girl."

Arlie waited, standing beside the table. Reluctantly Pillow nodded his head and the girl sat down.

During the meal Chance Pagan studied his guests. Pillow was a snarled, warped, knot of a man. His humped back made his body thick through the shoulders, and although he had said that he could not carry much, his corded arms, heavy with muscle, belied his words. His blue eyes were thin and slitted and they shifted constantly. Twice Chance, looking up from his plate, found Pillow staring at him, and each time the man looked hastily away.

When they had finished eating, Chance produced papers and tobacco and Pillow brought out a pipe. Chance, forming a cigarette between his fingers, watched as Pillow stuffed the pipe. "You came into the Basin when, Mr. Pillow?" asked Chance.

"Two years ago," Pillow answered. "I run a little store up there."

Chance wet the cigarette, lit it, and inhaled. "That used to be a pretty tough country," he commented.

"It is a hard country to make a living in," Pillow said, striking a match and setting it to his pipe. "I don't know why I stay there."

"Used to be a tough bunch up there." Chance pursued his thoughts. "There was Silvertip Upton and a gang of bad ones. That Badlands country makes a mighty nice hideout if a man don't want to be found. Any of them there yet?"

Pillow shrugged. "I just run a store," he answered.

Arlie was moving about the table, removing the

dishes. The heat seemed to have filled the girl's cheeks, and Chance, watching her idly, was surprised to note that she was almost pretty. Her eyes, big and blue and wide apart, were beautiful, but there was a haunted, almost a hunted, look in them. Chance, catching her eyes, became suddenly alert. The girl was afraid, afraid of her father.

"Well," said Chance, rising, "that's the way to get along. If I ran a store I wouldn't be too prying about my customers' business. I'll help with those dishes, girl."

"She can do 'em," snapped Pillow. "You'll spoil her."

"Not this once, I won't." Chance grinned. "I'll wash, and you dry. How's that?"

Arlie smiled timidly at him.

The dishes were disposed of in short order. When they were done Pillow, who had not moved to help, knocked out the dottle from his pipe into the stove, stretched, and yawned. Chance took the hint.

"We'll give the girl the bed," he said cheerfully. "You and me can do mighty well on a couple of robes on the floor." He did not wait for Pillow's answer, but busied himself, opening his roll of bedding, hanging a blanket from nails on a log rafter, and putting the other quilts and blankets on the bed. When he had finished he went out of the room, returning with an armload of wood. Pillow had slipped off his shoes and Arlie had retired behind the blanket curtain.

"Got a wood comfort here," remarked Chance, dumping his armload in the woodbox. "Either of us gets cold we can throw some on the fire."

Pillow grunted an affirmative and sat down on a buf-falo robe that was spread beside the stove. Chance like-wise threw down a robe, and he too sat down.

Neither man did much undressing. Chance pulled off his boots and loosened his belt. Pillow had already removed his shoes and simply stretched out and pulled the robe over him.

"You ready for the light to go out?" Chance called.

From behind the blanket Arlie said, "Yes," timidly.

Chance blew out the lantern, lay down on his robe and pulled the sides over him. The floor was hard but Chance Pagan made nothing of that. He had slept on many a hard bed. He settled himself, pillowed his head on his arm, and prepared for slumber. Just before he dozed off he heard movement and, partially wakening, asked a sleepy question:

"Everything all right?"

Pillow's answer came: "Yes." Chance grunted and relaxing again let sleep take him.

When Chance wakened the room was cold. From behind the blanket came a rhythmic snore. Chance sat up in his robe. Just on the other side of the stove was the other robe-wrapped figure. Getting to his knees Chance peered across the stove top. Arlie Pillow lay in the buf-falo robe that her father had occupied. A scowl crossed Chance's face. That was no way to treat a girl! He would tell Pillow . . .

Chance shrugged. After all, what business was it of his? He reached for his boots and the girl stirred. One white arm was flung out of the robe and, with the leather falling away, Chance could see the sweetly curved, girlish torso, hugged tight by the skimpy calico dress. With a smothered grunt Chance averted his eyes. Arlie Pillow wasn't just a little girl, after all. She was almost a woman.

4

FOR A WEEK after his arrival at the J Pen, Chance Pagan saw no one. The Pillows, father and daughter, left early on the morning after Tully Pillow usurped his daughter's bed, the girl smiling shyly at Chance and the man waving away Chance's proffered payment. During the week Chance rode the vega fence, rode the country west of the ranch, followed Tomcat Creek, the little stream that bisected the meadow land, and watched the snow melt off the range. During that week he had more of Chance Pagan's society than he liked.

He found things at the J Pen in perfect order. He had expected as much when he heard that John Comstock had held down the place. Everything was all right, there wasn't a thing to find fault with, and that irked Chance. He would have liked to find some fault with the Spear.

During the week, too, he rode the horses he had borrowed from Nowlen. The two summer horses, the bay and the black, came around easily and the buckskin was not hard to handle, but the sorrel was a fighting, pitching fool. Chance got a kick out of working the sorrel, and he got a surprise when he put his saddle on Farmer. Farmer pitched, not very hard but some. Chance chided the big bay horse.

"Here," he scolded, "don't you go bad on me, Farmer.

Don't you go outlaw!"

Snow melted during the week and water ran down the draws, for March was done and April was beginning. In another month or less, the swift spring of the range country would be in full command. Flowers would bloom in the dead grass and the range would turn from bronze to green. Chance waited for spring, relishing the thought.

But spring was not yet established. On the Monday following his arrival a major calamity befell. Chance found himself out of tobacco. He scraped his pockets and searched the cabin, sure that he had brought a box of Dukes Mixture from town, but of tobacco there was none. That must be corrected. The Basin being nearer than Cassidy, Chance resolved to ride up and get a supply. And too, Chance wanted to see Pillow again. Or *was* it Pillow he wanted to see? A pair of hurt blue eyes had been haunting Chance.

On the morning of his departure for the Basin he roped Farmer out of the horses, put on his saddle and turning the other loose, mounted. Again Farmer pitched, a little more roughly, a little more wickedly than he had the first time. The horse was so big and so fast that even his crow-hopping shook Chance up. But the flurry did not last long and putting the J Pen behind him, Chance rode south, heading toward Tomcat Creek and the pass to the mesa top. He had not been in the Badlands atop the mesa for years, and he was eager.

Had he been less eager he might have looked back and noticed that the clouds, hovering above Two Buttes to the north, were boiling. But had he done so he would have thought only of rain, for this was April.

Chance made five miles from the ranch before the snow struck. It came lazily at first, and then with more vigor. Still he kept on and it was not until the storm suddenly reached blizzard proportions with the wind howling and the snow a white blanket across the earth, that he halted. He would have to turn back. There was no use of going further, no reason for going further. Reluctantly, for Chance wanted that tobacco, he turned Farmer into the wind and pushed back for the cabin.

Landmarks were gone. Sense of direction alone kept Chance on his course and that failed to a degree. He found himself suddenly in Tomcat Creek bottom when he should have been on the bank, and seeking to correct his error he set Farmer at the bank. As horse and man reached the top, Chance wiped the snow from his eyes and Farmer stopped short. Something came at Chance out of the storm, something that drifted with the wind. It was a horse, and as the animal approached, Chance saw that the horse was saddled! Somewhere out ahead of him, somewhere in the sweep of wind and snow, was a rider, a man afoot, perhaps a man hurt, and certainly a man helpless!

The drifting horse made no effort to escape Chance. That told that the horse was gentle, that he had not pitched his rider off. Chance, holding the bridle reins of the stray, thought furiously. A riderless, gentle horse drifting with the storm! Horses drift downwind. The wind was from the north. One of two things had happened then: somewhere north of him was a man afoot, put afoot because the horse had fallen and got away before his rider could catch him; or it might be that the rider was dead. But Chance could not take that last risk. He had to find the man.

No rider would be careless in a blizzard of this fierceness. That meant that the horse had fallen and the only logical place for such a thing to happen was along Tomcat Creek. That was the only rough country in the immediate vicinity. Again Chance swung Farmer into the wind, and leading the stray, went north. As he rode he called, throwing his voice against the deadening snow and the wind, and he might as well, for all the good it did, have been back at the J Pen cabin, shouting at the walls. Still he called.

Farmer plowed ahead, head low against the storm. Chance rubbed snow from his face and kept his eyes clear of the furry whiteness. He couldn't see far, couldn't see but perhaps fifty feet. The stray horse, slack on the reins and following willingly, swung toward the creek. There was a break in the creek bank. Was this a trail that was familiar to the stray? Chance thought perhaps . . . He turned Farmer into the creek.

Down beneath the cut banks the wind was gone and the snow came straight down. The creek bed was fairly wide. Chance could not quite see the other side. Farmer broke through the icy water and, stumbling, almost fell. The big horse recovered, staggering on the slippery footing. Just on the far side of the creek there was a big black rock, and water shone. It wasn't a rock. It was a man! Farmer stopped and Chance dismounted stiffly, holding tightly to the reins. As Chance approached the man stirred.

"I've got you!" exclaimed Chance Pagan.

The man in the creek was big. He groaned when Chance bent over him, and moved his head. His hair was longish and gray, and his beard was big and bushy and streaked with white. Chance knew the man: Silvertip Upton, the outlaw!

"My horse fell," Upton said weakly. "I can't get up. I crawled here." Chance noted the straggling depression in the snow made by that struggle.

"I'll get you up," Chance promised. "I'll get you in." Silvertip's beard parted. The man was grinning!

It was a task to get Silvertip up and on his horse. It seemed that Silvertip had no use of his legs at all. Chance tied the bridle reins of both horses and looped them over his arm. He was not going to lose the horses if he could help it!

Silvertip was enormously strong in the arms. When Chance had pulled him up he could cling to his saddle and give some help. The outlaw pulling and Chance boosting, Silvertip finally gained the saddle. He hung on with both hands, his legs refusing to function. Chance mounted Farmer and again he took the reins of the lead horse.

"We've got about two miles to go," said Chance. "I'll get you in." He did not know how far they had to go and he wasn't at all sure that he would get in himself.

But Farmer was certain. Farmer went down the creek steadily, the lead horse following. Farmer turned off to the right and stopped, and there was a fence in front of the horse.

The fence helped. All Chance had to do was follow

the fence to the corner, turn right once more, and still following the fence, reach a gate. Inside that gate was the lane that led to the J Pen. Chance knew exactly where he was and he followed the fence.

At the corner, recognized by instinct alone, they turned again, and then still following along the wire, went east. Twice Chance thought that he had found the gate and twice was deceived. But the third time he was right and dismounted, opening the wire. Now the direction was south again and, so suddenly that it seemed almost like a card trick performed by a magician, the J Pen was about them. Chance dismounted beside the cabin.

Silvertip, his water-soaked clothing frozen, was glued to the saddle, his hands locked on the horn. The old man was unconscious and Chance had to pry loose the clutching fingers. Hauling the big body from the saddle, Chance dragged the man inside the house. Then, leaving Upton on the floor, he went out again, led the horses to the barn, and turned them in.

Back in the house once more Chance busied himself. First a fire and water in the teakettle and in a bucket on the stove. Then, even before the house warmed, he stripped the clothing from Silvertip and getting the man on the bunk, rubbed the gleaming white torso with a piece of coarse sacking.

Upton, stripped, was a Hercules. Muscles lay like dormant ropes beneath the white skin, their full roundness belying the man's age. It was while Chance was using the sacking that Silvertip opened his eyes, big, grey-blue eyes that held a twinkle.

"Made it, didn't you?" whispered the man on the bed. "You made it, didn't you, Jack?"

Upton was mistaking Chance for his father, Jack Pagan. Somewhere in the past this old giant had known Jack Pagan, must have known Jack Pagan.

Chance answered him. "We made it."

The water in the teakettle boiled. Chance mixed whisky, from a pint bottle, with the hot water and forced Upton to drink the scalding fluid, then warming a blanket he covered the man and Upton lay quiet. Chance put coffee in the pot and set it to heat.

From the bunk Silvertip spoke again, his voice stronger. "You're not Jack Pagan. Jack Pagan's dead."

"I'm his kid."

"I remember. Jack's kid, Chance. My horse fell with me crossing the creek. Hurt my back and I couldn't catch him."

"You're all right now," Chance assured. "This is the J Pen. You're all right. Take it easy."

There was whimsical amusement in Upton's voice. "I always figured I was too ornery to freeze to death. Always thought I'd be shot or hung. I reckon I was right."

"I'd started up to Pillow's store in the Basin," Chance said, prosaically. "Run out of tobacco and wanted some. That's how I came to be out in the storm."

A chuckle from the bed. "Pillow is out of tobacco too. I was comin' back from Cassidy with a box of it. On my saddle."

Chance grunted, settled the coffee with cold water, and carried a cup to the bed. "Drink this," he ordered, "then take it easy."

Upton swallowed the burning coffee without a grimace. When Chance took the cup again the man on the bed closed his eyes and relaxed. Chance went back to the stove with the pot. When he returned to the bed and spoke, Upton did not answer. Evidently Silvertip had checked out again.

Chance went to the barn, unsaddled the horses, and gave them both a feed from his meager store of grain. He located the wood pile, a mount of white in the yard, and brought in wood and the ax. He made the fifty-foot trip to the spring and carried water. All during that time Upton lay quiet, his face waxy-white and his eyes closed. Rolling a smoke from the supply he had found on the old man's saddle, Chance settled down to wait. At noon he cooked a little and ate. Upton, rousing, drank some coffee but wanted nothing to eat. During the afternoon Chance replenished his wood box and tended to the horses, putting hay in the rack. All the horses had come in, seeking shelter. The storm was lessening and when dark fell, Chance made a pallet on the floor and lay down.

Close to midnight he was awakened by wild mutterings from the bunk. Chance rose and lit the lamp, freshly cleaned and filled with kerosene. Upton's face was flushed and his eyes were wild and bright.

"It's a lie," Upton snarled, staring up at Chance. "A lie! Jack Pagan was fifty miles away. I took them!" He muttered incoherently a moment after that, and then staring at Chance whispered craftily. "I will lie for you, Jack, but you must stop."

"I'll stop," assured Chance, realizing that the older man was raving. "I'll stop, Silvertip."

"You never called me that, Jack," said the man on the bunk, and then: "I won't lie for you. I will for Molly. But you must quit because of her."

Chance, crossing the room, got a clean dishtowel and wringing it out of the waterbucket, put the damp, cold cloth on Upton's head. That seemed to soothe Silvertip. He relaxed after a time and muttered only occasionally. Finally he slept, but Chance did not sleep. He sat watching the man on the bunk. Silvertip had talked to Jack Pagan in his delirium. He had warned Jack Pagan to stop something, and he had said that he could lie, lie for Molly. Chance's mother had been named Molly. He did not remember her.

With morning the storm broke. The sky was clear steel gray and cold. With morning, too, Chance found himself with a very ill man occupying the bunk. Upton's breath was hoarse and rasping. His head was hot to touch and his body burned. Occasionally he muttered into his beard and turned on the bed. Seemingly he had recovered the use of his legs, but that was the only hopeful sign that Chance could see.

For a time Chance debated the advisability of going for help, but put the thought aside. There was no doctor in Cassidy, none nearer than Fort Logan, thirty miles north of Cassidy, and he was afraid to leave. If he went for help Upton might die, might even get out of his bed and wander away, for the man was in delirium. Chance stuck to the cabin.

There was but little he could do. He stewed jerky, of

which he had a supply, and forced Upton to take some of the broth. He bathed the old man with tempered water, trying to lower the fever that raged in the giant body. He did what he could and it seemed to him that he was constantly falling back, that little by little the fight was going against him. So, for four days Chance stayed and worked, sallying out only to care for his horses, to get water, or to replenish the wood supply.

At about one o'clock in the morning of the fifth day, Upton lay quiet. His eyes were closed and his breathing shallow. Chance sat beside the bunk, the lamp on the table nearby shedding a yellow glow. Suddenly Upton opened his eyes. They were clear and the fever was gone from them. He looked at Chance.

Chance returned that look and Upton spoke. "You stuck by me," he said weakly but rationally.

"You're coming all right," Chance assured him, strength in his voice.

"No." The word was almost a gasp. "You're Jack Pagan's kid?"

"I'm Jack Pagan's son."

"Good man . . . Jack . . . Good man."

There was a pause then. Chance waited, listening to the shallow breathing, watching the eyes grow bright with fever again. Suddenly Upton spoke once more.

"Don't take my trail, Jack. Don't go to the Badlands." The bright eyes closed.

For a moment Chance listened, scarcely daring to breathe. Then Upton took another breath, a gasp, and then another. During that instant Chance thought the old man gone.

But now the breathing came more steadily. Chance, putting his hand on Upton's head, felt a little dampness there. He kept his hand on the old man's forehead, sitting stiffly, frozen in his chair. The breathing came more regularly and the moisture grew until Upton was sweating. Chance relaxed. This was the corner. They had turned it. Weariness, the strain of his ceaseless vigil, crept upon him. His head tilted forward to his chest and his eyes closed. In its chimney the ill-trimmed wick of the lamp smoked and the kerosene in the bowl grew lower, diminished, and disappeared. The lamp went out.

Later in the morning Chance, coming out of the chair, his body stiff and cramped, found sunlight streaming into the room. Water was already beginning to drip from the eaves. On the bunk Upton was relaxed and resting. He wakened while Chance was kindling the fire and his voice, while weak, was rational when he spoke.

"I've been pretty sick," said Upton.

"Pretty sick," Chance agreed, coming over to the bunk. "But you're all right now."

For a time Upton considered that statement, then he grinned. "As all right as I'll ever be," he said.

"Hungry?" asked Chance. "I'll make some soup."

"I reckon I'm hungry," said Upton. "I reckon I can eat some soup."

He did eat the soup that Chance prepared and after eating fell asleep. Chance stood looking at the old man. Upton had lost flesh in his illness. The portion of his face that Chance could see above the beard had fined.

Chance grinned. "You had pneumonia, old timer," he

said half to Upton, half to himself. "And you've got the guts of a grizzly or you'd never have pulled through. The Lord knows I didn't do much to help you." With that he turned and walking to the door took his coat from the nail where it hung.

"And you'll want a little beef, I reckon," Chance observed. "I could use some myself. Maybe there's a J Pen steer around here close, and if there is we'll have steaks for supper."

With no weight on his mind for the first time in six days, Chance put on his coat, pulled his hat down and went out.

He found the horses close to the corral and caught the bay that Nowlen had lent him. The bay was the gentlest horse in the bunch and the easiest to ride, now that Farmer had taken to pitching under a cold saddle. After a final look at Upton, sleeping on the bunk, Chance mounted the bay and rode a little circle from the ranch. The snow was going fast, the roofs of the buildings were already bare, and riding down to the stack yard north of the house, Chance came upon a spot where all the snow was gone. There was a small white blossom in that bare spot and Chance grinned at the flower. Spring was sure enough come.

At the stack yard he found a few cattle. There were several Spear cows, a Spear bull, half a dozen steers that carried the Spear. There was also a little NOW stuff and, just the thing that Chance was looking for, a J Pen yearling steer. Chance took down his rope, cut the steer from the bunch, and dropped his loop on it, and with the animal fighting and bawling, started back for the ranch.

Reaching the corrals he snubbed the steer up short beside the butchering scaffold and, fastening his rope, got the hammer from the barn. He came back, carrying the hammer and the single tree that was used in butchering. The yearling had ceased to fight the rope and was about choked down. Looking at the beef Chance grunted. That steer looked familiar. He had seen it some place, and recently. Cowmen know stock as other men know people, and Chance was a cowman.

Unable to recall where he had seen the animal, and thinking perhaps he had spotted it during a ride along the creek or in the roughs on the mesa benches, Chance advanced again. The hammer came down with a whack and a crunch, the steer folded up and dropped as far as the rope would permit, and putting the hammer aside Chance got out his knife and the small stone he carried, and set about the business of dressing the beef.

When the carcass, skinned and drawn, was hanging from the scaffolding, Chance went to the house with a bucket containing the heart and liver. Upton greeted Chance when he came in and Chance put the bucket on the table.

"I killed a steer," he announced. "Liver for dinner, and I'll feed you a steak tonight. How do you feel?"

"I feel all right," Upton answered. "Whose steer did you kill?"

"Mine," answered Chance stoutly. "Some fried spuds would go good with the liver, huh?"

"Most anything would go good," returned Upton. "That steer . . ."

"Say." Chance quit rummaging in the potato sack and

straightened up. "You talked some while you were sick. You kept talking to Jack. Was that my dad, Jack Pagan?"

"I've knowed lots of Jacks," Upton evaded the question and averted his eyes from Chance. "So I talked out of my head, did I?"

"Seemed to me that you were talking to Jack Pagan," Chance pursued. "You said something about him quitting and about lying for him, and you mentioned my mother's name, Molly."

"Did I?" Upton's voice trailed away. When he spoke again he looked squarely at Chance. "I knew your dad," he said. "I knew your mother, too. I reckon there's no harm in sayin' I was in love with her, but a better man got her. I want to tell you this: there never was a whiter, squarer man lived than Jack Pagan, and you ought to be proud, bein' his son. Nobody ever looked back to see if Jack was along."

Chance flushed. "I *am* proud," he defended.

"That's good." Upton's voice was flat. "Were you goin' to peel potatoes to go with that liver?"

So reminded, Chance went to work again and the subject was dropped.

But that night, when the promised steaks had gone the way of all good beef, and Chance had rolled Upton a smoke, the old man spoke again. "I was pretty sick," he said abruptly. "I'm obliged to you for seein' me through."

"I didn't do much," said Chance.

"I'm a horse-thief." Upton disregarded Chance's words. "I've stole horses, leastwise I've spent time in

60

the pen for that. Accordin' to what I hear I've stole other things, too. You put yoreself in a hole, bringin' me here. Why did you do it?"

"Why not?" Chance asked. "I own this place."

Upton nodded. "But yo're sidin' an outlaw," he reminded. "That'll class you with the wild bunch. You got to be careful."

"I got to do the right thing," Chance insisted.

"It's never right to ride the Badlands, kid."

Chance made no answer and after a moment Upton spoke musingly. "Funny how debts get paid," he said. "Someway they always do."

"What do you mean?" Chance looked sharply at the man on the bunk.

"I mean that's my tobacco yo're smokin'," drawled Upton. "You might at least roll me one."

Grinning, Chance produced papers and tobacco. "That's a debt that's easy paid," he said, twisting the brown cylinder. "I hope I can square myself as easy always."

"And so do I, kid," drawled Upton, and then more slowly: "So do I."

5

THE PROCESS OF CONVALESCENCE was a slow thing for Silvertip Upton. He had pulled through a siege of sickness that might readily have killed an ordinary man. Silvertip was not ordinary. In the week that followed the passing of his crisis, the old man proved that to Chance Pagan in more ways than one. Silvertip Upton had covered country in his day. He could and did talk of the far places, of the outlying lands where cattle ran and the cowman was King. Chance listened, enthralled. His own experiences seemed meager compared to those of his guest.

Sometimes the tales grew personal with word of a man here, a man there, a friend or an enemy. Without being told, Chance gathered that Silvertip had been through the mill, that he had looked through gun smoke and not come out second-best. Chance shared a thrill when the old man spoke of battle in some little town, beside some lonesome butte or in a sun-baked draw. That thrill was more real because Chance himself had looked through gun smoke. Once Chance Pagan, driving a jerkline team for a mining company in Mexico, had squatted behind an ore sack and worked a Winchester until its barrel was hot. The bandits, seeking to raid the train, had been driven off, leaving sundry of their companions. The dead bandits had been directly opposite Chance Pagan's wagon. Again, in Arizona, in a little fight along the border, Chance had rounded a rock, thrown his gun up, and slung lead into a man; but these had been fights in which there were many. Chance had never, standing on his own feet, without backing, gone up against another man who meant to kill him.

It is not to be supposed that Chance spent all his time at the J Pen waiting on Silvertip Upton or listening to his tales. He rode daily, covering the rough country along the Calico Mesa and following the course of Tomcat Creek to see that there were no cattle down in the bog. In the course of his riding he cut sign. There was another horseman in the country, a man who duplicated the work that Chance was doing. Seeing that sign Chance grinned. He knew that it was a Spear rider who had made the tracks, knew that the Spear was not trusting him, that Fahrion had put another man in the country. Chance did not bother to hunt that other rider, was not even particularly curious who it was. If the Spear man wanted to see him he could come to the J Pen, and Chance let it go at that.

Toward the end of the week Chance rode back to the J Pen from his bog riding. He was, at the moment, feeling particularly virtuous for he had rescued two Spear cows from the sucking bog and had stopped to act as midwife to a Spear cow that was having trouble with her calf. When he reached the cabin he saw two horses in the yard and set the black NOW horse along, anxious to meet his company.

One of the horses wore a Spear, the other carried a Quarter Circle M, Tom Melody's brand. Chance let the black horse stand in the yard, and walked into the house.

Silvertip was propped on the bed. The old man had insisted on dressing that morning, and except for his boots, he was fully clothed. On the box opposite him Bill Fahrion sat stiffly upright, and Tom Melody lounged in the single chair. Chance greeted them.

"Hello."

Melody got up to shake hands but Fahrion made no movement and Chance did not venture an overture toward the Spear foreman. He grinned at the sheriff, put his hat on a bench, and squatting against the wall, rolled a cigarette. "First time we've had company," he commented as he rolled the smoke.

"We ain't company exactly," drawled Melody. "I was on my way up to the basin and picked up Fahrion, so we stopped here. Won't have to make the trip now. How goes it, Chance?"

"Pretty good. I'm riding bog and working the roughs like a thirty-a-month hand." Chance threw the hook into Fahrion. "Helping Wayne out a little," he finished innocently.

"You wasn't asked to!" snapped Fahrion.

"No," agreed Chance, "I wasn't asked."

"I was just talkin' to Silvertip here," drawled Melody. "How come him to be with you, Chance?"

Chance looked sharply at the sheriff. Melody was serious and Chance saw an opportunity. "I ran out of smoking," he said, eyeing Melody. "Upton happened along and he had a boxful. We decided to sit right here till we smoked it up."

Tom Melody disregarded the facetiousness. "I want to know," he said soberly. "How did Silvertip come to be here an' how long has he been here?"

Chance also sobered. "We had a storm," he reminded. "Silvertip had some trouble that day it hit. I brought him in here and he was sick for a while. He's been here ever since."

"I told you how long and why I was here, Tom," interrupted Upton quietly. "Chance dragged me in or I'd have frozen to death. I had pneumonia. I've been here since the day of the storm. Now you let down your hair.

Why all the questions?"

"Because," drawled Melody slowly, "Charlie Kelleher, down below Cassidy, is missin' fifteen head of blooded horses."

Upton flushed. "I've told you," he said, "that the Basin lets the Calico Hole alone. You've known me a long time, Tom."

"I have," agreed Tom Melody, "and you've been fair," he added, his voice thoughtful. "Still there's new faces in the Basin an' new talent."

"An' you ain't forgotten that I served time as a horse-thief," snapped Upton. "Tom . . ."

"Now, wait," Melody admonished swiftly. "I've known you a long time, like you say. You've played fair with me an' I aim to be fair with you. There could be things happen in the Basin that you don't know about. But yo're boss of the Basin. Keep it straight or *I'll* do it."

"You mean that you'll clean the Basin?" Silvertip's voice was level. "It's been tried, Tom."

"But never by me. Line 'em up, Silvertip, or line 'em out!"

Chance Pagan stared at Tom Melody. He had not known that the sheriff could be so direct, so hard.

"Another thing, Silvertip," Melody's drawl continued. "Let Chance here alone."

Upton's face flushed. Chance came to his feet. "Silvertip's visitin' me . . ." he began.

"Sit down, kid," ordered Silvertip, his voice deep. "You've served yore notice, Tom. I heard you."

Melody nodded. He had served his notice; he had

nothing more to say. In the flat quiet and the tension, Bill Fahrion threw in his voice. Bill Fahrion, fool!

"I never thought that you'd harbor an outlaw, Pagan," he stated. "Maybe that's why the Spear steers disappear so easy. We've lost some."

Chance, who had not seated himself as commanded, whirled to face the speaker. "Meaning?" he snapped.

"Meanin' that the Spear has mislaid some steers," drawled Melody. "Bill . . ."

"Keep out of this, Tom!" warned Chance. "Meaning what, Fahrion?"

Fahrion did not answer. Instead he asked a question. "I see a fresh steer hide on the corral fence. You butcherin' much these days?"

"A J Pen steer!" snapped Chance. "The brand is on the hide. What did you mean by that other crack, Fahrion?"

Old Tom Melody got up stiffly. Here, right under his nose, was grief. Chance carried a gun on his hip, a gun that swung high and apparently out of easy reach. Bill Fahrion had a gun in the trouser band of his Levi overalls. It lay right at his hand.

"Chance . . ." Melody began uneasily.

But Fahrion interrupted. "That's another thing that's on my mind," he said. "The Spear has been brandin' calves each year to pay you for your vega hay. The Spear fenced the vega and you've never paid 'em for that. I want to tell you, Pagan, that we'll brand you no calves this spring."

"You owe me for the hay you cut last year," Chance stated flatly. "You'll brand calves or pay money."

Fahrion grunted. "Show me the writin'," he said. "I'm responsible for the Spear now."

"But . . ." Chance began.

"You've rooked the Spear long enough," snapped Fahrion.

Chance was mad, all the way through. Deliberately he walked two steps and stood, looking at Fahrion. Fahrion's hand was on his lap, scant inches from his gun.

"You come in here and tell me that I'm letting Spear steers leak through," said Chance quietly. "You tell me that I've rooked the Spear and that you won't pay me for the hay that you've cut and used. If you hadn't had the hay your cattle would have winter-killed, but that's all right with you. You used it, and now you tell me you won't pay. Now I'll tell you, Fahrion! You'll pay me for the hay you cut. I'll see to that. You'll cut no more off the J Pen vega until Wayne gets back and I've seen him. As for me takin' Spear steers . . . you are a liar!"

That was the fighting word. Fahrion dropped his hand to his gun, twisting on the box as he did so. Bill Fahrion had killed a man and he was ready and more than willing to kill another. Tom Melody, with the trouble at a head, also reached for his gun. Melody was fast, had been forced to be fast more than once, and he wanted to avert a calamity. But he was not fast enough this time. Chance Pagan slapped at that gun, so awkwardly placed at his hip, and it was in his hand, cocked and pointed, before Melody or Fahrion could move.

"Get out!" snarled Chance Pagan. "Get out, both of you!"

Tom Melody let go a long sigh. If there was to have been a killing it would have been all over by now. Chance would not have talked; he would have pulled and shot. Bill Fahrion, face losing its color, got up from the box, his hand clear of his gun.

"It looks to me like we'd better go, Bill," drawled Melody. He waited until Fahrion moved to the door. Chance, gun still drawn, turned to watch the Spear foreman. When the door had been opened and Fahrion was outside, Melody spoke once more.

"I reckon," he said cryptically, "that you'll do to take along, Chance." Then, with a smile, he walked after the other man. Pausing at the door he flung back a parting word. "I'll be back to visit with you, Chance. Silvertip, don't forget what I told you." The door closed after him.

For perhaps five minutes after the two were gone, Silvertip Upton and Chance were silent. Then Silvertip asked a question. "Why didn't you shoot, kid? You had it on him. He'd reached."

"I don't know," said Chance. "He looked so damn' helpless, someway . . ."

"Jack wouldn't of shot, either," commented Upton. "How the devil did you snake out yore gun so fast? It looks like you couldn't reach it where you wear it."

"Holster," answered Chance. "I got a new kind from Myres, down in El Paso. It's got an open front."

"Let's see," ordered Upton.

Obligingly Chance showed the old man the holster on his belt. It was of heavy, carved leather, the work of a master hand. The front of the holster was open and the gun was held in place by a steel spring, shaped to it, and leather-covered.

"Hmmmmm," grunted Silvertip. "We live an' learn, don't we? Man goin' up against that might not live, but he'd learn a heap."

"They're new down along the border," observed Chance.

"But their use is goin' to spread," said Upton. "You know, I been sort of worried about you."

"Why?"

"Because of knowin' you. I ain't worried no more."

"I can look after myself if that's what you mean."

"That ain't exactly what I meant but it amounts to the same thing." Upton stroked his beard. "I reckon," he continued, "that I'd better pull out of here. Tom gave me fair warnin'."

"You can stay as long as you like," snapped Chance. "No man can be run off my place!"

"I know." Silvertip nodded. "That ain't it. I got things to do. I'll be leavin'."

"You ain't strong enough to ride," objected Chance.

"I ain't strong enough not to ride," corrected Silvertip. "Would you humor an old man an' have a can of them apricots for supper?"

Brought back to earth, Chance assured Upton that they would have the fruit for supper, and picking up his hat went out to look after the black horse.

Riding away from the J Pen, Tom Melody and Bill Fahrion also held their peace for some time. Indeed they had covered a mile before Melody spoke. "Bill," he drawled, "yo're livin' on borried time. If that kid had shot . . . shucks!"

Fahrion made no answer and Melody drawled on. "Why did you want to rile him? What's he done to you?"

"He came back here expectin' to run the Spear," growled Fahrion.

"An' why not?" Sharply. "Wayne had sent for him. Wayne brought him up, an' sent for him to come. He quit his job an' come a-runnin'."

"Because of what was in it."

"Because he likes Wayne Elder," corrected Melody. "Listen: he came back here. Wayne tells him that you're to run the Spear. The kid said that it was all right, that he'd go hold down the J Pen for the rest of the season and that he'd make Wayne a hand without pay. He meant it, too. What do you do? You rub him the wrong way every chance you get. I don't figure you, Bill."

"He's up there on the roughs an' we found Upton with him."

"An' we know he pulled Upton in out of the blizzard an' nursed him through a siege of pneumonia."

"That's what *they* say."

Tom Melody gave an impatient shrug. "An' that's what happened," he snapped. "Bill, yo're a fool! There's no use arguin' with a hard-headed idiot like you. You leave Chance alone; don't you go near him. When Wayne gets back he'll straighten all this out."

"If he straightens it out with Pagan he can give me my time."

"I wouldn't blame him if he did. Yo're jealous an' yo're hot-tempered an' you can't keep yore mouth shut.

You make me tired!"

Melody, his indictment done, waited for Fahrion to speak. Fahrion was moodily silent. In the back of his head Bill Fahrion knew that Melody had spoken the truth and that the right thing to do would be to go back, tell Chance Pagan that he had made a mistake, and own up to his fault. He couldn't do it. There were other men in the Calico Hole with stiff-necked pride, other men beside Chance Pagan.

"One thing you want to remember," Melody drawled again, "yo're sittin' there danglin' yore legs over leather because Chance didn't pull the trigger. Better keep that in mind, Bill."

At the J Pen there were apricots for supper, apricots and sour dough biscuits and steak and coffee. After supper Silvertip Upton talked. He talked while the dishes were washed and he talked while cigarettes were rolled, and he talked even after the lamp was out and they were in bed. Not once during the conversation did he refer to the happening of the afternoon and when Chance brought it up Silvertip turned the subject.

In the morning when they got up, Silvertip dressed and put on his boots. He walked around the cabin and seemingly was a well, strong man. Chance warned him not to try to ride, not to leave the J Pen for a day or two, and was tempted to stay and see that his warning was heeded. But when he spoke of staying Silvertip reminded him of the Tomcat bog and was so insistent, so urgent, that Chance saw that the old man would think he was spying if he stayed. He knew that Silvertip was going to leave, knew it and could not stop him, and so, when he ran in the horses, he left Silvertip's mount in the corral.

Chance left on his ride, bidding Upton a casual good-bye. Upton, too, was casual. When Chance had gone a mile he chose a knoll for a vantage point and stayed there, watching. He saw Silvertip come out of the cabin, saw the old man catch his horse, saddle, and ride away. Silvertip did not ride south, toward the mesa, but northeast toward Big Muddy. That puzzled Chance but he shrugged and turned to his own business, a little hurt by the treatment he had received from the man whose life he had saved.

That hurt was healed when, coming back to the J Pen early in the afternoon, he found a scrawled message on the table.

"I won't forget it, kid. So long and thanks. S. Upton."

Chance grinned and put the note on the shelf. It was so typical, so like the man who had written it, that he wanted to keep it.

6

WHEN SILVERTIP UPTON left the J Pen he rode northeast toward the Big Muddy. He had not wanted to leave the J Pen, had not wanted to go at all. Indeed he was in no physical condition to do the things he had laid out for himself to do, but he knew that he could not wait longer. Upton occupied an odd position in the Basin. Known as an outlaw, he had paid a debt to society by serving four years in the penitentiary. Since that sentence Upton had indulged in a good many lawless activities and had not been caught.

In the Basin he was a leader, *the* leader. The Basin, atop Calico Mesa and in the heart of the badlands, was an ideal hiding place. Upton had found it. Upton had settled there and gradually a little cluster of shacks had grown up about his original cabin. Men came and went from these shacks, riding out on secret errands and returning, sometimes wounded, sometimes flushed with success. There was one unwritten law in the Basin: no man led a posse to it and no man living in the Basin tampered with the livestock or with the activities of the lawful citizens in Calico Hole. That law Silvertip Upton enforced to the hilt. Tom Melody knew of that law and, respecting it, let the Basin alone. Other officers had tried their luck with the Basin and had given it up as a bad job. The men they sought were never to be found when they rode into the quiet settlement, and hard-eyed men watched their every move, placid, cool, as ready to kill as a rattlesnake on the hunt. The officers rode out again.

But the Basin was changing. Upton was putting on age. There were new men in the hole, for not all of the original settlers returned from their riding. Tully Pillow had come, throwing up a long log store building and stocking it . . . humpbacked Tully, with a sawed-off shotgun that he slung under his arm, his twisted grin and his ability to collect what was owed him. Tully made a link with the outside world and now, occasionally, riders came directly to the Basin from whatever piece of lawlessness they had performed. Tully was a fence, a way of disposing of goods and money. The Basin grew, Tully prospered, and Silvertip Upton watched anxiously, still trying to enforce his unwritten law.

When he crossed the Big Muddy, Upton kept on northeast and some two hours and a half after leaving the J Pen reached the NOW. He was almost exhausted by his ride but he fought against showing it. It would not do, on his present errand, to appear as anything but strong. Leaving his horse to stand before the NOW house, the old man walked to the door and pushed it open.

There were three men in the room he entered. Cliff Nowlen, Art Ragland and a smoothly built, black-haired man, Sam Pasmore. Upton nodded to the three, came on into the room, and sat down in a rawhide-bottomed chair.

"I thought mebbe I'd find you here," he stated.

"You been gone, Silvertip," Ragland smiled at the old man. "What happened to you? Have a good trip?"

"Good enough," answered Silvertip. "I got caught in the blizzard, lost my horse, and if it hadn't been for Chance Pagan I wouldn't be here."

The three exchanged glances and Nowlen, smiling at Upton, spoke. "We heard that there had been some horses missin' down below," he stated. "We thought that maybe . . ."

"That maybe I'd stolen 'em?" finished Upton. "I'm out of the horse business an' you know it."

Ragland nodded. "Banks an' trains are more yore

line, ain't they?" he asked innocently.

"Never mind my line," grated Upton. "What I'm here to see you about is somethin' else. Tom Melody come out to the J Pen. There's Spear steers missin'."

"Pshaw," Pasmore's voice held a little amusement. "Now, that's too bad. Reckon they winter-killed?"

"They was stolen," Upton stated bluntly.

Nowlen sat with a fixed grin on his face and Ragland made a little clucking sound with his tongue against his teeth.

"I know you fello's," Silvertip said slowly. "I've never butted into yore business no more than you have in mine, but I know you. I thought we might talk a mite."

"About what?" Nowlen's voice was innocence itself.

"About steers an' such," Silvertip matched Nowlen's smoothness. "Cliff, yo're a cowman an' you know how it upsets a man to find steers missin'. Art, you an' Sam have dealt in cattle in the past. You ought to feel for the Spear. I just wanted to remind you that the Basin is a hideout, not a place to work from. We live in the Basin an' we let the Calico Hole alone. *All* of us let it alone!"

"Tom Melody must have throwed the fear of God into you," commented Pasmore, smoothing the tip of his small mustache.

"Tom Melody told me to straighten out the Basin," stated Upton bluntly.

"Then you *are* scared?"

"How scared do you think I am?" snapped Silvertip. "I knew where to find you, didn't I? I came in here."

"And that's somethin' I don't understand." Nowlen spoke smoothly. "How could you hook me up with any stolen cattle?"

Upton grunted. "Easy. You an' you," he leveled a blunt forefinger at Pasmore then at Ragland, "stole a hundred head of O Slash heifers last year. You," the forefinger indicated Nowlen, "marketed 'em. They all wore a NOW when they went into the cars at Cassidy. You split the money three ways. That was none of my business. The O Slash is a hundred miles south. But the Hole *is* my business. Lay off the Hole!"

With that command Upton got up and holding himself stiff, stalked out of the door. He had served warning that the law of the Basin would be enforced.

Left alone the three men in the room stared at each other. Ragland was the first to speak. "How in hell did he know about that O Slash deal?" he demanded.

"How do I know?" Pasmore's voice was wrathful. "I didn't leak, Nowlen, if you talked . . ."

"An' hang myself?" demanded Nowlen. "Do you think I'm a fool?"

There was silence for a moment and then Ragland spoke again. "What do you aim to do?"

Pasmore grunted. "Talk to Pillow," he said. "He's got brains . . ."

"If you think I'm goin' to be bluffed by that old devil, you made a mistake," Nowlen blurted. "I've got a chance to make some money. The way we've figured, it's perfect. With the hay to feed an' all . . ."

"Upton's too big for his pants," snarled Ragland savagely. "He don't run the Basin. He used to, maybe, but he's got some competition now."

Nowlen turned to the others. "You started too early,"

he accused. "I told you we couldn't handle any cattle till fall. I told you . . ."

"Shut up!" snapped Pasmore. "Come on, Art. Let's ride up an' see Pillow."

"I'm going with you," Nowlen stated. "Wait till I get a horse."

Silvertip, leaving the NOW, rode toward the south. He had done part of what he had set out to do, but there was still more. Silvertip knew Tully Pillow, knew him for the grasping, cold blooded, brainy devil that he was. Silvertip knew that it lay between himself and Pillow. There was a showdown coming and riding south Silvertip wondered if it were wise to precipitate that showdown. Should he act at once, or should he wait? That, he decided grimly, would depend upon who was in the Basin. The Basin was really made up of two camps. There were those who dealt in cattle and horses and who looked with longing eyes upon the fat cattle in the Calico Hole; and there were others, men whose activities were not with livestock, who wanted the Basin to remain as it was, a peaceful hiding place. Silvertip could count upon those last if they were in the Basin.

The old man's ride had exhausted him and he had not rested at the NOW. Indeed, that interview had been more tiring than the ride. From time to time he rocked slightly in his saddle, but he kept grimly on. If he stopped, if he dismounted, he feared that he could not climb back on his horse, and there was distance to make to the Basin.

For almost two hours Silvertip rode and at the end of

that time he was clinging to his saddle, only determination keeping him going. He had by now reached the roughs at the foot of the mesa and was making for a horse trail that went up through a break in the rimrock. He could not see well through his bloodshot eyes and consequently he failed to discern a rider coming down the trail until that rider was almost upon him.

Startled, Upton let go his grip on the fork and reached back for his gun. The movement was almost his undoing for he was weak. He swayed in the saddle and nearly fell, reaching back to clutch the horn again and so saving himself. In the next moment the rider was beside him and Arlie Pillow was holding him up.

"Silvertip!" exclaimed Arlie. "Are you hurt? Have you been shot?"

Silvertip managed to grin. "I'm all in," he said weakly. "I been sick. Reckon you could help me down, girl?"

"Of course." Arlie made a quick movement as though to dismount.

"Not here," Silvertip was quick. "Get me off the trail."

The girl took the dangling reins and leading Upton's horse, left the trail. With native caution she proceeded until they were hidden in a wash, and then dismounting, helped Silvertip down from the saddle. The old man sprawled on the dry sand of the wash bank and the girl tied the horses to scrub oak and returned to him.

"Is there anything . . . ?" she began.

"Rest a minute," muttered Silvertip. "All right after I rest a minute."

Arlie sat down beside the old man, watching him anxiously. Silvertip was relaxed, flat on the sand, his chest rising and falling slowly as he breathed.

For perhaps fifteen minutes man and girl were quiet. Arlie arranged Silvertip's hat to shade his eyes from the sun and then stayed quietly beside him.

Finally Silvertip spoke. "Who is at the Basin?"

The girl thought before answering. "There's Ragland and Pasmore," she counted, "and Bert Ladeaux and Conroy and two new men that came in with Conroy."

"The Kid and Blaney and Poncho?" questioned Upton.

"They aren't there."

"I'll have to wait." Silvertip's voice was low.

In the silence that followed there came a clatter of hoofs. "Who is that?" breathed Upton.

Arlie got to her feet, peered over the edge of the wash, and then sank down again. "Ragland," she said. "Ragland and Pasmore and Cliff Nowlen."

Silvertip grunted.

"Shall I call them?" asked Arlie. "They could take you in . . ."

"No!" Hoarsely.

The sound of the horses diminished. Arlie looked her anxiety. Silvertip lay quiet.

"Girl," he said suddenly, some strength in his voice again, "there's trouble comin' in the Basin. Have you got any place you could go?"

Arlie shook her head. "No," she answered, "my mother's folks wouldn't have anything to do with her after she married Pillow. I couldn't go to them. I haven't seen any of them since I was five years old. I don't even know where they live."

Upton thought that over. "Then you got to stay with yore step-dad," he said. "Look, Arlie: if anything happens to me, you light out of the Basin; you get away from Pillow an' go to Chance Pagan. Tell him that I sent you an' that I asked him to look after you."

"Chance Pagan?"

"Yes. Him. I got a kind of a claim on him." A smile parted the heavy gray beard momentarily. "He saved my life for me an' I reckon that gives me a claim. You go to Chance, will you?"

"I will," the girl promised unhesitatingly. "I will, Silvertip."

"I reckon I can make it the rest of the way in now," said Upton. He struggled to a sitting position, straightened his hat, and looked at Arlie. "You stay with me till we're almost at the Basin, then let me go in alone."

"But you're sick," Arlie protested. "You . . ."

"I'll be sicker if you don't," answered Silvertip. "Will you do it?"

The girl nodded.

"Then bring the horses," Silvertip directed. "You'll have to help me up, I reckon."

The girl arose to obey. Helping the old man into his saddle she watched him as he gathered the reins and started his horse, and anxiously rode behind him as they took the trail again. But the rest had strengthened Upton. Grimly he held to his saddle, and rode steadily. Just before the two reached the Basin, Silvertip spoke again.

"I'm goin' to have to stick close to home awhile," he said. "I'll show myself though. Arlie, if you could come over an' visit me once in a while, you'd help a heap."

"I'll come, Silvertip," assured the girl.

"Good. Then you split off here. Circle around an' come in from the south—an' Arlie, you ain't seen me an' you don't know a thing about me."

"Of course," Arlie said simply. "And I'll come tonight, Silvertip."

She waited until Silvertip's horse, walking ahead, was out of sight around a clump of cedar, then turning her horse she rode west so that she would circle the Basin. Arlie Pillow loved Silvertip Upton and obeyed him unquestioningly. Of all the men in the Basin he was the only one who was kind to her, who treated her as a woman, to be respected and guarded. The rest . . . Arlie shuddered as she thought of the others. Pillow, her step-father, was brutal; Art Ragland treated her as a small girl, a nuisance to be tolerated; the Kid and Blaney, taking their cue from Upton, let her alone; but Sam Pasmore . . . Sam Pasmore was aware that she was a woman. Only the day before Sam Pasmore had stopped her outside the store, his eyes bold and his voice soft. Arlie had fled from Sam Pasmore. Circling the Basin, staying to the rim above the half-mile hollow, Arlie came to the south end and then riding the trail that so many lawless men had ridden, she entered the little set-tlement. As Arlie Pillow came in, Cliff Nowlen rode out to the north. The girl, seeing him go, had no idea as to his errand.

Cliff Nowlen, leaving the Basin, had a very definite

mission. He, with Ragland and Pasmore, had talked with Pillow, and the little humpbacked storekeeper had heard them through in silence. When they finished, Pillow shrugged.

"Silvertip's bluffin'," stated Pillow flatly. "The men that might back him ain't here now an' he won't turn a hand till they get back." He paused after that statement and tittered a little. "Hee, hee, hee. They ain't comin' back!"

"What do you mean?" asked Pasmore.

"I mean that they planned to hold up a bank in Las Cruces," answered Pillow. "Know who's sheriff in Cruces?"

"Jose Gonzales," Ragland answered. "He's . . ."

"He's poison," stated Pillow, "an' he knows they're comin'."

"He knows what?"

"Knows they're comin' an' why." Pillow tittered again. "I wrote him a letter. Mailed it in Cassidy. Jose will be waitin' with about twenty of his relations. The Kid an' Blaney an' Poncho ain't comin' back to the Basin."

"You turned 'em in?" Ragland, his eyes narrow, looked at Pillow. "You put 'em right square against it?"

Pillow shrugged and suddenly his voice was sharp. "I turned 'em in," he stated. "From now on I'm runnin' the Basin. It wouldn't have been so easy with them backin' Silvertip. An' what are you goin' to do about it, Art?"

As he spoke Pillow's hand swung at his side and stopped. Art Ragland considered that stationary hand. He knew that Pillow carried a sawed-off shotgun, slung under his shoulder by a strap. He knew that, with a flip of the now motionless hand, Pillow could swing that shotgun up, that the other hand could dart across from the suspender strap it now held, and that in a split second two charges of buckshot could belch from the muzzles of the shotgun. Art Ragland had seen that shotgun in action. He thought he could beat it, but he did not want to try.

"I'm goin' to move into Blaney's cabin in a couple of days," Ragland said, answering Pillow's question. "It's a better shack than mine."

Pillow grinned. "I thought so," he said, and the motionless hand resumed its little swing. "Cliff, you ought to ride down an' see what happened when Melody talked to Silvertip. You work it right an' Pagan will tell you. I want to know."

"I'll stop there tonight," assured Nowlen. "Want me to bring back word?"

"How else will I get it?" demanded Pillow. "Now you boys wait until I give the word. I'm runnin' this an' I'll tell you when we'll skin out our Silvertip. Hee, hee, hee."

So it was, when Cliff Nowlen left the Basin, he had a very definite mission and objective. He headed straight for the J Pen as soon as he was below the hill.

Chance, having finished his ride along Tomcat Creek, was at the ranch when Nowlen came in. He greeted Cliff warmly and when Nowlen announced that he would stay the night, Chance quit his work at the wood-pile and began supper preparations. Nowlen, efficient and friendly, aided in the work and the two sat down to a good meal.

"How things been goin', Chance?" asked Nowlen across the table. "I ain't seen you since you came to the ranch. How are the horses doin'?"

"Fine," answered Chance, spearing a piece of steak. "That sorrel bucked like blazes but he's goin' to make a good horse. The buckskin is comin' all right, an' the other two always were good horses from the way they act. Only one thing that bothers me is Farmer has decided he can buck. He makes a man ride."

"Goin' outlaw, huh?" asked Nowlen. "How'd you make out through the storm?"

"All right," Chance answered. "I had company. Silvertip Upton was here holed up with me."

Nowlen raised his eyebrows but Chance did not elaborate and Nowlen let it go. "Anybody else drop in?" he asked innocently.

Chance grunted. "Tom Melody an' Fahrion," he said. "Say, Cliff, you been missin' any cattle?"

Nowlen shook his head. "The boys ain't reported any," he said. "A few winter-killed every year. If I had some hay I could come through better, but I ain't got but a little jag. Why?"

"The Spear's lost some steers," said Chance, "and Charlie Kelleher some horses. Melody was on the prod."

Nowlen chewed a mouthful and swallowing, spoke. "I don't like that," he stated.

"Melody didn't either."

"Was Fahrion friendly?" Nowlen asked.

"No!" Chance scowled. "He said that I was lettin'

stolen cattle leak through and into the Badlands. He seems to think that the Basin is working the Hole country, and so does Melody."

"The Hole!" Nowlen made his voice express incredulity. "The Basin has always let the Hole alone."

"That's what Silvertip told Melody," said Chance. "Melody didn't seem to believe it."

Nowlen, his eyes narrow, asked another question. "What do you think?"

"I think that Fahrion's not cowman enough to know whether he's had cattle stolen or winter-killed!" Chance answered. "Know what he did? He came in here and told me that the Spear wouldn't brand me calves this spring to pay for the hay they cut; that's what he told me!"

"Well I'll be damned! What did you say, Chance?"

"I told him I'd collect for the hay," snapped Chance. "I will, too!"

"How?"

"Never you mind how. I'll collect. And another thing: there'll be no more hay cut from my vega by the Spear until they get this straightened out."

Here was opportunity. Nowlen took it. "Look here, Chance," he said, "I don't know exactly how your dicker was with the Spear, but I could use the hay off your vega myself. How about makin' a deal with me?"

"With you?" Chance looked up from his plate. "Why Cliff, there's two sections of this vega and we cut half a ton to the acre. Your bunch of cattle wouldn't eat that much hay in two years."

"I'm goin' to have more cattle," said Nowlen. "What

kind of deal will you make with me, Chance?"

"I can't make a deal," Chance announced slowly. "The Spear had first call on the hayland and . . ."

"After the way Fahrion's treated you?"

"Fahrion isn't Wayne Elder. I'll wait till Wayne comes back. If Wayne an' me can't get together I'll come to you. How is that?"

"I reckon it'll have to do." Nowlen hid his disappointment. "Pass the steak, Chance."

There was nothing more said concerning the vega land that night nor was the subject mentioned when, the following morning, Cliff Nowlen saddled his horse and rode away from the J Pen. Nowlen was hearty, cheerful and good natured, and his visit served to implant him more firmly in Chance Pagan's mind as a real friend.

7

SILVERTIP UPTON was of the old breed. He could go until he dropped and then be dangerous. There was one way to put Silvertip down: kill him! When he left Arlie Pillow he stuck to his horse until he reached his cabin situated on a knoll above the store. He managed, grimly, to stay on his feet until he had his horse in the stable behind the shack. Stable and living-room were in one building, for Silvertip did not believe in being separated from his horse. In the stable Silvertip managed to loosen his cinch, and then sprawled out.

For awhile he lay where he had fallen. The old man was done with pneumonia but it had left him weak and his wrenched back pained like fury. After a time he caught hold of a post, pulled himself up and clinging first to the post and then leaning against the wall, made it to the door that connected the stable with his living quarters. Inside the dark little room in which he lived, Silvertip took two staggering steps and fell flat on the bed. He was lying there when, later, Arlie Pillow came.

Arlie, having left Silvertip, rode a circle around the Basin. She expected to be scolded when she came in, railed at and cursed, for it was late. Arlie was a drudge, a slavey for the humpbacked little man that kept the store. Arlie had one freedom, only one relief from drudgery: her pony. Pillow loved horses. The big Clydesdales were the pride of his life and let something happen to one of them and Pillow was up and out, ready to spend a day or a night or a week serving the animal. That was the little man's weak spot, his horses, and being weak in that manner he said nothing against Arlie's having a horse. Silvertip had given her the pony that she rode and Pillow allowed her to keep it. Indeed, he even condoned her absences when she rode the horse, snarling at her when she returned from a ride, but going no further so long as she had performed her work about the place.

There were other occasions when Pillow was not so kind. He had struck the girl, slapped her, and twice had taken a whip and lashed her quivering back until there was blood on the thin calico.

With her pony cared for Arlie went to the house and set to work. She was there when Pillow thrust his head into the kitchen and snarled at her. But he could find no real fault. The kitchen was clean and a meal was almost ready. Still snarling, however, the little man withdrew.

Arlie had no chance to slip away until after supper. After the meal Pillow was busy in the store and Arlie, piling a plate full of food, went to Silvertip's cabin. There she fed the old man, made him comfortable on the bunk, pulled off his boots, and brought a bucket of water and a dipper to put beside the bed. That was all she could do, and promising that she would return in the morning, she went back to her work.

The next day was a busy one for the girl. Pillow was unusually vicious and the girl had no surcease from him through the day. She managed to steal time from her tasks to visit Silvertip, and found the old man better; but when she returned to the kitchen and living quarters back of the store, Pillow was waiting for her with a bitter tongue.

Toward evening Pillow left her alone. He spent his time in the store and when Arlie, beginning supper preparations, peeked through the door to the store she saw that Pillow was with Ragland and Pasmore. Accordingly she put three places on the table, and when supper was ready called the men.

The three came at her summons, seated themselves, and disregarding Arlie, thinking no more of her than they might of an extra chair, they continued their conversation. This concerned Cliff Nowlen, the vega, and possible sources of cattle. Arlie heard them but could make nothing of what they said.

Having finished the meal Pillow and his companions

went out, and Arlie, snatching hasty bits for herself, placed food in a pan preparatory to carrying it over to Silvertip. As she busied herself she heard a disturbance in the store and went to the door to listen. Pillow was berating someone.

"Why didn't you tell me Buck was down?" rasped Pillow as Arlie opened the door a crack. "Why didn't you come in when he got to actin' sick? I've told you to watch that horse. Damn you, Benito!"

Pillow was snarling at Benito Piaz, the man who looked after the Clydesdales and who acted as handyman about the store. Arlie could see Benito cringing before the angry hunchback, and the grinning Ragland and Pasmore standing beside the counter.

"He's got the colic again," grated Pillow. "Where's that laudanum? Damn you, Benito! I told you . . ."

Arlie closed the door. She knew now what had happened. Buck, one of the Clydesdales, had broken into the grain box the week before and had almost foundered himself. Pillow had spent a night and part of the next day with the horse. Now Buck was sick again. The girl let go a relieved sigh. She would not have to slip away to Silvertip's. Pillow would be at the stable for a long time, watching his favorite, and she would be free.

The little hunchback, followed by Benito, came stamping out through the kitchen. With no word to Arlie he snatched tea towels from the rack, picked up the kettle of hot water from the stove, and growling over his shoulder at Benito, went on out. Arlie watched him. When Pillow was gone she put more water on the stove in a bucket and dipped dishwater from the well beside the stove, putting it in the dishpan. Pillow would be back for more hot water and she must wait.

As she worked, washing the dishes and drying them, she heard the door from the store open and, looking up, saw Pasmore in the opening. Arlie continued with her work, avoiding Pasmore's gaze. Pasmore came into the kitchen. "Let the dishes go awhile," he ordered. "I want to talk to you."

"Father will be mad if I don't get my work done," Arlie answered, trying to keep the tremor from her voice.

Pasmore laughed. "He'll never know," he said. "He's down at the barn workin' with a horse. He won't be back till mornin'. You and me got the night ahead of us, girl. Come here."

As he spoke the man extended a hand. Arlie, moving around the table, avoided it.

"What's the matter with you?" Pasmore demanded.

"Let me alone!" Arlie could no longer control her voice.

Pasmore laughed again. "Why won't you be nice?" he asked. "Afraid of me, are you? I'll treat you right. All you got to do is . . . ." Again he made a swift movement. This time his hand touched the thin calico that covered Arlie's shoulder. There was a ripping sound as the girl pulled free. The sight of that rounded, white shoulder inflamed Pasmore. His eyes gleamed and his teeth, even and white and small, showed as his full lips parted. He started around the table. Arlie fled from him.

"Let me alone," she cried again, fear in her voice and

eyes. "You let me alone!"

"Damn you!" Pasmore snarled, "I've wanted you a long time. Now I'll have you. You . . ."

The table was between the inflamed man and the girl. Desperate, Arlie gave the table a shove. The dishpan, full of water, clanged to the floor. For a moment Pasmore was balked, and in that moment Arlie jerked open the back door of the kitchen and fled. There was but one place where she might be safe. Instinctively she sought it. Running from the kitchen she made her way up a rise to where Silvertip's cabin stood, a black block in the dusk. In another instant Pasmore came through the door, hesitated an instant, and then seeing the running girl, came after her.

Arlie screamed then, once, a terror-stricken cry. On his bunk in the cabin Silvertip heard that scream, heard it dimly through the lassitude that held him, and fighting against that debility, struggled to a sitting position. He was there on his bunk, amidst the tumbled bedding, when the door of his cabin was flung open and Arlie Pillow ran through.

"What . . . ?" began Silvertip, dazed. "What . . . ?"

Arlie came to that voice. She flung herself at the man on the bunk, her arms about his neck, her body hampering his movements. The force of her assault almost sent Silvertip back on the bed. He pushed at the girl, striving to free himself, but Arlie clung with the strength of desperation. Another figure showed in the doorway. A man stood there, black against the gray of the sky. He paused there and then came in, came stealthily, like some jungle cat stalking its prey.

"An' now, by God," snarled Pasmore, "I've got you!"

"Pasmore!" Silvertip's voice stopped the advance. "Pasmore!"

"So yo're here, too?" snarled Pasmore. There was a swift movement and from the darkness beside the door Pasmore laughed.

"That's fine. We'll just make this unanimous. I been wantin' a bear hide a long time, Upton: A Silvertip's hide!"

"Let go, girl!" Silvertip's whisper was a fierce rasp. "Let go an' get to the floor!" The arms about his neck clung all the tighter. Pasmore moved a little and there came the three distinct clicks of a cocking single-action Colt.

In front of Pillow's store a horse stopped and a man dismounted, and in Silvertip's cabin Arlie Pillow screamed, a long rising wail of terror.

In the morning after Nowlen had ridden away toward the east, Chance caught a horse and went about his own business. He rode that day, the country west of the vega, and in his riding he again cut the sign of another rider.

Chance was not pleased with himself. He was worried, first concerning Nowlen's offer, and again concerning Wayne Elder. He had, of course, received no word from Wayne. He was worried too about Silvertip. Chance knew that he should have kept Silvertip at the J Pen, blamed himself for letting the old man go, and in the afternoon he cut his ride short, turned and went back home.

At the J Pen he ate a hasty snack, caught a fresh horse,

and saddling, set out toward the south. Chance had decided to ride to the Basin and see that Silvertip had got home all right. The decision relieved his mind and he was cheerful as he took the wagon road west of the vega and started up the hill.

Riding along the road Chance saw several Spear cows and a few Spear calves. They were pretty high up, he thought and he was tempted to give them a push back toward the flat, but refrained. Some of the calves were sizeable, for this was an open range country and calves came at all seasons of the year. Eyeing one of those big calves Chance grinned to himself.

He was sore at the Spear, sore and angry at the treatment he had received from Fahrion. Fahrion had declared that the Spear would not pay for the hay they had cut from the J Pen vega, and Chance had replied that he would collect for that hay. Chance knew that he had only to await Wayne Elder's return and all the difficulty would be settled, but that did not suit him. He wanted to collect from Fahrion, wanted to show Fahrion up as a poor cowman, wanted to get even, which was a very natural feeling under the circumstances.

Big calves figured largely in the plan Chance had concerning that collecting. Riding up the wagon road Chance wished that he had asked Nowlen concerning the time when the round-up wagon would go out. That date was essential to his scheme. Chance planned, as a collection measure, to take the calves owing him. This he could do simply enough. He had only to wait until the round-up began and a section of country about the J

Pen had been worked. Then when things were right he would pick up twenty head of Spear cows, cows that were nursing big calves, December and January calves. These he would drive around behind the round-up, into the country that had already been worked. He would pen the calves in a canyon, building a brush fence to cut off the cows and leave them there. In three or four days the cows would have finished their bawling and he could go back, give the cows a good long shove into the worked country, and then run his J Pen iron on the calves. In that way he would collect from Fahrion, would put one over. Chance grinned. He had the very canyon in mind. It lay some ten miles from the J Pen, a cul-de-sac in the mesa with a big spring in it. A brush fence across the end of that and he had a corral! It would be a good idea to look it over, but it would be best not to build the fence until the round-up had passed. Another good wish would be to spot the cows and calves he wanted, spot them someplace off to the east where the Spear cattle were thick. Chance wished that he knew when the round-up wagon would start and which direction it would go. Perhaps he had better talk his plan over with Silvertip. That wise old hoot owl might know of a better way.

The wagon road climbed up, Chance climbing with it, and the sun climbed down. Chance reached the mesa top, scarred and furrowed, a badlands. He put aside his scheming, for he was almost at the Basin.

Dusk was in the Basin when Chance reached it. A lantern glowed in the stable behind the long, low, log building that was Pillow's store. That was the only visible light. Chance rode on down, the way growing darker as he descended. He would, he thought, stop at the store and inquire as to the whereabouts of Silvertip's cabin. Perhaps he might see the girl at the store. Oddly Chance wanted to see that girl. She was . . . Chance felt guilt. What business had he to think of any girl other than Lois Elder? Still . . . he wondered if Arlie's eyes were as frightened as they had been, if they were still as haunted. He hoped not.

Stopping in front of the store Chance dismounted, tied his buckskin horse to a porch post and hitching up his belt, set foot on the porch steps. He was halted there. A scream, a woman's scream, muffled, but distinct enough, came from the cabin a hundred yards south of the store and up on a little knoll. Chance turned toward that sound, and paused. It came again, terror-filled: a woman screaming. Chance Pagan slapped forward with his hand, reaching for the gun at his hip, and running, he made for the cabin.

As he reached it he heard Upton's voice: "Let go! Let go, Arlie! Damn you, Pasmore . . ."

Chance went through the open door like a bat following a dodging insect. There was a block of black across the opening and he was inside.

Upton's voice came from his left. To his right there was movement. Chance leaped toward it. He struck flesh, a gun roared, powder burning his shirt. Then Chance swung his forearm in a short, swift arc. His Colt thudded down, rose end fell again, and the body he was against went limp.

"Silvertip!" Chance snapped. "You all right?"

From the bunk Silvertip Upton gasped: "Chance, you . . . Damn it! She's fainted."

Chance fumbled in his shirt pocket, reaching for a match.

When the match flamed Chance could see Silvertip on the bunk, and with him, huddled and limp, Arlie Pillow. Pasmore lay on the floor, blood trickling down the side of his head and his eyes rolled back until only the whites showed. Chance bent down, assured himself that Pasmore's heart was beating strongly, and, as the match went out, caught Pasmore by the collar of his shirt and dragged him to the door. A lantern bobbed down by the barn behind the store and he could hear excited voices.

"Somebody coming," he said to Silvertip, turning back to the room.

Silvertip's voice was a harsh whisper. "Duck! Duck out back! Let me handle this!"

Bewildered, Chance stood just inside the door. Again came that insistent whisper: "Duck out into my shed!" Chance heard the old men move and, obeying the command, followed the movement. Silvertip's hand caught at his shoulder and hurried him. He was shoved through an opening, smelled the sweat of a horse, manure and leather, knew that he was in a stable, and then a door closed in his face. Chance stood there. Feet pounded up. A man's voice, Pillow's rasped: "What's happened here? We heard a shot!" Then light was seeping in around the cracks of the doorway and Silvertip was answering.

"Seemed like Arlie had a scare," Silvertip said

smoothly. "She came bustin' in here with Pasmore after her. I had to hit Pasmore a lick to keep him sort of quiet."

Chance repressed a grunt. Plainly Silvertip did not want his presence known, wanted to take the whole affair upon himself. Chance wondered why.

"Pasmore after Arlie?" Pillow rasped the words. "Damn him! I'll teach him to suck eggs! I'll . . ."

"I've already took care of that." Silvertip kept his voice smooth. "Natchully Arlie come to me. After all, I run the Basin."

So that was it! Silvertip was throwing a bluff. He was carrying out his role of leader. Chance grinned in the darkness. Far be it from him to spoil Silvertip's game. With a start he thought of his horse in front of the store. It would never do to let that horse be found. Chance glanced back, saw the gray of an open door, and slipped away. Behind him angry voices jangled in the cabin.

Back at the store Chance untied his buckskin, mounted, and leisurely rode back toward Upton's cabin. He was not going to be cheated of hearing the end of this. He felt his shirt, found that it was not burned through, and stopping the buckskin in front of the cabin, dismounted.

Pillow was talking inside: "I drenched Buck an' . . ."

"Hello, the house!" Chance called.

Pillow's voice stopped. There was a brief pause and then Silvertip called: "Who's there?"

"Pagan," Chance answered. "Can I come in?"

There was a hurried consultation inside the cabin. Pillow appeared at the door with the lantern in one hand, and a shotgun, the barrels short, in the other. He raised the lantern so that the light fell on Chance.

"Come in," Pillow ordered ungraciously.

Letting the buckskin stand, Chance entered the cabin.

Arlie was sitting on the bed, eyes wide with fright. Art Ragland stood, looking down at Pasmore on the floor. Pasmore's face was bloody but his eyes had returned to normal. Silvertip leaned against the table watching Pillow.

"Looks like a man had been hurt," drawled Chance, enjoying the situation. "Have a ruckus?"

"Not much," Silvertip's voice was casual. "A man got out of line a little."

"I'd say he'd been put back," drawled Chance.

Pasmore stirred on the floor, sat up, and put his hand to his head. His eyes stared about the room, his face dazed. Art Ragland reached down a hand and hauled Pasmore to his feet. Pillow, putting the lantern on the table, took a step, and Silvertip spoke:

"Leave it lay, Pillow!"

Pillow stopped, glared at Silvertip, and then subsided.

"What . . . what hit me?" demanded Pasmore. "What . . ."

"I hit you!" snapped Upton. "Next time you come bargin' in here I'll kill you. Get out! Take him out, Ragland, an' keep him away from me. I'd as soon beef him as not."

Silvertip Upton was in command. There was no doubt of that. Chance, wary and ready to back any play that the old man made, could not but admire the poise of the outlaw.

"Somebody came in the door . . ." Pasmore began, regaining his senses, in a measure. "Somebody . . ."

"Nobody came in the door except you," snapped Upton. "I'll kick you out of it in a minute. Git!"

Ragland had his hand on Pasmore's shoulder. He pushed the bewildered man toward the door. Pasmore went, docilely enough, all the fight knocked out of him. "I'll cool him down," promised Ragland at the door. "I'll cool him off."

"Do that!" snapped Silvertip. Ragland went on out.

Upton turned to Pillow. "If I was you, I'd look after my girl a little better," he drawled. "She was scared."

Pillow's face was a contorted mask. "I'll look after her," he snarled. "If that . . . I'll kill him!"

"No, you won't kill him," snapped Silvertip. "There'll be no killin's in the Basin!"

Pillow let that sink in. Gradually he relaxed.

"Did he hurt you, girl?" Silvertip looked at Arlie.

Arlie shuddered. Her eyes were fixed on Chance. Chance, behind Pillow, shook his head imperceptibly. It wouldn't do to tell it now. "He didn't hurt me," said Arlie, her voice tremulous. "He tore my dress . . ."

"Come on, girl," ordered Pillow. "You come on home. I'll see Sam. *I'll see him.*" There was a peculiar significance in the last words.

"I . . ." began Arlie.

"Yo're safe," assured Silvertip. "I reckon yore father will look after you."

Chance wondered why Silvertip seemed so anxious that Pillow and the girl leave. Pillow picked up the lantern. Chance, bringing a match from his pocket, advanced and lit the lamp on the table. Arlie was staring her bewilderment at Silvertip.

"Go on with yore father," Silvertip ordered gruffly.

Pillow went to the door, paused, and looked at Arlie. Arlie, with a final look at Silvertip, followed her father. The two went out.

Silvertip stood motionless, leaning on the table. He stood so for several minutes, Chance watching him; then carefully the old man straightened, put his weight on his feet, and took the three steps back to his bunk. He sank down on it. "Lord!" said Silvertip.

Chance closed the door.

Silvertip lay back on the bunk. His eyes closed and he was inert, seeming scarcely to breathe. Chance walked over and looked down. Through slowly moving lips Silvertip spoke. "I come near not making it," he whispered. "I reckon you got here about right, Chance."

Chance hurried across the room, got a dipper of water from the bucket, and holding the old man's head up, gave him a drink.

"I've got to be the boss," said Silvertip, after he had swallowed the water. "I've got to run 'em. You . . ."

"I could just as easy have shot that fellow," interrupted Chance, regretfully. "Fooling with a kid like that! He needs shooting!"

"Pillow will take care of him," answered Silvertip, his voice stronger, "he'll put the fear of God into Pasmore."

"Pasmore, huh?" snapped Chance, filing the name in his mind for future reference. "All right, let Pillow take care of him. Me, I'm going to stay here and take care of you."

Upton shook his head. "You can stay tonight," he answered, "but you'll have to go back in the mornin'."

"Why?" demanded Chance.

"Because I can't look like I needed help," Silvertip answered. "I'm runnin' a bluff, Chance. I've got to run it by myself."

"Just the same I'll stay and back your play," argued Chance, obstinately. "I'll . . ."

"You'll go in the mornin'." Silvertip was insistent. Chance grunted. "Well," he said reluctantly, "maybe I'll go."

8

BEFORE HE LEFT the next morning, Chance exacted a promise from Silvertip. He made the old man say plainly that if he, Silvertip, became sick or if there were trouble in the Basin that he could not handle, he would send for Chance. Silvertip was reluctant to comply but Chance refused to leave until Silvertip's word was given; so, unwillingly enough, the old man promised.

Riding out of the Basin, with the early morning sun warm upon him, Chance was fairly content. He knew that he had helped his friend and he knew too that he had helped Arlie. That made Chance particularly pleased, the fact that he had helped the girl. He was well down the trail before he recalled that he had not spoken to Silvertip concerning his plan of exacting payment from the Spear. Chance shrugged and let it go. Silvertip had enough worries!

Just before he came to the break in the rimrock, followed by the wagon road, he saw a rider coming briskly toward him from the left, and reined the buckskin to a stop. The rider came on and when Chance recognized Arlie Pillow, he went to meet her. Some distance from the trail they stopped and Chance, smiling at her, spoke his greeting.

"Morning," said Chance cheerfully. "How are you?"

The girl flushed. "I didn't sleep," she answered. "My step-father was out in the barn all last night. He had a sick horse and . . ."

"And you'd been upset," Chance completed. "I reckon you must have been."

"I want to thank you for what you did last night." There was gratitude in Arlie's voice and her eyes met Chance's and then were lowered quickly. "I went to Silvertip's this morning. . . . He told me I fainted and you . . . Well, I hurried right after you when he said you'd just gone."

"Why don't you get out of the Basin?" Chance asked, his face flushing with embarrassment. "It's no place for a girl. Why don't you go to Cassidy? I'll take you there, if you want."

Arlie shook her head. "I can't go," she answered. "Pillow . . . Well, I can't go. There are reasons."

Somehow Chance did not like Tully Pillow. "Well," he said, "it's your own business and I don't want to butt in, but you can take that offer any time."

"I don't think I'll have any more trouble." The girl looked up at Chance shyly. "Silvertip is there and Pillow was awfully angry last night. He threatened to kill Sam Pasmore."

"He ought to have done it," said Chance warmly. "I should have done it myself last night."

Chance swung his horse around then and started back toward the trail. Arlie started her pony and half a length behind Chance, spoke again. "I wish I could do something for you," she said. "I could wash your clothes and I . . ."

Chance reined in and laughed. "You don't owe me a thing," he stated. "I just happened along, that's all. Forget it. I'd be a fine sort of skunk letting you wash my clothes!"

"I'd like to do it," Arlie's blue eyes were earnest. "I'd like . . . I'd do anything."

Chance grinned. "You just keep out of trouble," he said. "Kind of keep an eye on Silvertip and if either of you need help you get me. I ain't so far off."

The girl made no reply to that and Chance was about to ride on when he heard a clatter of rocks on the road. Instinctively he kept quiet, preventing his horse from moving. A man rode by up the road, a man who was making time and paying no attention to the country on either side. When the rider had passed Chance looked at Arlie. "That was Cliff Nowlen," he stated.

Arlie nodded. "He comes to the Basin often," she said. "He and my step-father have some sort of business together."

Chance grunted. Remembering Pillow's actions, Pillow's twisted face, he thought that there might be better men for Cliff Nowlen to associate with in a business venture. "Pillow ain't your father then?" he asked.

"No," Arlie answered. "He's my step-father. He married my mother when I was little. My father and mother are dead."

"And you've got to stick with him," mused Chance. "You poor kid."

There was no more said for a moment and then Arlie, her eyes steady on Chance, made answer. "I'm not a kid," she said. "I'm . . . I'm nineteen and I . . ." Shyness overcame her. She reined her pony around.

"Wait!" commanded Chance. "You . . ."

"Good-bye." Arlie called the words over her shoulder. The pony's feet clattered on rock as the girl kicked with her heels. Chance half turned to follow her, then stopped, straightened out the buckskin and, with an amused grin on his face, watched her disappear around a point. She was an odd one, Arlie Pillow. A mighty odd girl.

Back at the J Pen he found things just as he had left them. The cabin had not been disturbed and everything was in order. Once more Chance settled down into the routine he had made for himself.

That routine was unbroken for the rest of the week but on Monday, finding that he was out of coffee, salt pork, and a few other necessities, Chance resolved to go to Cassidy. There was an old pack-saddle in the shed and putting it on the bay horse he had borrowed from Nowlen, and with his own saddle on the sorrel, Chance made an early start. He made the journey in six hours and was in town by one o'clock, eating his dinner at the restaurant.

With his purchases made at Apfel's store Chance had

nothing more to do. He could, of course, go back to camp, but camp was thirty-seven miles away, and seventy-four miles in one day was too much for his horse. Consequently he decided to stay in town overnight and return to the J Pen in the morning. Leaving his horses at the livery until the next morning, Chance went back up the street.

Perhaps two blocks from the livery Chance was hailed by Tom Melody, who came across the street to speak to him. "How you makin' it, Chance?" asked Melody as they shook hands. "Pretty lonesome?"

"I manage to make out," Chance replied, "even when you do come in an' run off the folks that are staying with me."

Melody frowned and then laughed. "I should have talked to Silvertip long ago," he confessed. "I've been fallin' down on the job."

"How is that?" Chance was curious.

"Well," Melody drawled, "I've known all along the kind of men that were in the Basin. I've let 'em stay there, mainly on account of Silvertip, and because they let us alone down here in the Hole. I've gone up there a couple of times with a posse when some other sheriff wanted to look for a man, but we never found the man we wanted and the folks in the Basin seemed to take it all right. It's been a sort of let-me-alone-an'-we'll-let-you-alone proposition, an' that ain't any way to be a law man."

"Come in and have a drink," Chance invited. "I'd like to talk to you, Tom."

"I'll drink a little beer," agreed Melody. Side by side

the two entered the Longhorn.

When Con Rady had attended to their orders, Chance and Melody carried their drinks to a table in the rear of the room and sat down together. "Tom," said Chance when a little beer had been sipped, "just how did Silvertip get to be an outlaw anyhow?"

Tom Melody looked over the rim of his glass, drank, and put the glass down. "Well," he said slowly, "I'll tell you what I know about it. Your daddy and Upton and me was all pretty thick. We worked together on several round-ups. The OXC ran cattle all over this country then and we worked with that wagon. Wayne Elder came in along during the last years the OXC ran cattle in here, and him and Jack—yore daddy—an' me, we each taken a place an' homesteaded some water. Yore daddy got the pick of it all. He got that vega."

Chance nodded. "I knew that you all settled about the same time," he said. "Why didn't Silvertip take up land?"

Melody shrugged. "I don't know," he replied. "We didn't call him Silvertip then. We called him his name: Ruff."

"Well?" encouraged Chance.

"He got the name Silvertip when he come out of the pen," Melody digressed. "He wasn't an old man but he was grizzled as a badger an' someway he got to bein' called that."

"But how did he get to the pen in the first place?" asked Chance impatiently.

"I'm comin' to that." Melody sipped his beer. "Don't crowd me." He sipped again while Chance waited.

"Along after yore daddy an' mother married," resumed Melody, "there was some trouble down here in Calico Hole. There was a bunch in the Badlands then, like there is now. Ruff Upton was ridin' for yore daddy, holdin' down a line camp over to the east by Dripping Springs."

Chance nodded. He knew where the Dripping Springs line camp had been located.

"Well," Melody went on, "I don't mind sayin' that it had been a nip-and-tuck race between yore daddy an' Ruff for yore mother. Yore daddy got her, an' Ruff was best man at the weddin'. They was all friends. Wayne got married about that time, too."

"Yes?" encouraged Chance.

"Yeah." Again the old sheriff sipped his beer, finishing it. "Well, there was some horses stolen down below Cassidy. Abe Mulvaney was sheriff then an' I was his deputy in here. Abe got a hot lead an' followed the horses an' we run into 'em just above the J Pen vega."

"On the way to the Basin," Chance surmised.

"I don't know where they were goin'," said Melody. "Whoever was with 'em dropped 'em before we caught up. We took the horses an' turned around and started back. When we came to the J Pen it was dark so we put the horses in the trap an' went to the house. Yore daddy an' mother an' Ruff Upton was there."

"And . . . ?"

Melody frowned. "Don't crowd me," he complained. "We went in to supper. Of course everybody knew why we was there an' where we'd been, an' just for a joke

Abe spoke to yore daddy. 'Yo're goin' to have to do some explainin', Jack,' he said. 'We picked up some stolen stock right above you. Where you been keepin' yoreself?' Of course, it was all in fun. Yore daddy was just new married an' he hadn't stirred from the house, we allowed."

Chance leaned forward over the table. "What happened?" he demanded.

"The funniest thing I've ever seen," Melody answered. "Yore mother turned white as a ghost an' yore daddy started up, mad as a hornet, an' Ruff Upton spoke right up. 'It's a lie!' he said. 'Jack Pagan was fifty miles away. I took the horses!'"

Silence followed Melody's words. Chance moved his glass. The old officer drawled on once more. "That upset it," he said. "Ruff confessed the whole thing. He told Abe an' the rest of us, all about it; just what he done an' how he done it. Jack started twice to butt in, but Ruff stopped him. They were friends, you see, and Jack was mighty upset about what Ruff had done. We taken Ruff and the horses back to Cassidy with us. Ruff pleaded guilty an' got four years out of it. When he come out he was Silvertip Upton, an outlaw. We heard of him around. He was mixed up in plenty, we knew, but he never was caught. Then he drifted back, settled down in the Basin, an' he's been there ever since. I guess he ain't been long ridin' for ten years or more."

Chance Pagan sat stock still at the table. Old Tom Melody, his tale done, saw a chance to impress a point. "That's what comes of runnin' with the wild bunch," he said. "Silvertip done it an' he's been in the Badlands, one way or another, ever since. You keep away from the Basin an' the folks in it, Chance. Don't neighbor with 'em or they'll get you in bad."

"Thanks, Tom," said Chance absently. "Thanks, I reckon . . ."

He did not finish the sentence but stood up, and hardly looking at Melody walked out of the Longhorn. Tom Melody stared after him.

"Now what the dickens?" demanded Melody. "What's got into him, anyway?"

"Nothin'," answered Con Rady, "but yo're stuck for the beer, Tom. Want me to put it on yore bill?"

Out in the street Chance Pagan stood like a man bemused. So that was it? So that was what the ravings of Silvertip Upton, outlaw, meant! The whole thing was explained to him. Silvertip had relived that story in his delirium at the J Pen cabin, and had added a chapter to it, a chapter that neither Tom Melody nor anyone else knew.

"I would lie for you, Jack," Silvertip had said, "but you must stop." Stop what? Horse stealing, of course. Chance Pagan, son of Jack Pagan; son of a thief, of a man that had let another take the blame for his misdeeds. Chance hardly noticed the steps that came up behind him, hardly heard the deep ring of a voice:

"Chance, you old son-of-a-gun! Chance . . . What's the matter with you, kid?"

Chance turned then. John Comstock stood facing him, a grin on his square, homely face.

"John!" exclaimed Chance, and their hands met.

It had been a long time since Chance Pagan and John

Comstock had been together and they spent the first few moments looking each other over. Then each grinned and John laid his hand on Chance's arm once more. "Doggone but I'm glad to see you, Chance," he said. "I wrote you a note . . ."

"And I got it," Chance finished. "You were right, too."

"You always were hot-headed," said Comstock. "I knew you'd just flew off the handle."

"I reckon that was it," Chance agreed. "What brings you to town, John?"

"We're getting ready to start the wagon," Comstock answered. "Going out Wednesday."

Chance was alert. For the moment the shock he had received was forgotten. "That's day after tomorrow," he announced. "Awful early, ain't you?"

"Some," Comstock nodded. "Bill has been riding us. He's sour as a pickle: being boss had gone to his head. I reckon he wants to get the brandin' started before Elder gets back."

"That may be it." Chance nodded.

"Anyhow," continued Comstock, "the grass is early and there's plenty of big calves. I reckon it's all right to start the wagon. You going with it?"

"No." Chance shook his head. "I reckon I wouldn't be welcome with the Spear wagon right now."

John Comstock laughed. "You might not, at that," he said. "Well, I'll look after yore stock for you, Chance. Maybe I'll earmark a few J Pen calves to my own brand."

It was Chance's turn to laugh. Tom Melody came out

of the Longhorn and seeing the two together, walked rapidly toward them. "I wondered what had got into you, Chance," he said. "You walked right out on me. I reckon you clear forgot me when you saw John."

"I guess I must have," Chance agreed. "And I forgot to pay for that beer. We'll go back and have another." He linked his arm through Comstock's, put the other hand on Melody's arm, and pushed them along back toward the Longhorn.

For the remainder of the day Chance and Comstock were together. John Comstock had come to Cassidy with the Spear wagon and a list of supplies. He had time on his hands and he had found his friend, Chance Pagan, once more. They had a good time together, visiting and recalling old experiences they had shared. Tom Melody stayed with them awhile and then left, but they did not note his going. Late in the afternoon Comstock spoke of going to the wagon yard to see about his teams, and Chance, agreeable, accompanied the bigger man. The wagon yard was next to the livery barn and when Comstock was sure that his rig was all right for the night, they went into the stable to look at Chance's horses.

"I'm riding NOW's," Chance explained as they walked back between the stalls. "I had just one horse when I lit here, and Cliff loaned me a string."

"Bronks, I'll bet you," Comstock announced. "Cliff Nowlen knows that you can handle horses."

"There are two bronks," grinned Chance. "I've got one of them with me. The other two were summer horses."

They stopped beside a stall and Chance advanced gingerly. The sorrel in the stall kicked at him and reared against the tie rope. Dodging back, Chance grinned. "That sorrel is still bronk," he said.

John Comstock laughed. "Cliff bought him from Elder," he said of the sorrel. "We had two of 'em, one five an' one six years old, alike as two peas in a pod, both out of the same mare an' stud. You've got the six year old. He's hell on wheels an' our peeler gave him up as a bad job. The other horse is gentle as a kitten. Wayne sold this one to Cliff because somebody was always makin' a mistake in the corral an' ropin' out the bronk horse. This horse throwed Wayne himself twice when he made that mistake an' tried to ride him."

Chance chuckled. "Had to split 'em," he said. "I haven't found him so bad. He's sure a showy horse."

"You could tell either of them a mile away," said Comstock. "That bright sorrel sure shows up. Trouble would be to tell which was which. How do you like the bay horse?"

"Good."

"He's a good ropin' horse," agreed Comstock. "Babe Wilmot had him with the wagon when he repped for the NOW last year. What do you say, Chance, let's go eat supper and then see what we can stir up in the way of excitement. There's a poker game down at Quinn's, and there's a new waitress at the restaurant."

"I'll vote for the poker game," said Chance. "I'm not interested in waitresses."

"You wouldn't be," grunted Comstock. "I'm not sure that I'd be either if I had Lois Elder on my side."

With a start Chance realized that he had not thought of Lois Elder for weeks. "When is Wayne coming back?" he asked.

"I wish I knew," Comstock answered. "I've had enough of Bill Fahrion running the spread. Come on, let's go and eat."

Arm in arm the two left the livery and went down the street. At the restaurant they ordered from the new waitress and when she was gone Comstock commented upon her charms, which were few. After the meal they repaired to Quinn's Exchange Saloon and there found the poker game they sought. Both sat into the game and both lost a little money to the cold-eyed gambler who ran it. When they had had enough of that they left and went to the hotel where Chance had a room. Sitting on the bed, side by side, they pulled off their boots. Each man was occupied with his own thoughts.

Comstock stopped in his undressing. "It's mighty good to have you back, Chance," he said, boot poised in hand. "Mighty good."

"It's good to be back," answered Chance.

Comstock let the boot thump on the floor.

In the morning after breakfast the friends parted. John Comstock had a wagon to load and drive back to the Spear. Chance, packing the bay horse with a saddle load of groceries from Apfel's, subdued the sorrel and started for the J Pen. Before he mounted he bade Comstock good-bye.

"Come up, John," he urged. "When the wagon gets up around the place, you ride over."

"I sure will," said Comstock. "We're workin' the

southeast end of the ranch first so I'll see you in a day or so." With that assurance they shook hands and parted.

Riding out of Cassidy the warmth of John Comstock's friendship was still with Chance. He grinned now and then as he rode along, and when the sorrel shied at a yucca and dodged four feet to one side in a single jump, Chance did no more than chide him. But as the miles dropped away and Cassidy was left behind, the warmth departed. Gradually, as he rode, the talk with Tom Melody came uppermost in Chance Pagan's mind and by the time he reached the J Pen all the good feeling was gone. Chance dumped his pack saddle by the door, rode out, and caught the black for a wrangling horse, then turned the bay and the sorrel loose.

Back at the house he carried in his groceries, a black mood holding him. He put the groceries on the shelves, pulled off his coat and hat, and without building a fire, sat down beside the table. For the first time he looked around. The cabin was neat and clean, much neater and much cleaner than Chance had left it. Someone had scoured and scrubbed the place. Chance got up to survey the room.

On his bunk there were three pair of socks, neatly washed and darned. The bed had been freshly made. Further search brought to light a pie, placed in the meat safe to keep cool. Chance went back to the table and sat down again.

Who had cleaned the cabin? Who had darned those socks and baked that pie? Chance had the answer simply enough. Arlie Pillow. Arlie Pillow, poor little kid, seeking to repay a favor. For a time Chance sat there, motionless, then once more he got up and going to the stove shook down the ashes.

Arlie Pillow had ridden over and done all these things, had come in spite of her curmudgeon of a step-father, had stolen time to do them. And for whom had she done them? For Chance Pagan. For Chance Pagan, a fool with a hot temper, and the son of a coward and a thief!

9

ON WEDNESDAY MORNING Chance got up, early as usual, and after breakfast left the J Pen. The Spear round-up was starting and it was time for him to begin his own round-up. There were J Pen cows with calves at heel out on the flats and those calves needed a brand and an earmark. As Chance was not represented with the Spear wagon, for his request to Comstock had been purely a jest, it was up to him to brand those calves. He could work from the J Pen, covering the adjacent country, the breaks along the mesa, and the country about Two Buttes to the south. Later he might have to take a small camp outfit and ride the country north of the Spear. Such riding was legitimate and very desirable. Not only would he pick up his calves, but he could keep an eye on the round-up crew and keep track of where they were. In view of his plan to collect for his vega hay, that last was desirable.

All that day Chance rode and during the day he

caught and branded three J Pen calves. That was not a bad day's work considering the country he had to cover and the scarcity of J Pen in it. The next day, too, he rode and again on Friday. On Friday evening returning to the cabin he saw smoke north and west and knew that the round-up wagon was nearby.

After supper that night, just before the moon rose, Chance tied his ax to his saddle and went out again. Riding northwest he definitely located the Spear wagon and grinned when he saw the fire. The wagon had come far enough. It was time to put his plan into action.

Swinging back south Chance struck the country just below the mesa and went on west. Canyon after canyon running down from the rim he passed and then turned into a dark canyon mouth. This was the Dripping Springs, the site selected for his brush corral.

For a long time then, as the moon climbed and slid down its invisible hill, there was the sound of an ax and of dragging brush in the Dripping Springs canyon. The moon was almost down when Chance finished, but there was light enough left to see his work. Across a narrow neck of the canyon was a stout brush fence, almost closing the way. There was a pile of brush beside the opening he had left. Up above that fence water dripped softly into a pool. Chance, again tying his ax to his saddle, mounted his horse, and tired but content with his work, rode out of the canyon and back toward the east. The moon was gone before he reached the J Pen and he turned his horse into the dark corral and went to bed.

The next day, Saturday, Chance rode the river. Innocently enough he was looking for J Pen calves to brand. Not so innocently he sized up the Spear cattle that he saw. Late in the afternoon he put a little bunch of Spears together, cows that had big calves at foot. He threw them loosely into a draw that ran to the Muddy, and leaving them, went back home.

At the J Pen he ran in the horses, roped out Farmer and turned the others loose. Farmer, big and tough and a cowhorse, was the mount Chance needed for his job that night. In the dusk, a lamp glowing on his table, Chance cooked and ate a hearty supper and then forced himself to wait.

The night settled down. Chance sitting on his stoop, waiting for the moon, rolled a cigarette. When it glowed before his face he locked his hands around a leg and watched the stars. They were close, crowding down to the earth. The cigarette glowed and faded, only to glow again. Someplace in the brush along the Tomcat Creek an owl hooted. How many men, riding at night, had heard the owl hoot? Chance wondered. Had Silvertip heard it? Had Jack Pagan?

When a man has built his whole life, his whole foundation upon one thing, he is in for trouble. Chance had so built. At first his father, and then his father's memory, had been his guide, his foundation. Now, by the words of an old man, incoherent and delirious, mumbled through a gray beard, and by the slow story of a cowtown sheriff, drawled across a saloon card table, that foundation was wrecked. What should have been solid incorruptible granite had proved to be sliding shale. The props had been knocked out from under

Chance Pagan.

Bitterly Chance thought of Tom Melody and of Silvertip. Chance wondered how Silvertip was making it. He should have gone to the old man but he had not been able to force himself to that. Jack Pagan had wronged Silvertip. Chance could not just ride up to the Basin, go to the cabin and say: "How are you, Silvertip? Say, my father stole some horses, didn't he? And you took the blame for it? I'd like to know about that." No, that wouldn't do.

The moon peeked over the mountains to the east and the cigarette described a glowing arc. Chance got up and walked to the corral where Farmer waited. It was time to go. At that, he wished he had gone to see Silvertip. He wished . . . He was worried about Silvertip.

Chance Pagan was not the only one whose mind was troubled about the old outlaw. Arlie Pillow also worried. Of all the people in the Basin she alone had an idea as to his real condition. Silvertip was aging rapidly, that was apparent to all, but Arlie knew why. She knew that he had been desperately ill and she knew too that he had a back injury that tortured him day and night.

The girl did what she could for the old man but it was little enough. Her own tasks kept her busy and when she managed to slip away from the store and visit her friend there was little in which she could aid him. Silvertip was waiting, waiting for something, just what, Arlie did not know. He asked her, at each visit, as to the men in the Basin, and Arlie answered him.

There were new men coming into the place, thin-faced, furtive-eyed fellows that came to Pillow's store and then went away to inhabit one of the disused shacks in the Basin or its side canyon. Arlie told Silvertip of these and the old man shook his massive head.

"What about the Kid or Blaney or Poncho?" he would ask, and Arlie, truthfully, was forced to tell him that she knew nothing of the three.

Conditions worried the girl and she had another and secret worry, a longing rather. Arlie had gone to the J Pen, daring Pillow's wrath, and had cleaned up the cabin, washed and darned some socks for Chance, and left him a pie. Chance Pagan was the first man, the first young man, that had treated her as a girl should be treated. Arlie did not know it but she was in love with Chance Pagan. She thought of him constantly and when she thought of him there was a dull ache within her. She hoped that he would come to the Basin to see Silvertip, hoped that he would come, and yet was afraid that he would come.

On Sunday Arlie finished her work early. Pillow had taken his teams and wagon to Cassidy and the girl was free for the day. She went out to the stable, saddled her pony, and mounting, rode toward the north. At first she planned to ride to the J Pen, but when she had been gone from the Basin for perhaps half an hour, shyness overcame her and she changed her course. There was a canyon in the rim that Arlie often visited, a canyon with a spring that dripped from the rock wall into a basin. Arlie did not know its name but she loved the quiet beauty of the spot. Accordingly she turned and rode toward it and as she rode another rider followed her.

Sam Pasmore, knocked into insensibility by Chance Pagan's Colt, threatened by Pillow, angry and sore and furtive, laid his downfall to Arlie Pillow. Where he had, at one time, occupied a place of confidence with Tully Pillow, he now was suspected and kept away from the councils that took place in the log store. Hating the girl and yet with his body aching for her, Sam Pasmore had made it a habit to spy upon Arlie. The man had become almost a maniac, but a cunning, clever maniac hiding his insanity under a smooth exterior. When Arlie saddled her pony and rode out of the Basin, Sam Pasmore saddled his horse and followed, keeping back out of sight.

Reaching the rim above the Dripping Springs canyon, Arlie followed a small side canyon to the flat where she could turn and ride back up to Dripping Springs. As she reached her turnoff she heard cows bawling and, curious as to the cause, rode on further until she was on the rim above Dripping Springs. Looking down into the box she saw a brush fence. There were calves on the south side of the fence, quite a little bunch of them, perhaps twenty-five, and on the north side of the fence were the bawling mothers of those calves. As Arlie looked down a rider appeared beyond the cows, a rider that even at that distance, she knew to be Chance Pagan.

For a long moment Arlie watched the rider, then hastily, lest she be seen against the skyline, she reined her pony back and, circling, rode away. Arlie did not know much about the cattle business but she knew enough to realize that there was something amiss in the

Dripping Springs canyon.

The girl had hardly left the rimrock before Sam Pasmore appeared on it. To his knowing eyes the scene below was easily explained. Pasmore knew just what was going on but he did not recognize the rider below the cattle. There were strict orders to the men in the Basin that they should make no move against the Calico Hole for the time being. It looked to Sam as though one of the newcomers had disobeyed those orders and, anxious to reinstate himself in Pillow's good graces, he decided to investigate. Accordingly he sought a way down from the rim, found the trail, and was in the canyon next to Dripping Springs when Chance Pagan, his inspection done, started back to the J Pen. Pasmore saw Chance ride by the mouth of the canyon he occupied. He recognized him, but to make sure there was no mistake he waited until Chance was gone and then rode into the Dripping Springs to verify his suspicions, carefully following the tracks of Chance's horse. Sure, after his reconnaissance, that there was no mistake, that Chance Pagan was the man who had built the brush fence and put the calves behind it, Pasmore pondered as to his next move. With his discovery he had entirely forgotten his pursuit of the girl Arlie.

Pillow was in Cassidy and would not be back until Monday afternoon. Pasmore would have liked to report to Pillow but that was impossible. Cliff Nowlen was next in importance and accordingly Pasmore left the canyon and set out to the east. He would ride to the NOW, tell Nowlen of what he had discovered, and so put himself back into the position he had occupied.

Arlie rode directly from the rim above Dripping Springs to the Basin. She stopped her horse at the barn behind the store and without waiting to unsaddle went to Silvertip's cabin. Silvertip called: "Who is it?" in answer to her knock, and when the girl replied, bade her enter. The old man lay on the bunk, his head propped up, and he smiled at the girl.

"I didn't look for you till late," said Silvertip. "How come you could get away?"

"Father is in Cassidy," Arlie answered. "Silvertip, I've just come in from a ride. I saw something."

"What?" demanded Silvertip.

The girl launched into a recital of her ride and Silvertip listened carefully. When she finished he withheld comment for a moment, then, "You sure it was Chance?" he asked.

"I'm sure," Arlie answered.

For a while Silvertip lay looking at the ceiling, one hand stroking his beard. Suddenly he spoke. "I can't ride," he grumbled. "I'm crippled when I need to be free. Will you do somethin' for me, girl?"

"If I can, Silvertip."

"You can. You go get Chance Pagan an' bring him here. I've got to see him. If some of that Spear bunch found them calves . . ." Silvertip broke off abruptly.

"What would happen?" Arlie asked breathlessly.

"Chance Pagan would take to the roughs, like I done," growled Silvertip. "The young fool! When will you go, Arlie?"

Arlie thought a moment. "I've got to go back to the

store," she said. "If Benito told father that I'd been gone all day I don't know what he would do. I can slip away in the morning, Silvertip."

"I reckon that'll have to do," grumbled Silvertip. "You tell Chance I want him, want him right away."

Arlie agreed to that. "I've got to go now," she said. "Benito saw me come in. I'll come back when I can get away, and bring you some supper."

"Yo're mighty good to an old man, girl," answered Upton. "Mighty good. Run now an' don't get into trouble on my account."

Arlie smiled at him and went out.

At the NOW Sam Pasmore reined in his horse and dismounted beside the corral. There was another saddled horse there, a NOW horse. Evidently someone had just come in. Pasmore recognized the saddle as belonging to Suel James and went on to the house.

James and Nowlen, drinking coffee in the kitchen, greeted Pasmore as he came in. "I just came out from town," said James. "Been tellin' Cliff the news. Wayne Elder has come back."

Pasmore looked from James to Nowlen. Nowlen was scowling. "He's got a ranch buyer with him," announced Nowlen. "Young Carl Terril of Terril & Blake."

"A ranch buyer?" asked Pasmore inanely.

"An' that means that Cliff has got to get a wiggle on if he wants the J Pen vega," stated James with unction. "Ain't that so, Cliff?"

Nowlen grunted sullenly. Pasmore pushed back his

hat. "Say," he commenced, "you ain't got all the news. Guess what I seen today."

"A ring-tailed elephant," answered James. "You been drunk enough this last week to see pink ones."

"I saw Chance Pagan rustlin' cattle," stated Pasmore definitely. "That's what I saw!"

"What?" Nowlen came up out of his chair and James leaned forward over the table, spilling a little coffee in his excitement.

"Just that." Pasmore enjoyed the stir his announcement had caused. "He's got a bunch of Spear calves behind a brush fence in the Drippin' Springs canyon. The cows are bawlin' on the other side of the fence. I saw it."

"Yo're crazy. It wasn't Pagan!" This from James.

Nowlen held up his hand. "Wait!" He commanded. "Let Sam finish."

"I was on the mesa an' heard the bawlin'," said Pasmore. "When I rode over to see what was makin' the racket I saw the cows an' calves an' a brush fence. There was a rider down below the fence. I thought mebbe it was one of the boys an' rode down to see, but it was Pagan."

"He see you?"

"Naw. I stayed hid in the canyon next to the Springs. I saw him ride past an' then I went in an' took a look."

"An' they was Spears?"

"A Spear on every cow."

James said, "Well, I will be hanged!" Slowly.

Nowlen, his eyes narrow, looked from one man to the other. "Pagan said he aimed to collect for his vega hay,"

Nowlen spoke slowly. "I reckon this is the way he done it."

"Well," James looked at his boss, "what are we goin' to do about it?"

Nowlen shook his head. "Shut up an' let me think!" he snapped.

"I'm goin' to tell Pillow . . ." began Pasmore.

"Shut up!" snarled Nowlen. "You'll tell Pillow nothin'. Suel, is Babe still out in the bunkhouse?"

"You know he is," answered James. "He come over from the wagon this mornin'. Fahrion don't work his crew Sunday. Babe's out there now playin' pitch with the rest of 'em."

"You get him!" directed Nowlen. James left the room and Nowlen, staring at Sam Pasmore, rocked contentedly in his chair.

"How well do you like Pillow, Sam?" he asked.

"You know," growled Pasmore.

"Not very well," Nowlen laughed. "Pillow has been whippin' you around the stump, ain't he? You ought to have left that girl alone."

"Damn Pillow!" grated Pasmore. "He . . ."

"Pillow got pretty salty with me," mused Nowlen. "Tellin' me that gettin' the vega was my look-out. All right, I'll get it. An' you string with me, Sam. Keep this business to yoreself. When we get it wound up you'll be well fixed."

"How do you mean?"

"I mean that Pillow an' Silvertip are fixin' for a showdown. We'll let 'em have it an' then step in an' clean up the pieces. Here comes Suel an' Babe."

Babe Wilmot, slight, wiry, the smallest man in the Calico Hole, entered the room in front of Suel James. He came directly to Nowlen.

Nowlen nodded. "Yo're kind of tied to me, Babe, ain't you?" he asked.

"You know I am," Wilmot answered grudgingly. "Are you goin' . . ."

"I'm goin' to ask you to do somethin'." Nowlen nearly purred. "There's a whole bunch of Spear cattle over in the Dripping Springs. Somebody is weanin' some calves in there. Now tomorrow, Babe, when you come in from yore mornin' circle you go to Elder . . ."

"Elder ain't in the country," expostulated Wilmot.

"He got back today," Nowlen stated. "He'll go to the wagon in the mornin', chances are. You go to him an' you tell him that you followed tracks to the Drippin' Springs an' that you seen his cows an' calves there, the calves behind a brush fence an' the cows bawlin'."

"We're ten miles from the canyon." Again Wilmot entered objection. "I won't be any place close to there. We're workin' the Two Buttes . . ."

"Never mind where yo're workin'! Yo' do like I say."

Wilmot nodded sullenly. "All right, an' then what?" he asked.

"Then go with Elder if he wants you to," smiled Nowlen. "That's all, Babe."

Wilmot, still sullen, retired. Nowlen smiled at Suel James. "It pays sometimes to have kept a man out of jail," he announced.

"I don't see what that'll get you," announced Pasmore. "Elder will ride over there an' they'll try to catch

Pagan, but Pagan ain't a fool. He'll look that canyon over from top to bottom before he ever rides in."

"Likely yo're right, Sam." Nowlen appeared to be uninterested. "You stayin' for dinner or are you goin' back to the Basin. Our cook's laid up an' Suel an' me are gettin' the meals. Of course yo're welcome, but we ain't much on cooking."

Pasmore stared at Nowlen. "I reckon I'll ride back up," he decided.

Nowlen came to his feet. "We hate to have you go, Sam," he said, putting his hand on Pasmore's shoulder. "But if you think you'd better, it's all right. You just keep still about what you saw an' everything will be fine." The hand on Pasmore's shoulder urged him toward the door.

When Sam Pasmore, somewhat bewildered, had departed, James and Nowlen went back into the house. Suel James stared quizzically at his boss. "I'm like Sam," he said. "I can't figure what it'll get you. Elder an' likely Fahrion will go up there an' find those cattle. They may set a trap, they may just turn 'em loose an' go lookin' for the man that took 'em. I can't figure it, Cliff."

"No," Nowlen agreed, "you wouldn't figure it, Suel. I don't want you to, but I do want you to ride over to Pagan's this afternoon an' borrow that sorrel horse of ours he's got."

"You want me to ask Pagan . . . ?"

"Who said anythin' about askin'? You won't see Pagan. You'll get that sorrel an' bring him here. The sorrel, mind you. He's the showy one of the bunch."

A light dawned in James' eyes. "I'll get him," he promised. "I reckon mebbe Elder will see that sorrel an' . . ."

"Just get the horse," directed Nowlen, quietly.

1 0

ASURREY from the livery barn in Cassidy brought Wayne Elder to the Spear. Wayne rode in the front seat beside the driver and in the seat behind Lois Elder and Carl Terril sat. Lee Su and the luggage followed in a livery buckboard.

When the party reached the ranch Elder climbed down stiffly and turned to face the pair in the back seat. "This is the Spear, Terril," he said needlessly to the dark-haired man. "Light down an' make yoreself at home."

Carl Terril smiled and alighting from the buggy held up his arms and swung Lois out. The girl was flushed and laughing as she reached the ground.

"Where is everybody?" Elder demanded. "I don't see a soul around the house . . . Oh, there you are!" Tony, the roustabout, had come around the corner of the house and was staring with unbelieving eyes at the group beside the porch.

"Where is everybody, Tony?" Elder demanded again.

"Round-up." Tony waved his hand. "They out with the wagon."

"Dang, Bill!" Elder fumed. "He didn't say a word about startin' the round-up when he wrote me. Help Lee get that truck off the buckboard, Tony. Lois, take Mr.

Terril on into the house. I got to pay these drivers."

Lois, her hand tucked under Terril's arm, went on into the house; Elder turned and pulled out his wallet, and Lee Su and Tony, grumbling, pulled luggage from the buckboard, among that luggage being a sacked saddle.

When Elder joined the two young people in the living-room Lois had thrown off her wraps and Terril was standing before the cold fireplace, his hands locked behind his back.

"Roundin' up," grumbled Elder. "Bill never said a word . . ."

"Probably didn't want to bother you, Mr. Elder," suggested Terril. "You round up early in this country."

"We got open range," explained Elder. "Calves comin' all the year. We got lots of big calves right now."

Terril nodded. "This is pretty new country," he said. "Most of our land is under fence. I suppose you fence nothing but your horse pastures and hay land."

"That's right," agreed Elder. "Wish I could go out to the wagon today, but it's too late. We'll go in the mornin'."

"And you'll go in now and lie down until supper time," announced Lois firmly.

"I'll do no such thing! Think I just came home to take a nap? I . . ."

"The doctors said for you to lie down a while every day!" Lois exercised her prerogative of spoiled daughter. "You'll go lie down now or you won't be fit to go out tomorrow. Now . . ."

"Doctors!" grumbled Elder. "That's all I been hearin' for the last month. Doctor this, an' Doctor that. I'll . . ."

"You'll go lie down!" Lois pushed her father toward a bedroom door and after he had grumblingly entered it, returned flushed and triumphant to Carl Terril.

Terril smiled down at her. There was more, considerably more, than friendliness in that smile and the flush on Lois' cheeks did not come entirely from her exertions with her father.

"Are you glad I came?" demanded Terril, still smiling at the girl.

Lois looked up from beneath demure eyelids. "Of course," she said. "I want father to sell the Spear and get to a warmer climate."

"And is that the only reason you are glad?"

The girl did not answer that. "I'll show you your bedroom," she proffered. "All the bedrooms are right off the living-room. This house is dreadfully old-fashioned." Turning, she crossed to another door and opened it. Terril had followed her and looked into the neat room that was disclosed.

"You are making me far too comfortable," he said. "I'll never want to go." He laughed then and Lois Elder joined him.

"Do you want to go in?" she asked.

Terril shook his head. Suddenly his voice was serious. "See here, Lois, you know why I came with you, don't you?"

"You wanted to see the Spear. You thought that perhaps it would do for a northern steer ranch for Terril & Blake. Wasn't that it?"

Terril caught her arm. "Look at me!" he commanded. Hesitantly the girl looked up. "Do you think that the ranch was the attraction?" asked Terril.

Lois Elder was honest. She lowered her eyes and answered the question. "No. I know why you came, Carl."

"Then was I wrong in coming?" Terril was insistent. The girl shook her head. "I don't know," she answered. "I . . . Carl, don't ask me now."

Light came into Terril's eyes. "I'll wait," he promised. "But Lois, I can't promise how long I'll wait."

In his hand the girl's arm stirred, pulled away. Terril released his hold. "I shouldn't have spoken," he said contritely. "I . . ."

"I must go and see to supper," Lois interrupted. "I'll . . . Oh, I must go." She turned away then and swiftly crossed the room, not to the kitchen door but to the door of her bedroom. Terril, waiting until that door closed, smiled slowly and entered the room that had been assigned him.

In her own room, the door closed safely behind her, Lois Elder sat down on her bed. Her eyes, large and dark, looked blankly at the wall opposite her and thoughts raced through her mind. She knew, had known for two weeks, that Carl Terril was in love with her. The two had been thrown constantly together at Hot Springs, a pair of youngsters in a company of elderly cripples. At first she had gone about with Terril just to escape the deadly dullness of the place. Later she had been glad of his company for its own sake. She was of two minds about Carl Terril. He was a gentleman, polished, smooth, and courtly. He was a man occupying a place in the world, an active partner in the big outfit of Terril & Blake. Terril & Blake owned ranches all over the state of Texas. They were big, so much bigger than the Spear that the latter ranch was insignificant. Carl Terril could write a check to pay for the Spear and never feel it.

But that was not the whole attraction nor the chief one. The chief attraction was the man himself and the fondness he displayed for her. Terril had not tried to hide that feeling and Lois had thrilled to it.

But what of Chance Pagan, Chance Pagan whom she had known always, whose ring she wore on a chain about her neck? What about Chance Pagan? Lois did not know, and thinking of him her eyes grew somber and her hands folded together tightly. She had to be fair to Chance; had to be. She must see Chance and tell him . . . What should she tell him? That she loved another man? It would be hard to do that, hard to see the hurt look in Chance's blue eyes and to hear him drawl an answer. She knew what Chance would say. He would tell her that it was all right, not to think of him. But it wouldn't be all right and she must think of him.

It was a strangely silent girl that answered Lee Su's call to supper. She sat at the table, eating little and keeping her eyes on her plate. Elder made conversation with Terril, trying to draw his daughter into it. In the course of that conversation he mentioned Chance Pagan.

"I reckon somebody will tell Chance that we're back," he said jovially. "He's up at the J Pen." Then, turning to Terril: "Chance Pagan is the son of an old friend of mine. I pretty near raised him after his father died. Him an' Lois used to team around together. The scrapes those two would get into . . . !" Elder chuckled. Terril, watching the slow flush rise on Lois' cheeks, was apprised of a situation.

After the meal when Elder had gone out for a moment, Terril snatched at his opportunity. "Is that it?" he asked. "Is it Chance Pagan?"

Lois looked at the man. "I don't know," she answered honestly. "Chance and I have been friends for years. We were raised together. When he left here he gave me his father's signet ring to wear. I've kept it."

"Do you love him?" Terril's voice was quiet.

"I like him. I've known him a long time . . ."

"Then I'm going to stay," said Terril. "I love you, Lois, and I won't give you up until you tell me that it is useless to stay longer. Will you see Pagan?"

"Of course." Simply.

"Then you will make your decision." Terril's voice was still low. "And remember that I love you . . ."

He broke off. Wayne Elder was coming back into the room, boots thumping on the floor. Entering the room he glanced sharply from his daughter to Terril. Wayne Elder was not blind and he had a good idea as to the status of things. That bothered him, for he loved his daughter, had raised Chance Pagan, and was genuinely fond of Carl Terril.

"It's 'most bedtime, I reckon," Elder announced. "We'll want to sleep some after our trip, an' I'm goin' to take you out to the wagon with me in the mornin', Mr. Terril."

"I'll be glad to go," assured Terril. "Good night, Mr. Elder. Good night, Lois." He turned and entered his room.

"Lois," said Elder when the door had closed, "what . . . ?"

"Don't ask me, daddy," wailed Lois. "I don't know. I just don't know!"

Wayne Elder did not get up too early the next morning. He slept until six, his own bed a comfort to his tired body. When he did arise and dress he found the living-room deserted. Elder went out to the kitchen. Lee Su was busy over the stove. The scent of frying bacon, of good coffee, and of flapjacks filled the air.

"Monin'," greeted Lee Su. "Mis Lois she gone. Tell me tell you she not be home for breakfast. You ready for hot cakes?"

"Where'd she go?" demanded Elder.

Lee Su shrugged. *"Quien sabe?"* he answered, lapsing over into Spanish. "Hot cakes good."

Without answering Elder went back through the kitchen door. In the living-room Carl Terril, bright-eyed and smiling, was waiting for him.

"Breakfast's ready," said Elder gruffly. "Let's eat an' get along out to the wagon."

"Is Lois . . . ?" began Terril.

"She won't eat with us," Elder announced. "I reckon she's tired."

Terril glanced toward the bedroom door and then followed Elder to the table. Wayne Elder sat down, speared a stack of cakes, and poured cream into his coffee. He did not know surely where Lois had gone but he had a good idea. It was up to Lois, he thought, as he munched his hot cakes. She would have to do her own deciding and if she wanted to see Chance Pagan . . . well, that was the right thing to do.

The two men left the Spear after breakfast. Tony had run in horses and put Elder's slick old A forked saddle on one, and the newer, swelled fork saddle of Carl Terril on the other. The men mounted and rode away toward the south.

"Tony said that the wagon was at Two Buttes," Elder announced as they rode. "You'll get to see some of the range as we ride out an' you'll get a look at some of the cattle today."

"This early grass looks good," Terril commented. "You must have plenty of snow."

"Plenty," Elder answered and launched into a discussion of range conditions and climate as they affected the Spear.

"The hay you cut must be a life-saver," said Terril when Elder paused. "That is the thing that makes the ranch attractive. Plenty of hay and a man can get through the late storms."

Wayne Elder did not answer for a moment. The hay that the Spear cut came from the J Pen vega and the Spear did not own the J Pen. If Terril found the hay so attractive then perhaps Elder had better not mention the fact that the Spear leased the meadows. "Some winters we don't feed hardly at all," Elder said at length.

"I wouldn't want to risk a winter here without hay." Terril was definite.

Elder nodded. "It's best not," he agreed. If hay was what Terril wanted with the Spear, then Wayne Elder would get it for him. He would see Chance and talk it over with the boy. Chance, he knew, would do anything that Elder asked. If the selling of the Spear depended on the J Pen vega, that was all right, and Wayne Elder would see that Chance didn't lose by it.

When Elder and Terril reached the wagon the crew was out and only the cook remained, laboring over his fire. Fahrion had started at five, the cook said. The crew was out on circle and would be in with their gathers just about noon. They were making two circles a day and branding twice, and it was damn' hard work if you asked him, so said the cook.

That left time to kill. Elder and Terril rode on south from the wagon, inspecting the range and looking at cattle. "I'll show you the vega this afternoon or tomorrow," Elder promised.

When they came back to the wagon there were cattle bunching on the round-up grounds. Three drives were in and even as Elder and Terril stopped their horses, Bill Fahrion threw a bunch into the growing herd. He came loping over to the wagon then, dismounted, and with hand outstretched, walked over to greet the Spear owner. "I wasn't lookin' for you for a while yet," said Fahrion after he had shaken hands with Elder and been introduced to Terril. "I thought that you'd stay at the Springs a while."

"I got fed up," said Elder. "How is it goin', Bill?"

"Good. Do you want to go over the tallies?" Fahrion reached toward the tally book in his hip pocket.

"Not right now. You started early, didn't you?"

"Yes. The grass was early and good and we had a lot of big calves. We didn't lose much in that blizzard after you left."

"That's good." Elder spoke absently, his eyes on the growing herd. "Where's Chance, Bill? I want to see him."

"At the J Pen, I reckon," answered Fahrion shortly.

"Why ain't he with the wagon?" Elder's question was sharp.

"I had trouble with Pagan, Mr. Elder," answered Fahrion. "I . . ."

"We'll talk about it later." Elder threw a sharp glance at Terril. He did not want Terril to know who owned the vega and Bill Fahrion was about to tell something.

Terril caught that glance. "I think I'll ride out and see if I can be useful," he declared. "I haven't handled cattle for over a year." Without waiting for an answer, Terril rode off.

"Now," said Elder to Fahrion.

"I had trouble with Pagan," Fahrion began again. "After you left he got on a high horse. We had Comstock at the J Pen an' Pagan ordered me to pull him out. Said that he wanted the cabin. There wasn't anything else for me to do."

Elder nodded. "What got into Chance?" he asked.

"He was sore because you'd left me here to run the Spear." Fahrion spoke bluntly. "I went up there to see him an' he had Silvertip Upton in his cabin. Silvertip had been stayin' there. Seemed to me like he was mighty friendly with that Basin bunch."

Elder shook his head. "I'll have to see Chance," he said.

"I ain't branded any calves for him this year." Fahrion grew bolder. "I told him I wouldn't. We been payin' too much for that vega lease."

"I told you to brand 'em, didn't I?" snapped Elder. "You give him those calves. We've got to have that vega."

Fahrion looked startled. He had been getting along pretty well, getting his story across nicely. Here was a hitch.

"Sure I'll brand 'em, if you say so," he agreed, "but I wasn't goin' ahead without orders."

"I've got to have that vega." Elder spoke more to himself than to Fahrion. "Terril won't buy without the hay."

Fahrion grunted. "We've missed some stuff," he said. "Pagan claimed to be ridin' the lower end but we missed some so I put Ben Godman down there to look after it. We ain't missed any since then."

"Dang it," Elder growled, "I'll have to see Chance. I've got to get that vega, an' here's this buyer with me that I've got to wet-nurse around. I wish . . ."

He did not say what he wished. A rider came in past the herd, a rider unencumbered with cattle. He came on at a steady lope, drew up to the wagon, and stopped. "Where's your gather, Babe?" demanded Fahrion. "Where . . ."

Babe Wilmot paid no attention to Fahrion. He spoke, low-voiced, his horse close by Elder's. "Mr. Elder, I just come from the Drippin' Springs. I . . ."

"What you doin' away over there?" growled Fahrion. "What . . ."

"Let be, Bill!" snapped Elder. "Now, what is it, Wilmot?"

"The Dripping Springs canyon. I found a bunch of tracks leadin' over there. I followed 'em. There's twenty-five head of cows in the canyon. Somebody has built a brush fence an' got the calves penned off from the cows, weanin' 'em. I come right on in to tell you."

Elder and Fahrion exchanged glances. Elder's eyes narrowed. "The Drippin' Springs, you say?"

"Yes, sir."

"I'll go over there . . ." began Fahrion.

"I'll handle this," Elder stated. "You stay here an' get this brandin' done, Bill. I'll take Wilmot here an' another man . . . I'll take Comstock, an' go right over."

The cook rose up from beside the fire. "Come an' get it!" he called.

From the herd, riders detached themselves and came loping in. Other men, left with the cattle, spaced themselves to hold the bunch. There was a rattle of tin plates and cups, the babble of voices. Men came to Elder, shook hands, and told him how glad they were that he was back.

Carl Terril came riding up and dismounted. Terril was smiling. "I'd forgotten how much fun a round-up can be," he said.

"It's fun if you don't have to work," Elder replied.

"That's why I'm enjoying it. Let's get plates before all those mountain oysters are gone. I haven't eaten any of them for three years."

Elder, accompanied by his guest, filled his plate, and when the two were seated side by side, some distance from the fire, Elder spoke.

"I've got a ride to make this afternoon," he said bluntly. "Somebody has got some cows of mine penned in a canyon an' is weanin' calves. I'm goin' to look into it."

Terril eyed the Spear man questioningly. "Do you want me to go along?" he asked quietly. "I'd like to, you know."

Elder shook his head. "I'd ruther you didn't," he answered. "I'll take two men from the crew . . ."

"Then I'll stay and help with the branding," offered Terril.

"That would be mighty fine," Elder praised.

When the empty dishes were in the pan and the men at the herd were relieved, Elder took John Comstock and Babe Wilmot aside.

"We're goin' now," he said. "Babe, you didn't spill what you saw, did you?"

Wilmot shook his head. "I just talked to you an' Bill," he assured.

"Good." Elder nodded his commendation. "John, you get the cook's thirty-thirty an' stick it in the saddle scabbard you drag around. We'll pull out."

"What is this?" questioned Comstock.

"Tell you while we ride," answered Elder. "Get that rifle an' don't make much fuss about it."

Comstock went to get the rifle and Fahrion came over to Elder. "I'd like to go with you," he said wistfully.

"Somebody's got to stay here an' handle this herd,"

Elder announced. "Bill, you go ahead like nothin' was wrong. Put the boys out on circle when you turn the herd loose, but you stick around the wagon. I guess you'd better keep Terril with you." Fahrion nodded as Comstock came back with the cook's gun.

The three—Elder, Wilmot, and John Comstock— were the focus of curious glances as they rode away from the Spear wagon. There were eleven men in the Spear round-up crew, counting the reps from the NOW, the Quarter Circle Bar below Cassidy, and the LK that was east of the Big Muddy. Every man in the bunch wondered why the boss was riding out from the round-up grounds with Comstock and Wilmot, and why Comstock had a rifle on his saddle.

When they were well out from the wagon, Elder told John Comstock what their mission was. Comstock swore incredulously. "Spear calves?" he questioned.

"Spear calves," Elder answered grimly. "That is, if Babe ain't seein' things. We'll go easy an' after we see the layout I'll decide what to do."

The men kept their horses at a sharp trot for they had ground to cover. The mouth of Dripping Springs canyon was fully twelve miles from the wagon. The pace was hard on Elder for he was soft, and too, while Hot Springs had helped him it had not entirely cured him. Only a softer climate and less work would do that.

Nearing the mouth of the canyon they slowed their pace. There might be someone in there with those bawling cows, but Elder thought not. Mostly a rustler visits his cattle at night. After reconnoitering to make sure the canyon mouth was clear they rode in. Well up the canyon, where it narrowed, they found the cows, the brush fence, and the calves trying to make as much noise as their mothers on the other side of the fence. Wayne Elder sat on his horse and stared at the scene.

"I'll be hanged," he said slowly. "I'll sure be hanged for a horse-thief if I'd ever believed it."

Leaving Comstock and Wilmot to follow, he rode slowly forward. The others started after him, perhaps fifteen feet of distance separating them from their leader. The cows moved away from the brush fence as Elder came up and stopped. Wilmot and Comstock also stopped. Elder turned to speak, and apparently seeing something on the canyon side, flung up an arm, pointing. At that moment a rifle crashed; the pointing arm dropped limp and Elder crumpled forward over his saddle horn. There was a sorrel flash in the brush on the canyon sidehill. Comstock, jerking out his rifle, saw a man in a black hat, mounted on a sorrel horse, going up the slope. He fired at that man, fired again and again, emptying the carbine, but without result. Wilmot had reached Elder and was holding him up. Comstock dropped the rifle and, controlling his frightened horse, reached the two.

"He's bad," announced Wilmot. "Help me get him down."

Comstock dropped from the saddle and, reaching up, took Elder in his arms and carefully lowered him to the ground. Elder was shot through the chest.

"You ride for help," directed Comstock steadily. "Get the wagon out here an' send somebody to town for Tom Melody an' the doctor. Have 'em come to the Spear.

You'll find somebody at the wagon."

Babe Wilmot, his face white and frightened, wheeled his horse. Babe Wilmot had had no idea that murder was implicated in the message that he had carried. His horse bounded under the thrust of spurs.

"An' *ride,* Babe!" called John Comstock.

A rattle of loose rock answered him.

Comstock, now that Wilmot was gone, knelt beside the wounded man. Carefully he bared the wound. It was bleeding profusely, and the wound in the back was even worse. Comstock began to tear Elder's shirt to strips, making a bandage of the lengths.

"Chance, Chance," said John Comstock beneath his breath. "To think you'd do this! I wouldn't believe it now, *but I know that sorrel horse!*"

11

LOIS ELDER was up at four o'clock. When Lee Su's battered tin alarm clock exploded, Lois got out of bed. She had slept little during the night, tossing restlessly on her bed, her mind consumed with the problem that confronted her. There was only one way to settle that problem and that was to see Chance. Once she saw him, once she talked to him, she would know definitely what she must do. She spoke to Lee Su in the kitchen as she went out, leaving a message for her father. There were horses in the corral and with the competency of the ranch-raised girl, Lois caught one of them and saddled. The morning was clear and sweet as she rode toward the south.

The girl argued with herself as she rode. Her affair with Chance had been a boy and girl infatuation, she told herself. They had simply been together so much that they imagined themselves in love. Still she could not forget Chance Pagan, could not throw him aside. And yet withal she knew deep in her heart that she loved Carl Terril. It was in a troubled frame of mind that Lois reached the J Pen.

She did not see a pony that stood in the corral. There was smoke coming from the chimney of the cabin and the door was closed. Dismounting, Lois walked to the door and knocked.

Hers was the second arrival at the J Pen that morning. Arlie Pillow, rising early, had cooked breakfast for Benito, washed the dishes and, taking her pony, informed Benito that she was going riding. Benito had grumbled but he could not forbid her and Arlie set out. Her destination was the J Pen and her mission, the delivery of Silvertip's message to Chance. Silvertip's last words to her, when she had taken him some supper, were to be sure to deliver that message, and Arlie had promised again.

Chance was not in the cabin when she arrived. There was a fire in the stove, but no breakfast in preparation, and the bed was unmade. The cabin appeared to be waiting for Chance to come back, as though he had stepped out for but a moment, and Arlie sat down to await his return. The delay made her uneasy. She got up, and went over to the bed and smoothed the covers, her hands lingering on the thin pillow. Chance used that pillow; his head rested there every night. Having made the bed and swept the cabin, Arlie sat down again. Waiting was hard. Numerous times she went to the door and looked out, but Chance was not in sight. The girl had no idea of how long she had been there when she heard a horse outside, and starting up from the box she occupied, Arlie hurried to the door. There was a knock and she shrank back from it. Chance would not knock at the door of his own cabin! Before Arlie could take a full step back the door opened, disclosing a girl in the opening.

The girl was dark haired, flashing-eyed. There was color in her cheeks and her full, red lips were parted in amazement. "Oh!" exclaimed the girl in the door, and then again, "Oh!"

Arlie said nothing, made no movement. She was like some small, trapped animal. Lois Elder advanced a step into the room.

"Where is Chance?" she demanded.

"I don't know," Arlie answered hesitantly. "He went out . . ."

"Who are you?" Lois Elder seemed to fling the words at Arlie's head. "What are you doing here?"

"Chance . . ." began Arlie.

"Never mind explaining!" Lois' eyes were flashing. "I can see for myself! So that is the way Chance Pagan acts when I am gone! He keeps a woman in his cabin!"

"But I . . ." Arlie tried desperately to stop the flood of words.

"Don't try to lie!" The tone was a whiplash. "I can believe my own eyes. Chance Pagan was engaged to me and this is the way he acts! You can tell him never to set foot on the Spear again! I never want to see him again! Tell him I know what he is and I know what you are! You're a common . . ." Her hand went to her throat, snatched at the slender chain that held the ring, and breaking the chain, jerked out the ring. With a sweep of her arm she threw it from her.

"Stop!" Arlie's voice penetrated the anger in Lois' mind. Arlie was advancing, cheeks flushed, blue eyes blazing. "You can say what you want to about me, but don't you dare touch Chance Pagan. Don't you dare!"

Before that angry advance, Lois retreated. She found herself at the door, her hand against the lintel. Still Arlie came on.

"You leave Chance alone!" flared Arlie.

Lois drew herself up. "You dare to defend him!" she cried. "You dare . . ."

"Chance doesn't need to be defended. He hasn't done anything. I came here to see him. I had a message . . ."

"And stayed here with him, I suppose." There was withering scorn in the words. "Never mind answering me. Give him my message." Her back rigid, scorn in her very posture, Lois turned and stepped out of the cabin.

Just short of the door Arlie stopped. "You don't believe . . ." she began. But Lois Elder was gone, almost running, to the patiently waiting horse. Arlie, hand on the lintel of the cabin door, watched the dark-haired girl mount, swing her horse, and go galloping away. Then she turned back into the cabin.

"What have I done to you, Chance?" wailed Arlie softly. "What have I done?"

She stood there a moment, collecting herself, her hands trembling, tears in her blue eyes. Then, steadily, she turned to the door again, went out of the cabin and to the corral to get her pony. Silvertip's message was forgotten. All that Arlie could remember was the scorn in those flashing dark eyes and the words: "Chance Pagan was engaged to me and this is the way he acts . . . !" Arlie mounted her little horse and slowly rode out from the J Pen, back toward the mesa.

Lois Elder kept her horse at a lope. She was furious. The inconsistency of her position did not occur to her. All that she knew was that Chance Pagan had been untrue to her, had betrayed her during her absence. She did not remember that she had ridden out that morning to tell Chance that she no longer loved him, that her heart was given to another man. She did not recall that she had allowed Carl Terril to make love to her, almost to propose to her. Like many a person who has wronged another, Lois forgot her own straying and raged against Chance Pagan. She was done with Chance, free of him, free of him forever! She could ride back to Carl Terril with her heart free and her mind clear. Carl Terril . . . Lois thrust with spurred heels. The sorrel, who had slackened his gait, took up a run.

And where was Chance? At that moment he was a mile behind Lois Elder, spurring the black horse and swearing because the black was slow.

That morning Chance had risen early as usual, kindled his fire, and gone out to wrangle horses. He had left the black up for a wrangling horse and after saddling he rode out to the horse pasture. He found the horses at the far end of the pasture, Farmer and the buckskin and the bay NOW horse. The sorrel was not in evidence. Chance wanted the sorrel horse and looked for him. He was not in the horse pasture. Chance scratched his head and looked again. The sorrel bronk simply was not there!

A ride along the fence disclosed that the wire was tight. The fence didn't leak. There was a confusion of tracks at the gate. No opportunity to single one track from another. Chance rode back into the pasture again, up over the rise beyond the cabin. Somebody had taken that sorrel, lifted him, and left. When Chance met that somebody there would be some salty conversation! He would eat a bite of breakfast, get Farmer, and go looking for the sorrel horse and the person that had taken him. It would go much against the grain to have to ride over to the NOW and tell Cliff Nowlen that his horse was gone. Chance picked up Farmer, the bay and the buckskin, and headed home.

Coming over the rise in the horse pasture Chance saw a horse and rider going down the creek. They were half a mile away but the sun glinted from a bright coat on the horse. There went his horse, there went the sorrel! Chance couldn't tell who the rider was—it was too great a distance for that—but he was sure of the horse. He dropped the horses he drove, and set out in pursuit.

The gate bothered him. He had to stop and open it and then close it again. He did not ride through the ranch yard and he did not see the pony in the corral. Cutting across, Chance headed for the river where now the sorrel horse and the rider were lost to sight. He picked them up again when he climbed a rise. The rider was heading straight north, making for the Spear as straight as geese go north in the spring. Chance kicked the black and the black kept up his run, dropping back and back from the running sorrel. The sorrel had wings; Chance swore! He just picked up and flew, but Chance kept right on. He would at least find out where the sorrel went and who had him.

Arlie Pillow, reaching the top of the hill, set her course toward the Basin. Somehow her journey had tired her, somehow she was weary and old. When she reached the Basin she saw Pillow's teams and wagon in front of the store and she hurried, slipping around to the barn and stabling her pony, then fearfully, entering the building from the rear. It was nearly noon and Arlie feverishly kindled a fire in the stove and set about preparing a meal.

Pillow came into the kitchen. Arlie shrank from him but Pillow did not scold her, did not even ask her to explain her absence. Indeed the little, warped man was strangely jovial, apparently in high spirits. Art Ragland came in with a dark-faced man that Pillow called Blair. The three sat down to the meal that Arlie had prepared. They talked over their food, entirely oblivious to the girl that waited on them.

"How'd he take it, Tully?" asked Ragland. "Did he rave around some?"

Pillow shook his head. "It knocked him off his feet," he said. "He just read the paper an' didn't say a word."

"Silvertip was always pretty salty," Ragland commented.

"He's done!" Pillow flung back his head and laughed. "His days of bein' salty are over. I run the Basin now. If he wants to take orders he can."

Ragland shook his head. "He won't take orders," Ragland said definitely.

"I don't want him to. I want him to take what I've got for him. More coffee!"

Arlie filled her step-father's cup, her hands trembling. Something had happened to Silvertip. Something awful had happened.

"What are you goin' to do about Nowlen?" asked Blair, looking at Pillow.

Pillow shrugged. "Nothin', now," he said. "He's after some hay land. He thinks when he gets it we'll furnish his steers. We will, mebbe; mebbe his own steers."

All three laughed. Arlie put the coffee pot on the stove. She had to get away, she had to find out what had happened to Silvertip. It seemed to her that the meal would never end.

But it did end finally. The men filed out of the kitchen into the store, and throwing caution to the winds Arlie fled through the back door and up the rise to Silvertip's cabin. A little discretion remained with her. In place of rounding the cabin and entering at the front she slipped into the stable and called:

"Silvertip! Silvertip!" The call was soft, barely rising above a whisper. There was no answer and for a moment Arlie's heart pounded in her ears. Then Silvertip's voice came.

"You, Arlie? Can you get in?"

Arlie opened the door from the cabin to the stable and

went into the room. Silvertip lay on the bunk, his body twisted, the bedding a tangled knot beneath him. The man's eyes were shrunken into their sockets and the face above the beard was lined and seamed with pain.

"Silvertip!" Arlie exclaimed and went to him.

She helped the old man straighten himself, holding stiff and strong while he grasped her arms and pulled himself up. She got the bedding from beneath him and straightened it. Not until that was done did she speak.

"What happened? Tell me!"

"I fell and twisted my back again," Silvertip answered, his voice low. "Did you get to Chance? Did you tell him to come here?"

Arlie shook her head.

"Good!" Silvertip growled the word into his beard. "The Basin is no place for him now. Yo're goin' to have to get out of it, Arlie."

"What happened?" Again Arlie made her demand.

"I've just heard my death warrant," answered Silvertip, grimly. "Reach me that gun on the table, girl."

Arlie complied, her face pallid. "Your death warrant?" she murmured.

"In that paper on the table." Silvertip took the long-barreled gun in his hands and opening the loading gate, inspected the cylinder. "Read it if you want to."

Arlie picked up the paper. The headlines blazed beneath the caption: *Las Cruces Examiner.*

"BANK BANDITS FOILED," the headlines read. "SHERIFF'S POSSE KILL THREE DESPERADOES!"

"Silvertip!" gasped Arlie.

"Read it aloud, girl," rasped Silvertip. Mechanically

151

Arlie obeyed.

"Sheriff Jose Gonzales of Dona Ana county today foiled a clever plot to rob the First National Bank of this city," she read. "Warned of the coming of the bandits, Sheriff Gonzales and a ten-man posse stationed themselves about the bank building in advantageous positions. About ten o'clock, after the bank had opened, three men rode up to the doors. Two went into the bank while a third remained with the horses. The bank officials, warned of the coming raid, made no resistance but passed out the money in the cages, and it was not until the two bandits retired from the bank that the trap was sprung. Met by a withering blast of gunfire from the sheriff and his deputies, the two men who had entered the bank were killed immediately, and the man who had held the horses died half an hour later.

"In questioning the wounded man, the identity of the bandits was learned. They were: Tom Blaney, 37, of Crookman, Arizona; Poncho, a Mexican, age and address unknown; and William Saunders, commonly called Kid Saunders, of South Dakota. All three were known desperadoes. A reward of one thousand dollars had been placed on Blaney by the Arizona authorities. This reward, coupled with the Bankers' Association reward of one thousand dollars for each bandit killed while robbing a bank, will be paid to Sheriff Gonzales and his deputies.

"The money was recovered intact and no damage was done to the bank, other than a broken window, shattered by a bullet fired by one of the possemen. Sheriff Gonzales . . ."

"That'll do." Silvertip's voice was grim. "I reckon that'll do, girl."

"But the Kid and Poncho and Blaney . . ." began Arlie.

"They ain't comin' back," Silvertip rumbled. "The fools! If they'd talked to me!"

"But Silvertip . . . !"

The old man's voice rumbled on. He was not so much talking to the girl, as thinking aloud, and Arlie stopped her words to listen. "It's the end of it. I've kept the Basin clean enough. It was a place to come when a man was crowded. We laid off the Calico Hole. If we hadn't, the Hole would have cleaned us long ago. I reckon they will now, but I won't be here to see it!"

"What do you mean, Silvertip?"

"I mean that Pillow has got the Basin. All these new men, Ragland an' Pasmore an' Nowlen, they follow him."

"My step-father?"

"Pillow. He's crippled an' he's crazy. He thinks that the Basin can stack up against them from below. He thinks that the Basin can steal cattle an' horses an' keep out the men from the Hole. He's crazy. I warned him. If I could walk . . ."

"Can't you?" sharply.

The gray head was slowly shaken. "My back's gone," answered Silvertip. "For good this time, I guess. I fell again."

"Oh!" A sharp exclamation of pity and pain.

"Don't be sorry for me. You've got to get out of here. It's comin', now; comin' as soon as Pillow gets ready. All I hope is that he's the first man through that door!" There was savage rage in the wish.

"But Silvertip . . ."

"As sure as if he'd pulled the trigger, he killed those boys!" The rage grew. "He crossed 'em. He wrote Gonzales that they was comin'. An' damn him, I'll pay him for it!"

Arlie shrank back from the fierce old man on the bed. There was silence for a moment. Silvertip's voice had calmed when he spoke again. "Set that water bucket over by me," he requested. "Put out the oven full of bread, close to the bed, then you get out, Arlie. Get out of here an' out of the Basin."

"I won't leave you . . ."

"You've got to leave me! Want Pasmore to get hold of you? Do you want to be dragged around an' handed from man to man? You've got to go. Get to Chance an' tell him I sent you, an' tell him to stay out of the Basin!"

Arlie stood trembling beside the table. Silvertip, eyes bleak and sharp, stared at her. "Will you get the water?" he asked, gently.

Arlie brought the water bucket. Beside it she placed the Dutch oven, heavy and full of bread. "Silvertip . . ." she said.

From the store came Pillow's angry voice:

"Arlie! Arlie! Damn you, come here!"

"Slip out the back," Silvertip directed. "Get around behind the store an' answer him. An' girl, get out of the

154

Basin. Get to Chance!"

Arlie gave the man on the bed one final piteous look. Silvertip shook his head. With a little gesture Arlie moved across the room and opening the door to the stable, slipped through. Then she called:

"I'm coming, father." Silvertip let go a sigh of relief and his shoulders sagged. The long-barreled Colt was cradled in his hands. Perhaps Pillow would come again to gloat. Perhaps Pillow would step through that open door. If he did . . . Silvertip Upton smiled into his beard. He could not walk, but there was nothing the matter with his hands.

1 2

WHEN WAYNE ELDER and Carl Terril left the Spear, Lee Su, in the kitchen, was left alone on the ranch with Tony. Lee Su did not bother about Tony. Tony had found a little fence down where he wrangled the horses and was, even now, riding out to fix it, fence pliers and a boot top full of staples fastened to his saddle.

Lee Su was engrossed with difficulties. He had, returning to the Spear, found things not exactly to his liking. There was a big nick in his favorite cleaver and Ch'en, his favorite game cock, was sick. Tony, curse his ancestors, had not looked after Ch'en. With his dishes washed and put away Lee Su collected the cleaver and a sharpening stone, a teaspoon and some pepper, and went down to the barn.

Ch'en, the Warrior, drooped in his coop. Next to him

Wing Tai, a Red Cuban game cock, pecked viciously at the bars that restrained him. Ch'en was old and sick; Wing Tai was young and untried. Lee Su sat down and began to work on the cleaver, the while he eyed his pets. Presently he put aside the cleaver, caught Ch'en and gave him a small dose of cayenne pepper. Maybe that would pick him up.

The pepper had little effect, but when Wing Tai came over to the side of the cage Ch'en showed some life. That gave Lee Su an idea. Ch'en was going to die, it seemed. Then why let him die without using him? Here was Wing Tai that needed schooling in the pit. Here was Ch'en, veteran of many battles. Why not use Ch'en's last remaining energy to teach Wing Tai? A good idea. A very good idea. Lee Su congratulated his ancestors in having so brainy a descendant. He reached into his sleeve, brought out two pairs of needle-sharp, three-inch, steel fighting gaffs and, holding them, opened Ch'en's coop. As he pulled out the bird a horse pounded into the yard.

Lee paid no attention to the arrival, but fastened the gaffs to Ch'en and returned him to the coop. Catching Wing Tai he performed a like service to that battling bird. With the chickens gaffed, Lee Su held the Cuban's head toward Ch'en's cage and carefully billed the birds. Their hackles rose. Ch'en was showing plenty of life now. Carefully Lee Su opened Ch'en's coop and holding the Red Cuban, let Ch'en come out. He placed the Cuban on the ground.

The first arrival at the Spear had been Lois Elder on the sorrel. She flung herself from the saddle and letting the horse go, stamped to the house. Her humor was furious, wild, and she was ready to vent her wrath upon the first person she met. The sorrel walked down to the fence and fell to cropping the scanty grass.

Chance Pagan, almost ten minutes behind the girl, rode the black into the Spear yard and stopped. There was his sorrel horse, cropping grass along the fence. Chance looked at the house and then at the horse. Surprise filled his eyes. What was Lois Elder's saddle doing on his horse? Chance had put that saddle on too many horses to mistake it. Well, there was a way to get an answer. With no idea as to what he was running into, Chance dismounted and walked to the back door of the Spear. As one long familiar he opened the door and called for Lee Su. Receiving no response he walked into the kitchen. He was halfway across that room when Lois Elder opened the opposite door and stopped.

"Lois!" exclaimed Chance. "When did you get back? I saw your saddle on my sorrel horse but . . ."

"I came back too soon, evidently!" The scorn in Lois' voice stopped Chance.

"I went to the J Pen this morning," Lois continued. "I found what you'd been doing!"

For a moment guilt flooded Chance. Had Lois found out about those calves? It couldn't be. She couldn't have found them.

"I saw the woman you've been keeping."

"Woman?" Chance could not believe his ears.

"Don't try to lie out of it! I found her there. I never thought it of you, Chance."

"What's all this about?" demanded Chance. "What

woman are you talking about?"

"As if you didn't know!" It seemed to Chance that all the bitterness in the world was packed in those words.

"But I don't know," he expostulated.

"I thought that you loved me!" Lois flung reproach at the man in the center of the room. "I thought that . . ."

"But I do," Chance urged. "You know I do. I wrote to you an' . . ."

"And as soon as my back was turned you take up with another woman."

Chance lost his temper. "Now see here," he said reasonably, "I came here following my sorrel horse. I spotted him at the J Pen. I find him with your saddle on him. Maybe that's all right, but I'd like to know . . ."

"That's my father's horse!" Lois snapped. "I rode him. There is no use of trying to get out of it. What was that woman doing in your cabin?"

"There wasn't any woman in my cabin."

"I saw her with my own eyes! I accused her of living with you and she didn't deny it. Get out of here, Chance Pagan. Don't dare come near me. Don't you dare set foot on the Spear again!"

"Are you crazy?" Chance demanded. "Where's Wayne? There ought to be somebody around here with some sense!"

"I'll tell my father about you when he comes back," Lois flared. "He'll attend to you . . . you . . ." Lois began to cry, not from weakness but from wrath.

Instantly Chance was contrite. "Lois . . ." he began, advancing.

"Get away from me! Get . . . away . . . ! I never want

to speak to you again!" The girl struck viciously at Chance as he advanced, her hand splatting sharply against his cheek. "You living with a woman and daring to come here!"

Chance recoiled from the blow and as he stepped back the girl, turning, flung herself from the room. The door banged shut.

Chance stood stock-still in the kitchen, a dull red imprint growing on his cheek. Things were happening pretty fast, too fast for Chance. To come riding in following a horse-thief, to be met by Lois Elder and accused of harboring a woman in his cabin, to be slapped! Things were just a little speedy. Chance turned toward the back door. If that was the way she felt about it, all right! He was done! He might have expected it at the Spear. The Spear, the whole outfit was against him. Chance stamped out through the door and banged it behind him. Over across the yard his black horse stood beside the sorrel. Chance stalked toward the horses. He would go back to the J Pen. He would leave that sorrel right where it was and Wayne Elder or Lois could explain to Tom Melody how the horse came to be at the Spear. Chance reached the black horse and catching the reins led him out. He twisted out a stirrup preparatory to mounting. Something sharp and cutting struck him just at the knee. With a yelp of surprise Chance jumped back. The black horse shied.

Down at the barn things had also been occurring. Lee Su, having billed his birds, and released Wing Tai, let go his hold on Ch'en and stepped back. In his oriental mind there was no sympathy for Ch'en, a sick chicken pitted against a bold young fighter. There was only curiosity and a desire that Ch'en, before he died, would teach Wing Tai some of the tricks of the trade.

But Ch'en did not intend to die. Ch'en met Wing Tai breast to breast. Wing Tai went high into the air, his feet shuffling in a rapid motion. Ch'en went higher in the air, the gaffs twinkling lightning. Like a quail shot in mid-air, Wing Tai fell, collapsing into a huddled heap of feathers. Ch'en alighting on the dead bird, cackled his triumph and shuffled his feet.

"Hai!" yelped Lee Su in surprise. "Hai!" One yellow hand reached out for the bird. Ch'en struck at that hand, struck and brought the blood, and eluded the clutching fingers. As Lee Su scrambled to his feet, clutching the cleaver, Ch'en ran from the barn. Lee Su pursued his rooster. He would have that chicken's head!

Coming from the barn Ch'en saw a man with his back turned. Ch'en attacked that man, leaping high and striking with the gaffs.

Chance, struck at the knee, turned and kicked viciously. The bunch of feathers he kicked at, dodged and seemed to poise above the extended foot. French veal leather is no protection against three inch gaffs. At the barn door Lee Su waved the cleaver and came on, running. "You kick chicken!" raged Lee Su and threw the cleaver.

The whirling weapon missed Chance by inches. Without benefit of stirrup Chance went into the saddle. The black, snorting, wheeled away, ran and then fell to bucking. In all his eight years, the black had never encountered the like of this. He bucked straight away from the corral, bucked in a straight line, and when Chance, struggling, got his horse's head up, the black had the bit clamped in his iron mouth. The black ran and Chance went with him. Beside the corral Ch'en, his work done, began a triumphant crow. In the midst of that pæan of victory, the bird slumped and then collapsed. His exertion had finished Ch'en. Lee Su bent over his dead bird, his black eyes hard and gleaming, and then reaching out, lifted his cleaver. The cleaver had two nicks in its blade now, two nicks, both deep.

"Damn it!" said Lee Su.

Lois Elder, having slammed the kitchen door, stood waiting for Chance to open it. She was still crying, so angry that she could not stop the flow of tears. There were more things that she wanted to say to Chance Pagan, and when she heard him stamp out of the kitchen and the outer door slam shut, her anger and resentment increased. She was tempted to follow him, to scream at him, but she did not. Instead she flounced across the room and flung herself down into the big rawhide-bottomed chair that was Wayne Elder's. She was sitting there, seething internally, when she heard Lee Su shuffle across the kitchen and, looking up, saw his impassive yellow face at the door.

"Chlicken dead," announced Lee Su. "You like chlicken fo' dinnah?"

"I don't want anything to eat!" Lois snapped.

"You sick?" The yellow face did not change expression. "Twelve o'clock. Dinnah time now."

"I'm not sick and I don't want anything to eat. Get out!"

Lee Su closed the door.

For a while Lois remained in the chair. She calmed gradually but the bitter, burning resentment against Chance did not lessen. Finally restlessness overcame her. She got up from the chair and going to her room changed from the riding skirt and blouse she had worn, into a dress. With that done, a fury of energy attacked her. There was no one for her to vent her wrath upon except Lee Su. Lee Su, stolid and impregnable, was no fitting object. Lois attacked the house. Beginning with her own room she turned things upside down. She swept, she dusted, she changed furniture about, and as she worked, the physical exertion relieved her mental stress.

At six o'clock Lee Su appeared again. Lee Su had lain low during the afternoon. He knew that Lois was in bad temper and he had no desire to clean house. Standing in the kitchen door Lee Su requested information as to the number that would be in for supper and if there were any particular dishes desired. Lois shook her head.

"Cook what you please," she directed. "I don't know how many will be here."

Grunting, Lee Su retired. Lois looked about her. She was flushed and tired. The living-room was swept, mopped, dusted, and came as close to glistening as a ranch room can. There was not another thing to be done.

As she surveyed the room Lois heard a horseman

come up outside. Leather creaked and then there was the slow thump of boots on the porch. With no preliminary knock the door was opened. Tom Melody stood looking into the room.

"Have they brought Wayne?" asked Melody slowly.

Lois Elder's hand flew to her mouth. Her eyes were wide. There was that about Tom Melody that spoke of disaster.

"What?" the girl gasped.

Melody came slowly into the room. "You didn't know?" he asked.

"Didn't know what?"

Tom Melody sat down in the rawhide-bottomed chair. "Yore daddy," he said deliberately, "was hurt this mornin'. They've sent the wagon to bring him in."

"Hurt?" she said uncomprehendingly. "Dad?"

"Shot." Melody had no finesse, nothing but bluntness. "The word was brought to me in town. I've sent a telegram for the doctor in Fort Logan. Babe Wilmot is waitin' in town to bring him out."

"But . . . but dad! He was all right this morning. He . . ."

"He ain't all right now," grated Melody. "I thought they'd have him here by now. You better get ready for him."

Lois Elder sank down, a little huddled heap on the floor. She did not faint, it was simply that her legs no longer would hold her up. Tom Melody came up out of his chair. "Here, that won't do," he said sternly. "Get up from there. They're bringin' yore daddy in in the wagon. You've got to get things ready for him an' for the doctor when he comes!" The old man reached down a long arm and caught Lois' shoulder, and the girl came to her feet. Some of the shock was gone. She stared steadily at Melody.

"Who did it?" she demanded.

Tom Melody shook his head. "We'll come to that when the times comes."

Lois turned from the sheriff. She hurried to the kitchen, calling to Lee Su. "Get a hot fire in the range. Heat a big kettle of water," she directed. Coming back from the kitchen she went to Wayne Elder's bedroom, entered it, and turned back the covers on the bed. "Now," she said to Melody, who had followed her, "tell me . . ."

"There's the wagon," grated Melody.

Wheels rumbled slowly just outside the Spear ranch house.

The men brought Wayne Elder carefully into the house. There was John Comstock, carrying the Spear owner as though Elder were a baby cradled in his arms. Behind Comstock came Bill Fahrion, face white and anxious, and moving on tiptoe and behind Fahrion was Carl Terril. Lois fled to Terril, straight as a homing pigeon, into his arms.

"Lois!" Terril breathed. "Lois girl! Don't worry. He'll be all right."

Comstock took Wayne Elder into his room and laid him on the open bed. The bearded and burly cook, having tied his chuck wagon team, came through the door. The cook went straight to the bedroom. Cal Davis, the cook, was a doctor of sorts. He had set many a broken bone, had given many a puncher a dose of soda and vinegar, and more than once he had bandaged a gunshot wound. Lois could hear Davis' voice rumbling in the bedroom.

"Don't stand there like a ninny, Bill. Help me get his clothes off!" The strong arms about Lois tightened. She sobbed against Carl Terril's chest.

John Comstock came out of the bedroom. His face was straight-lined and hard with determination. He walked up to Tom Melody. "I was with him. Did Babe tell you?"

Tom Melody nodded. "He told me that you an' him an' Wayne went up into the Drippin' Springs to see some calves that somebody was weanin' up there, an' that whoever had the calves, taken a shot at Wayne from the brush."

"Is that all he told you?"

"That's all he knew. I left him in town to wait an' bring the doctor out when he comes. I sent a telegram to Fort Logan. Do you know any more, John?"

John Comstock nodded. "I do," he said firmly. "It was Chance Pagan that shot Wayne!"

"What?" The word was jerked from Melody. In Terril's arms Lois stopped her sobbing. Bill Fahrion appeared at the bedroom door.

"Chance Pagan," said Comstock firmly. "I saw the horse he rode. It was that bright sorrel he'd borrowed from Nowlen."

"Are you sure?" Melody had a grip on Comstock's arm.

"I'm sure."

Dead silence followed that announcement. Then, from the door Fahrion spoke. "Why didn't you tell me? Why didn't you tell me, John? I'd have gone to the J Pen an' I'd have ripped Chance Pagan apart. By God . . . !"

"Hold it!" Melody's voice came, stopping Fahrion. The sheriff looked from one man to another in the room. "How many know this?" he asked Comstock.

"Us here. I didn't speak till we got in. I . . ."

"You wanted Pagan to get away!" accused Fahrion from the door. "He's a friend of yores, the black hearted . . ."

"I didn't want a lynching!" John Comstock broke through Fahrion's tirade. "I've told you, Melody. I knew the horse. Nowlen bought him from us. I saw him in the Cassidy livery barn and Chance was using him."

Melody looked around the room. His voice was deliberate as he spoke. "Nobody'll say a word about this, understand? Nobody!"

"If you think you can stop me . . ." blurted Fahrion.

"I can stop you," said Melody quietly, but with force in his voice. "If I have to lock you up an' keep you, I'll do it, Bill. There'll be no lynchin' in this county. Not while I'm sheriff. You done right, John, keepin' still until you got to me."

Again his eyes traveled over the group. "There's goin' to be a bunch of boys in here from the round-up pronto, now. They'll find the wagon gone an' they'll follow it. You'll say no word, none of you. You'll not speak until I have Chance Pagan in jail. Hear me?"

The driving force of the old officer, the strength of his

very being, was in that last command. One by one his eyes met those of the others and those other eyes lowered. Even Bill Fahrion, slowly, grumbling, gave his consent. "I'll keep my mouth shut," rumbled Fahrion, "but if Wayne dies . . ."

Behind Fahrion the bearded face of the cook appeared. "Say," Cal Davis spoke calmly around the chew of tobacco that bulged his cheek, "Wayne's got his eyes open. That slug went high. Looks like it just missed the lung. If some of you'd get me the turpentine . . ." Davis' eyes bulged. A flying girl thrust him out of the way, bursting past him to go to her father.

The others followed the girl. They stood about the bed, looking down at the wan man that lay there, and at the girl, on her knees, her head buried on the bedding. Wayne Elder's eyes were open. His lips moved, but even when he bent close Tom Melody could not make out the words that Elder tried to speak. The sheriff straightened.

"Yo're all right, Wayne," said Tom Melody strongly. "Yo're home. Yo're all right."

Elder's blue eyes closed. Lois, one arm across her father's knees, shook with her sobbing.

"If somebody'd get me the turpentine . . ." complained Davis.

"You lay off the turpentine," commanded Melody, "until the doctor gets here. Terril, get that girl up an' out of here. Bill, I'm countin' on you an' John to keep yore mouths shut an' keep the rest of 'em quiet. When yore crew gets in you hold 'em here till I give the word."

"Where are you going?" demanded Bill Fahrion.

Tom Melody looked at him. "I'm going to get Chance," he said simply. "I reckon I'll need a fresh horse. I might have to ride a piece."

13

CHANCE PAGAN, when he pulled the black down, rode on south toward the J Pen. After his first bucking and the run, the black was easy enough to handle. Chance had kept him up during the night and had brought him down from the J Pen at a hard lope. That had taken the ginger out of the black.

For awhile Chance did no logical thinking at all. Lois Elder had blown all the logic out of his head as effectually as though she had exploded a dynamite bomb therein. Chance revolved the happenings, tried to think, and got nowhere. He covered the first five miles from Spear without making any headway toward an explanation. At the end of those five miles the black went stone lame.

Chance got off the horse and looked him over. Somewhere, either in the run to the Spear, in the bucking, or in the run following the bucking, the black horse had bowed a tendon. Chance swore helplessly. That wasn't his horse. If the black was ruined then Chance had a horse to buy. He could not ride the black further, that was certain, and there was still about ten miles to cover to the J Pen. One thing for it: walk! walk, and like it! Chance walked but he did not like it.

A man walking can make four miles an hour. A man

walking in high heeled boots, towing a lame horse that hangs back on the reins, cannot make four miles an hour. Chance found that out. Chance had left the Spear at just about twelve o'clock. It was after five when he reached the J Pen and his feet and temper were worn to a frazzle.

At the J Pen, coming into the yard with the black limping behind him, and still leading like a stone boat, Chance stopped short. There was a horse in the corral, a sorrel horse. Chance towed the black over to the corral fence and with unbelieving eyes stared over the bars. Sure enough, that was his sorrel horse. There was no mistaking him. Chance rubbed his eyes, wiped the sweat from his forehead and stared again. It *was* the sorrel!

Automatically he stripped the saddle from the black and turned him into the pen. The black limped over to drink. The sorrel nervously circled the fence.

"How in time did you get here?" Chance demanded of the sorrel. The sorrel, normally enough, made no answer.

It took Chance some little time to unravel his puzzle. He had left that sorrel at the Spear but here he was. Chance had come straight back from the Spear and no one had passed him. Chance scratched his head. Then an explanation of this new mystery entered his mind. He swore gently. Of course! John Comstock had told him in Cassidy that the Spear had two horses, just about alike. They had sold one to Cliff Nowlen. The horse that Chance had seen at the Spear was the other sorrel.

"I made a fine fool of myself!" announced Chance.

"I sure did."

Leaving the corral he walked, limped rather, to the house. It had just occurred to him that he had had nothing to eat for about twenty-four hours. He had left the J Pen before breakfast, he had had no dinner and now it was supper time. His belly clamored for food.

In the cabin Chance kindled a fire and set about stilling the demands of his stomach. He put cold biscuits into the oven, he sliced salt pork into a pan of water and he opened a can of beans and made coffee. When the water over the salt pork boiled, he drained it off and let the pork fry. The smell was a pleasant agony, and when the coffee boiled that agony was redoubled. Chance carried his food to the table and sat down.

For the first few minutes he was occupied with eating; then as his appetite was quieted, he took his time. Things had certainly happened to him today. Plenty of things. Chance reviewed them. None of the memories were pleasant ones.

When he finished eating and had put his dishes in the dishpan, Chance sat down and pulled off his boots. Rolling up his trousers leg he examined the gaff jab at his knee. It was deep and painful. Chance got up and, searching, found a bottle of horse liniment. The liniment stung like fire in the cut and burned the two little stabs in his foot. Having his boots off felt mighty good.

Chance lit the lamp and walking over to the bunk lay down. Dusk was deepening outside. He would have to go out pretty soon and attend to his horses, but right now he wanted to think and rest his feet.

Lois Elder, down at the Spear, had laid him out. She

had just about knocked all the wind out of him. Chance raised a hand to his cheek and touched it. The girl had slapped him plenty hard. It seemed as though the cheek still burned. Certainly his mind burned. What had she meant about seeing a woman in the J Pen cabin? There wasn't any woman here. Chance raised up on an elbow. It occurred to him, suddenly, that the bed was made. He knew he had not made it. Arlie! That was it! Arlie Pillow had ridden over and Lois had seen her.

Thinking of Arlie calmed Chance. He eased back on the bunk. There was a girl! She wouldn't go spying on a man! She would believe in him and stick with him and back him up, no matter what happened. Chance did not know how he knew it; he just knew. He remembered the anxious blue eyes and the tremulous lips of the Basin girl. Remembering them he could not but compare the two. Lois Elder was imperious, she was demanding, and she certainly had told him off! She had said that she was done with him, with Chance Pagan. Well, he was done with her! No one could talk to him like that. He would not try to explain to Lois. She was just like the rest of the Spear outfit!

With a groan Chance sat up. He had to attend to the horses, and had to turn the black out. If the black really had bowed a tendon he would be laid up for a long time. And there was that sorrel in the corral. Had the sorrel got out and been brought back by someone, or had the sorrel been ridden, or what? Chance didn't know. Here was a first-class mystery. Chance pulled on his boots, wincing as they found the sore spots on his feet.

He walked out of the cabin and down to the corral.

The dusk was thick but it was not yet dark. At the corral fence Chance stood, meditating a moment. Arlie Pillow had come over from the Basin. Why had she come? Had it been a repetition of the scrubbing and socks and pie incident? Or had there been another reason? Chance wondered. Uneasiness grew in his troubled mind. Had Arlie brought a message from Silvertip? Was the girl in trouble? Chance had told her to come to him if she wanted to leave the Basin. He had said that he would take her to Cassidy. He remembered the night in Silvertip's cabin, the snarling, growling voice of Sam Pasmore, and the swift and sudden action there. There was only one thing for him to do: ride to the Basin and find out what Arlie's visit had meant.

Stooping, Chance took his rope from his saddle where it lay beside the fence. He would get the sorrel, run in the other horses, and then ride to the Basin. Tired as he was, he knew that he had to go. Carrying the rope Chance went into the corral.

There was still light enough to see. Chance estimated that he would have just about time to get the horses in before full dark came; then he would wait for the moon and make his ride. His rope circled and shot out, missing the sorrel.

On the second loop he caught the horse and held him. The sorrel did not fight the rope much. Chance went down it gingerly. Generally he had to tie up a foot before he saddled the animal. Now the horse stood. Somebody had taken the ginger out of the sorrel. He had been ridden that day. Chance slid his rope up until it was behind the sorrel's ears and led the horse out.

The animal stood for saddling. He accepted the bit and did not fight it. Chance mounted the horse and leaving the corral gate open, put the black out. He followed the limping black to the horse pasture, let the black in, and rode over the rise. Farmer, the NOW bay, and the buckskin were just over the hill. Chance drove them ahead of him to the corral.

When he had the horses penned, he unsaddled. The velvety darkness was coming now. Chance limped over to the shed and brought back the lantern. He sat down beside the fence, rolled a cigarette and lit it. The moon would come up in another half hour. Chance waited for the moon, letting his body relax and his tired feet rest.

When the moon came peering over the eastern hills he got up and lit the lantern. Putting it beside his saddle he went into the corral with his rope. Farmer, carefully handled, would let a man catch him. Chance, on aching feet, dodged back and forth until he had Farmer cornered, and then advancing slowly, got the rope over the big bay's neck. He led Farmer out and with the lantern to aid the moon, put on his saddle. Farmer stood, his back humped, his ears sullen. Chance led the horse away from the fence.

Twisting out a stirrup he caught the reins close to Farmer's ears and eased himself up. Farmer had been pitching a little at every saddle for the last few weeks. Chance caught the off stirrup and settled himself for the crow-hopping. Farmer ducked his head. Farmer went up high and wide and lit, sucking back under the saddle. Farmer started to do a real job. The lantern on the ground beside the corral fence was first on one side and then on the other side of Chance. On the fifth jump Chance was loose in the saddle, his balance gone. On the sixth jump he lost a stirrup, and on the seventh Farmer shucked his rider as clean as an ear of corn in an Iowa corn patch. Chance lit, all the wind knocked out of him. For a minute he lay, dazed. He could hear the thump of Farmer's feet, could feel the tremor of the ground as the big horse came down. Chance scrambled up.

"Damn you, Farmer!" he swore. "You've gone outlaw on me!"

Chance Pagan's head still reeled from his fall. There was still sparkling light going through his head, flashing before his eyes. He reached out a hand toward the corral fence, close by. As his eyes cleared he saw that the lantern was being held in the air. There was a man holding it up. Steadying himself by the fence Chance looked at the lantern holder. It was Tom Melody.

"Where did you come from?" demanded Chance, still dazed. "How did you get out here, Tom?"

Melody's voice was calm. "I came from the Spear."

Chance, his head clearing, let go his hold on the fence and moved toward Melody. "That horse has gone clear bad on me," he said. "He's a plumb outlaw."

Melody's voice was cold. "The horse ain't the only one that's gone outlaw. I'll take that gun, Chance."

Startled, Chance saw that Melody was holding a heavy, blue weapon in his right hand. The lantern held high was in his left. Behind Melody the sheriff's horse stood, head drooping. Farmer had quit bucking and was standing now, well along the fence.

"What's the matter, Tom?" demanded Chance. "What's wrong with you?"

"There's nothin' wrong with me, Chance," answered Melody sadly. "Just hand over your gun."

Slowly Chance reached back to the spring holster at his hip. His gun was gone. "I've lost it," he said. "Tom . . ."

"It's on the ground where you fell. Step aside, Chance."

Chance moved away. Melody, advancing, stooped and picked up the weapon from beside the corral. He put it in the waistband of his overalls, moving carefully, not taking his eyes from Chance.

"We're goin' to Cassidy," said Melody.

"You might tell me what all this is about," said Chance.

"It's about some calves," answered the officer.

Guilt flooded Chance. So they had found the calves! He had been seen then, when, so foolishly, he had ridden over during the day. Of all the fool things . . . !

"Those are my calves," Chance defended himself. "You heard Fahrion tell me they wouldn't pay for my hay. I was just collecting. When I see Wayne . . ."

"You've seen Wayne," Melody's voice was hard. "Did you have to shoot Wayne Elder to collect for your damned hay? Chance . . ."

"Wayne? Me shoot Wayne?"

Melody's voice went on, reading a cold indictment. "Do you think I'm a fool, Chance? You took that NOW sorrel you've been ridin' an' went over to look at the calves you'd stolen. When you saw John Comstock an' Babe an' Wayne you lost your head. You cut down on Wayne and dropped him. Comstock saw you when you left."

So that was where the sorrel had gone? That accounted for the sorrel's disappearance. "I haven't had the sorrel today," snapped Chance. "He was gone from the horse pasture when I went to wrangle this morning. I looked for him. I . . ."

"Do you expect me to believe that?" Still Melody's voice was cold. "You'll have to cook up a better story. I'll take you to Cassidy and you ought to thank God it's me that's takin' you. If the Spear crew knew about this they'd be out here an' you'd hang."

"But I tell you . . ."

"Get yore horse. I'm takin' you in, you Judas!"

Chance Pagan, looking at the hard old face lighted by the lantern, closed his jaws firmly. His mind was working like a well oiled spring. There was no use in trying to talk to Tom Melody. Melody had his mind made up. One false move and the old sheriff would shoot. The sorrel horse, stolen from the J Pen pasture, had been used to good advantage. Wayne Elder had been shot and that shooting was pinned on Chance Pagan.

"Is Wayne dead?" asked Chance calmly.

"No thanks to you that he ain't."

Relief flooded Chance. "Did Wayne say I shot him?" he demanded.

"Wayne ain't talkin'. Get yore horse!" Impatiently.

"I'll have to rope him," said Chance.

"Do it then."

Chance stooped and picked up his rope from where it lay coiled beside the fence. Farmer was down the fence. The moon was high now, high enough so that Chance could see. Melody's shadow was black against the corral posts. He had lowered the lantern so that it dangled beside him and the gun was held firmly in his right hand. Chance knew that once he had caught Farmer, Melody would handcuff him. "You'll have trouble takin' me in on that horse," Chance said, calmly shaking out a loop.

"I'll take you in," grated Melody.

It was now or never. Chance Pagan had no intention of being taken to the Cassidy jail. Once there, and he was done. He was an outlaw now, a cattle-thief, accused of dry-gulching the man who had raised him. It was whole hog or none. Holding the rope Chance moved down the fence toward Tom Melody and Farmer, beyond the sheriff.

"There's nobody to lie for me, is there?" asked Chance, remembering Silvertip.

Melody retreated, stepping away from the fence, to Chance's right. "What do you mean?" snapped Melody.

"If Silvertip hadn't lied for my father this wouldn't have happened," Chance answered. "You wouldn't believe me now on a stack of Bibles, would you?"

"You'll have every chance," answered Melody. "At least they won't take an' hang you out of hand."

"They won't hang me at all." Chance lifted his rope. Farmer pricked up his ears. Melody's horse moved to the right. "They . . ." The rope shot out, not toward the

177

big bay but at the sheriff. Chance was staking it all on that throw. If he missed, Melody would shoot.

But he did not miss. The rope lashed across the sheriff's face. Chance had not tried to rope Tom Melody, he had simply whipped out with the rope. Melody dropped the lantern. The gun in his hand spouted flame and lead, but that lashing rope had blinded the man. Chance, leaping after the rope, struck the officer, dropping him, crashing him to the ground. One flying hand swept down for the gun Melody held. The other swung in a blow. Down the fence Farmer snorted and whirled to run. Tom Melody's horse, better trained and more gentle, danced away. On the ground two bodies writhed as Chance Pagan fought desperately to hold the gun away from him. His right arm, free, pumped in short, chopping blows. Some of those blows went home, others did not. Tom Melody was old and wiry and tough. Chance Pagan was young and tough and wiry. Chance Pagan was desperate. That desperation did the trick. Melody, relaxing for a moment, unable to keep the pace, took a blow on the head. Chance's fist caught him on one side and his head struck a corral post. Melody went limp. Chance, twisting the weapon from the officer's hand, scrambled up. The lantern had rolled and gone out and there was only the moonlight.

Panting, clothing torn, breathless from the struggle, Chance still could not stop. Tom Melody was only dazed, not knocked out. It was Chance or Melody, and Chance knew it. The sheriff's gun swept down, the barrel striking true and hard against Tom Melody's head. There was no pity in the blow, given by a man fighting for his life. Tom Melody sprawled limply.

For a moment, then, Chance stood collecting himself. He bent down over Melody, took his gun from where it was caught in Melody's shirt and overalls and automatically holstered it. Melody's breath came raspingly. There was a dark trickle of blood from his scalp where the gun barrel had struck.

"It was you or me!" panted Chance. "You or me, Tom."

No time to wait now, no time to see how badly Melody was hurt, or to attempt to repair the damage. Chance Pagan, stooping again, caught up his rope. He penned Farmer in the corner between the corral and the shed and caught the big horse. He held Farmer tight when he mounted, pulling the horse's head up and going into the saddle. Farmer humped his back but made no effort to buck. Wheeling the horse about Chance looked down at Melody, lying there in the moonlight beside the dark corral. For an instant he looked and then Chance Pagan, outlaw, swung his mount and headed for the hills, headed for Calico Mesa and the Badlands.

After a time, after the pounding of Farmer's hoofs had faded and diminished into nothing, Tom Melody groaned. He lifted his hand to his head and groaning again sat up. The moon was high over him, coming straight down. Melody crawled to the corral, crawled the four feet that spread between him and the posts, caught a post and pulled himself to his feet. He stood there, supporting himself by the fence, collecting himself. Gradually, as he gained control over his reeling head, he relinquished his support. After a time he took a step or two, staying close to the corral, trying himself out. His legs functioned. His tough old body, resilient as rawhide, recovered from the shock. Tom Melody went into the corral and taking water from the trough, splashed it over head and face.

The water revived him. Chance Pagan had been gone three quarters of an hour when Melody, moving slowly but surely, drove his horse into the corral and caught him. Mounting the animal Melody looked up at Calico Mesa, black and tipped with the white light of the moon. The sheriff's face was hard, implacable. Melody swung his horse out of the open corral gate and steadily, without looking back, rode to the north. There was no sentiment in Tom Melody, nothing but a hard determination. Chance Pagan had got away, had taken to the mesa. Chance Pagan was in the Badlands, perhaps in the Basin. Tom Melody rode toward the Spear. He had failed once. He would return with the Spear riders and this time he would not fail.

When the sheriff rode into the Spear the moon was setting. There were lights in the house, and at the corral a cluster of horses were tied to the fence. The Spear riders had come in. Melody added his horse to the others and went in through the kitchen; there he paused to drink a cup of the hot black coffee that Lee Su had made. Lee Su followed the officer into the living-room.

All of the Spear crew was in the living-room. Men squatted against walls, their eyes hard and bright on the sheriff. These men knew what had happened; Tom Melody saw that, despite his orders, they knew what had happened. Over beside the door Babe Wilmot teetered on his heels and in a chair close to the fireplace Carl Terril stared at the smouldering logs. Every eye turned to Melody when he entered.

Bill Fahrion, coming from beside Terril, went to Melody. "What happened?" he demanded, keeping his voice low. "You've been hurt, Tom."

"Did the doctor get here?" countered Melody.

"Just come. Babe brought him out from town. He's with Wayne. What happened to you?"

"Pagan happened to me," Melody answered grimly. "I took too many chances with him. He got away."

"How?" The Spear men, the reps from the Quarter Circle Bar and the LK assembled in a tight little circle about the officer. They were breathing deeply, raspingly, as men will when under excitement or stress.

"He slapped my face with a rope," Melody answered, not sparing himself, "then jumped me an' got my gun. I reckon he slapped me with it, too."

"You've got a cut on yore head," said Fahrion. "We'll get the doc to look at it when he's done with Wayne."

"Has Wayne talked any?"

"Not to amount to anything. He don't know what happened to him."

Melody's eyes went around that circle of hard faces. "I reckon we'll go to the mesa in the mornin'," he said slowly. "Chance got away an' took to the hills."

"What's the matter with now?" asked a voice, Ben Godman's.

Melody shook his head. "When it's light," he said. "There'll be time enough."

"And Chance has gone clear bad?" That was John Comstock.

Melody looked at the speaker. "He told a cock an' bull story about somebody takin' that sorrel horse," he answered.

The voices of the men in the circle murmured. From that murmur came one voice, metallic, distinct. It rose above the others.

"Chlance Pagan bad," announced Lee Su. "He kick chlicken."

Melody looked at the impassive, yellow face. "So," he said, a grim smile twisting his lips. "I reckon that settles it, boys."

"Today noon he kick chlicken," stated Lee Su, making his case strong.

Tom Melody's eyes widened. John Comstock was staring at the Chinese.

"When?" rasped Melody.

"Dinna' time. He come here, have fight with Miss Lois. Kick my chlicken."

Comstock's eyes sought Tom Melody's. Sheriff and puncher stared at each other. "At noon?" questioned Melody.

"It was noon an' after when we reached the Dripping Springs," stated Comstock. "Where is Lois?"

"She's with her dad," rasped Fahrion. "What's this got to do with . . ."

"If Chance Pagan was here at noon he couldn't have shot Wayne," rasped Melody. "Not unless he was twins,

182

or could fly. Where's Lois?"

Comstock had already gone to the door of the bedroom. His voice was soft but seemed loud in the quiet room. "Lois!"

Lois Elder, her eyes red but chin firmset and defiant, appeared in the doorway. "Dad is bad but he's not going to die," she stated. "Doctor Grayson said so. He got the bullet out and . . ."

"Was Chance Pagan here at noon?" Melody interrupted.

The girl looked at the sheriff. "Why . . ." she said, her eyes narrowing as she thought, "he was here. He . . . I suppose it must have been about noon. Lee Su came in right after he left and said that it was dinner time."

"Tell me about it, girl," Melody came forward until he stood looking down at Lois. "Tell it careful."

Lois flushed. "I went to the J Pen this morning," she said. "I . . . I had a reason. I wanted to see Chance. He wasn't there and . . . well, I came back here as fast as I could. I hadn't been here ten minutes before Chance came in. He had some foolish tale about following a sorrel horse. He said that I'd taken my horse from his corral. I . . . we quarreled and he went away. That's all."

Her eyes turned appealingly to Carl Terril and Terril smiled at her. At the edge of the group Babe Wilmot moved stealthily away.

"And it was noon and Chance was followin' you because you rode the sorrel?" That was Comstock's question.

Lois nodded. The men in the group about the girl did not feel the draft of air as Wilmot opened and closed the door; they were too intent upon what was happening here. Comstock turned to Melody.

"The sorrel Chance had was a full brother to our horse," said Comstock. "They're alike as two peas in a pod."

Tom Melody was nodding slowly. "Chance was here at noon," stated the sheriff. "Wayne was shot in the Drippin' Springs, twenty miles away, an' that was noon." He looked around him. "It couldn't have been Chance," Melody completed.

Slowly the heads about the speaker nodded.

"But he didn't deny stealin' the calves," Fahrion rasped. "He slammed you over the head, an' ran. Are you goin' to let him get away?"

Tom Melody stared hard at the burly Spear foreman. "It's my head," he said slowly, "an' I've got the ache in it. Chance took some calves, yes. I reckon Wayne an' him can settle about that. Seems to me like Wayne owes him some calves. The important thing right now is to get the man who shot Wayne."

Again the heads in the circle nodded.

14

CHANCE PAGAN rode up the mesa road. He was branded now, there was no question as to what he was. Outlaw! He had stolen cattle, he had escaped from Tom Melody, knocked the sheriff on the head, and he was supposed to have shot Wayne Elder. This, Chance thought, was how a hunted man felt. This was the way it felt to be a long rider, a man wanted by the law. It was not a nice feeling, not a pleasant one.

Riding up the road, Farmer strong under him, he reflected bitterly on the events and occurrences that had brought him to this pass. Bill Fahrion was the man he singled out for his wrath, and the girl, Lois Elder. If it had not been for Fahrion he would never have taken the calves, never have ordered John Comstock from the J Pen. In place of riding up the mesa trail he would now be with the bunch of Spear hands, looking for the man who shot Wayne Elder. If it had not been for Lois he would be at the Spear, and while he would still be guilty of stealing Spear stock, he would not be accused of downing Wayne. That was the sum and substance of it. Bill Fahrion and Lois Elder: they were to blame!

Chance shook his head. They were not to blame. There was just one man at the root of all his troubles: proud, high-headed, hot-tempered, foolish Chance Pagan. Chance Pagan whose father had been a thief and a weakling, who had allowed another man to take the blame for his misdeeds. That was the fellow. Chance Pagan!

But there was no back-tracking now. No backing down. He had placed himself in this position, he could not get out of it. The boot fit; he had to wear it. He would go to Silvertip Upton. He was already in Silvertip's debt, or rather his father was in Silvertip's debt. Silvertip, perhaps, would help him, direct him to a hiding place, give him the lay of this strange country into which he rode. A man entering the Badlands needed a guide. There could be none better than

Silvertip Upton.

When he reached the mesa top Chance set his course for the Basin. There was no need to hide his trail. Tom Melody knew where he had gone and would follow him, that is if Tom Melody ever followed anyone again. That last blow with the Colt had been shrewd and hard. Perhaps he had really killed Tom Melody in place of just being accused of killing Wayne Elder. Chance laughed bitterly and Farmer cocked his ears back. There was no mirth in that laugh, that Farmer could discern.

When he reached the Basin, Chance looked down at the dark buildings. The moon was high and touched the top of Pillow's store with light. There was a lamp burning in the store, otherwise the Basin was dark. Chance wondered if Arlie was sleeping peacefully beneath that moon-touched roof. He hoped that she was. Poor Arlie, poor little kid. A tough life for anyone, the kind she led, let alone a girl, a sensitive kid like Arlie. Chance remembered how her eyes looked and how her lips had trembled.

He rode on down. Farmer made no sound after he left the rock of the road, and Chance, circling, kept away from the store and on toward Silvertip's cabin. At the foot of the knoll upon which the cabin rested he dismounted in the shadows. Climbing the knoll, still keeping to the shadows, Chance reached the back of the cabin. Purposely he was keeping hidden. He wanted to see Silvertip, not advertise his arrival to every man or any man in the Basin. The light in Pillow's store told him that men were still up and about. Chance left

Farmer behind the stable room of the cabin and entered that dark shed. In it he spoke softly: "Silvertip!"

There was no answer. The quiet was so intense that it seemed almost to scream. "Silvertip," said Chance again, "Are you there?"

He expected a light to flame in the cabin, to hear Silvertip moving about, but there was no sound. Chance, listening, ears alert, heard a faint clicking. There were three clicks, rapid and close together. Such a noise is made by a single action Colt when it is cocked and the trigger not held down.

"It's me. Chance Pagan."

A voice came from the cabin, a voice filled with incredulity. "Chance Pagan?"

"It's me, Silvertip," assured Chance again.

The voice was cautious. "Who's with you?"

"Nobody."

"Come in, then. Come in slow an' when you get inside light a match. If you don't show a light when you step through the door, I'll shoot."

Chance found a match in his pocket. Holding it he stepped to the wall where his searching hand found the door. He pushed on the door and scratched a match at the same time. The match flamed, tiny in the darkness.

"Put it out an' come in." Silvertip's voice showed his relief.

Chance shook out the match and stepped into the cabin. "What are you doin' here?" rasped Silvertip. "I told you to stay out of the Basin."

"I had no place else to come," explained Chance simply.

"Why? What's happened to you?"

"I took some calves to collect for the hay that was owed for," answered Chance. "I been accused of shootin' Wayne Elder an' I hit Tom Melody over the head with a gun an' got away." Chance put it all in that short, succinct statement.

In the darkness Silvertip laughed, a harsh, sharp bark. "You did it all, didn't you?" he rasped. "Did you shoot Elder?"

"No."

"Then," said Silvertip, "sit down, you young fool, an' tell me all about it."

Chance's groping hand found the bed. He sat down upon it, feeling Silvertip close beside him. "I'm a young fool, all right," confessed Chance. "I got into this jackpot all by myself."

With that confession as the beginning, he continued. He told Silvertip of taking the calves and putting them behind the brush fence in Dripping Springs canyon. He told the old man about Bill Fahrion and about Lois Elder and about the sorrel horses. Silvertip listened.

"So," commented Silvertip, "you took to the Badlands, did you? You couldn't have come at a much worse time."

"Why?" Chance demanded.

"Because I'm layin' here, a useless cripple, waitin' for Pillow to come an' kill me," answered Upton.

"There'll be two in here waitin'," reminded Chance. "Things have been happenin' to you, Silvertip. I reckon you'd better tell me."

"I'll tell you enough so that you'll get out an'

skedaddle," the old outlaw replied. "I've run the Basin for years, Chance. I'm all through now but I can tell you a place to go. I can give you a hideout where you'll be safe."

"I didn't come up here to hide behind you like my father did." Chance's words were clipped.

"What?" snapped Silvertip.

"I've put two an' two together," Chance answered. "I heard you talk when you were sick. Tom Melody told me the story in Cassidy. I figured it out."

"What did you figure out?" Silvertip's voice was curiously flat.

"How my father hid behind you."

"Yeah? An' how did he do that?"

"He took some horses," Chance spoke slowly. This was hard to do. "He had 'em up above the J Pen. Maybe he was coming here with 'em, anyhow he left 'em on the way when the posse pushed him close. The posse came down to the J Pen, and the sheriff, just kidding, accused him of stealing the horses. You jumped in and took the blame. They arrested you, took you to Cassidy and you pleaded guilty. That put you in the pen. When you came out, you went from there."

The silence that followed was heavy in the cabin. Silvertip's voice was low and calm when he spoke. "An' that's the way you figured it out?"

"That's the way."

"You are a young fool." No inflection, nothing but a flat statement of fact. "What did I say when I was sick at the J Pen?"

"You said that you would lie for my father. You told

him that he would have to stop."

"Did I say stop what?"

"No." Reluctantly.

"An' you put two an' two together, did you? An' that's the four you got? It looks to me like you got an even dozen."

"There's no need to protect Jack Pagan to me. I'm his son. I know . . ."

"You know nothin'! Listen to me. I was a wild-eyed, reckless kid. I loved yore mother. I loved yore daddy, too. I reckon they loved me, but yore mother loved me like I was her kid, not the way I wanted her to love me. I got into a jackpot in Cassidy. I lost a lot of money on a horse race an' I thought I'd been took. I had to pay though, an' I borrowed from Jack. Jack was in a tight but I didn't know it. He owed for a section of the J Pen vega an' he had to pay off. When I found out about that, I went crazy. Just about like you did over them calves an' yore fool hay. I went down below Cassidy and I lifted fifteen head of Cofeen's thoroughbreds. The easiest horses in the country to trace. I hadn't any sense."

There was bitterness in the old man's voice as he recited the indictment against himself.

"Up above the J Pen," Silvertip resumed after a momentary pause, "I got crowded an' left the horses. I hightailed it to the ranch. I told Jack an' Molly what I'd done. See? I was runnin' to them, tryin' to get behind Molly's skirts. Jack said not to worry; that he'd cover me. I'd been ridin' for Jack off an' on an' he could alibi me some. Old Abe Mulvaney who was sheriff, picked up the horses an' come back down to the J Pen. They all stopped for supper. I had to sit at the table with 'em an' eat, an' all the time knowin' I was the man they wanted."

Again there was silence, then once more Silvertip's voice rasped on. "After supper Abe got to kiddin' Jack an' told him that he reckoned they'd have to take him in. Jack went white an' I didn't know Abe was kiddin'. I blabbed out what I'd done. Natchully they took me. Before I left I asked for a word with Jack. I wanted to talk to him about the vega an' about that gamblin' debt. I wanted him to stop payin' it an' I said so. He said he wouldn't. The man I owed the money to was powerful an' he could help or hurt me. I told Jack I'd tell that the race was fixed and he wouldn't have to pay. I told him I'd say that me an' the other fellow were in cahoots to get his vega away from him. He asked me if I'd lie. I told him I wouldn't lie for him, but I would for Molly.

"When we went back in, Abe taken me on to town. I pleaded guilty an' got four years. When I come out I learned that yore daddy had paid that debt an' that he'd pretty near lost the vega. That put me kind of crazy. I didn't go back to see him. I figured that I'd make some money an' come back an' square up what I owed. I didn't know that he'd pulled through an' finished payin' for the land. That's when I started. I'd got in with a bunch in the pen, an' we held up a train an' made some money. I knew where the Basin was an' we come here an' holed up. Jack was dead by that time, an' Molly was gone, an' I stayed here. I've rode a time or two since then, but mainly I've held the Basin. An' that's the God's truth, so help me!"

There was no doubting the vehemence in the rasping old voice, no doubting the grip of the strong old hand that had settled, vise-like on Chance's arm.

"Jack Pagan an' Molly were the salt of the earth," rasped Silvertip. "Do you believe me, boy?"

"I believe you," Chance choked.

For a time the two men sat there, silent in the dark, then Silvertip spoke again, his voice petulant. "This waitin'," he complained. "I wish they'd come an' take me."

"You wish who would come?"

"Pillow an' the pups that follow him. They're comin' sometime but I wish they'd hurry."

"They won't take you," Chance assured. "We'll be waitin' for them."

"*You* won't be waitin'," stated Silvertip strongly. "Yo're goin' to take Arlie an' get out of here."

"Why can't we all get out?"

"Because I can't ride. I can't get off this bed. It'll be you an' Arlie that'll go. I don't want to."

"You don't want to?"

"I—want," Silvertip forced the words out one at a time, "to—get—Pillow. He's killed my friends and now he's got to pay."

That needed explanation to Chance. He knew Silvertip now, knew him for what he was: A man that wronged Silvertip's friends had Silvertip to answer to.

"Pillow turned 'em in," rasped the old outlaw. "He wrote to Gonzales at Las Cruces an' told him they was comin' to rob the bank there. The Kid an' Blaney an' Poncho. They're dead."

Chance had nothing to say. Why try to tell this fierce old man that his friends were outlaws and were better dead? Why indeed? Here sat Chance Pagan, an outlaw, talking to Silvertip Upton, another outlaw.

"You'll have to get Arlie out," resumed Silvertip, conversationally. "Mebbe she'll slip over tomorrow like she did this mornin'. I can tell you where to go then. She knows the Badlands an' you don't."

"Maybe I could get her," suggested Chance.

"No," Silvertip's voice was certain. "You'd just make it tough for her. We'll wait. One thing a man learns, growin' old: that's to wait."

Chance made no reply. After a time Silvertip asked a question.

"Tired, boy?"

"Some."

"Take a soogan from the bed an' spread it down. Get some sleep. I'll be awake."

"How about you being tired? Why don't you get some sleep yourself?"

"I don't get tired waitin'." Silvertip was cheerful. "I just want Pillow to come through that door. Then I'll rest."

"My horse is down the hill," said Chance.

"Get him an' put him in the back. I had a horse but I asked Arlie to turn him loose. There's a spring down the hill where he can water, an' there's a little hay in the rack."

Chance, moving cautiously, slipped out the stable door. His feet sounded for an instant and then there was quiet. Lying there in the darkness Silvertip asked a question. "Did I square myself, Jack? Did the kid believe me?"

When Chance came back Silvertip heard him moving in the shed. There was a rustle of hay as forkful after forkful was thrown down. Chance came in chuckling.

"Farmer," he said, "is clear banked up with hay. I found a little stack an' a fork and I just put a good-sized pile at the back of the barn. Nobody can see over it very well. He's had water and I'll get him some more if he needs it."

Silvertip grunted approval. "I'm glad you did that," he said. "It'll look like I'd been out. I haven't stirred out of here and I've bothered, because Pillow must know I'm laid up. Now he won't be able to tell. Spread down your soogan, son. This reminds me of one time . . ." Silvertip's voice droned on softly.

Babe Wilmot, slipping away from the Spear, went to the horses tied at the corral fence and took a hammer-headed roan. Babe had not brought his own horse back from Cassidy but had come out with Doctor Grayson in a buckboard. Babe had made time going into town and the horse he had ridden to Cassidy was all done. The stirrups were too long for Babe and the roan fretted, but Wilmot was a horseman. He led the horse away from the Spear, and then mounting, set out to the southeast. Babe was going to the NOW.

Once away from the ranch he rode as if the devil possessed him. Wilmot was no fool. He was putting two and two together. He had been given a message to deliver to Wayne Elder and had delivered it, not knowing that there was murder in that message. Now, still loyal but more than a little sick at his stomach, he rode to the NOW to tell Cliff Nowlen that Wayne Elder was not dead, and that Chance Pagan was cleared of trying to kill him.

When he reached the NOW there was a light in the house. Babe rode straight to the door and as he dismounted the door opened and the light streamed out. Cliff Nowlen was in the doorway, a gun in his hand and behind Nowlen, Suel James showed his anxious face.

"It's Babe," Nowlen announced needlessly. "Come in here. What are you ridin' for?"

"I've come from the Spear," explained Wilmot. "Wayne Elder is there. John Comstock brought him in after he'd been shot."

Nowlen's narrow face twisted into a grin. "So Elder got shot?" he said. He had stepped back from the door, making room for Wilmot to enter. Babe closed the door and stood with his back against it. He looked from Nowlen to Suel James and back again. Suel James' face was pasty white, so white that his mustache stood out like a black shadow.

"You know he got shot," Babe answered Nowlen's comment. "He ain't goin' to die. Doc Grayson from Fort Logan is out there now."

James stared at Nowlen. "Elder is goin' to live," said James, stating a fact.

"An' that ain't all," Wilmot continued. "Comstock seen the horse the killer rode an' it was our sorrel that Pagan has. Melody went up to the J Pen to arrest Pagan for shootin' Elder."

"So Pagan was the man that cut down on Elder." There seemed to be satisfaction in Nowlen's voice. "Now who'd of thought that? I reckon they had trouble about those calves that Pagan stole."

Wilmot shook his head. "Pagan didn't shoot Elder," he stated. "Melody knows it an' so do the rest. Pagan was at the Spear when Elder was shot. Pagan got away from Melody an' he's on the loose now."

Nowlen's ruddy face blanched. His eyes bored into Wilmot.

"An' they know that Pagan didn't do the shootin'?" he asked.

Wilmot nodded.

"Do they know who did? Are they . . . ?"

"I got loose an' come over here." Wilmot's voice was low and tense. "I owe you somethin', Cliff, an' I pay my debts. Tomorrow that bunch is goin' to scatter out. They're goin' to be ridin' the country. When they get here what are you goin' to tell 'em?"

Silence followed that question. Into that silence Suel James injected words. "Wilmot, you damned fool! They'll know you come here. They'll miss you an' they'll know!"

Nowlen's face was drawn and when he turned to James his eyes were frightened. "You think that . . . ?"

"They'll miss Babe an' they'll follow him. He'll lead 'em straight to us."

Nowlen whirled back to Babe Wilmot. "Suel's right!" he snapped.

"I had to warn you!" Babe Wilmot, back against the door, spread his arms until his hands pressed against the door panels. "I had to. You sent me with a message to Elder. You . . ."

"That damned sorrel horse!" James broke into Wilmot's words. "He'll pin it onto us as sure as the devil."

"Now wait." Nowlen tried to control the panic that was growing in the room. "That sorrel is back in the J Pen. You put him there, Suel. You . . ."

"But Pagan was at the Spear at noon when Elder was shot," snapped Wilmot. "Cliff . . ."

Cliff Nowlen looked from one to the other of his men. The panic that was in them spread. It was infectious.

"I didn't know you meant murder," stammered Wilmot. "When you told me what to tell Elder I thought that you wanted to hang that calf rustlin' on Pagan. Cliff . . ."

Suel James lost his head. "I didn't know you meant murder, either," he snarled. "I brought you the sorrel an' I put him back. You're standin' alone in this, Cliff."

That was the word that touched a spark in Cliff Nowlen. These two men, these men of his would leave him as rats run from a burning barn. These two were the only ones that had certain knowledge of what he had done. With Babe Wilmot and Suel James out of the way . . . "You stand alone . . ." James had said.

The panic seized Cliff Nowlen. He had not holstered his gun when Wilmot came in. Now that gun leaped up. Suel James, an incredulous expression on his face, pitched down to the floor and smoke trickled from Nowlen's gun. Babe Wilmot screamed and tried to get away from the door. Nowlen was turning, his face twisted until it was a distorted mask.

"I'll stand alone!" he snarled, and again the gun crashed. Wilmot's scream broke in two and became a whimper as he lurched forward, his hands reaching out for the floor.

James was trying to crawl, trying to get to the table. Cliff Nowlen stepped across to his foreman and deliberately pointed the gun. Suel James, whimpering, tried to shield his head with his arms. A forty-five slug crashed through those shielding arms and into his head. Babe Wilmot lay where he had fallen. Cliff Nowlen looked at Wilmot. The little man was motionless. Nowlen laughed, harsh, short, insanity in the note.

"You're right. I stand alone, you dogs!"

He stepped across Babe Wilmot's body. The open door sent light streaming out to where the roan horse stood. Nowlen caught the roan and mounted, turning the horse south. There was a refuge for wanted men, a refuge for murderers: the Basin. Tully Pillow was in the Basin and Tully Pillow wanted to prey upon the Calico Hole. Cliff Nowlen rode toward the Basin.

15

ARLIE PILLOW, sleepless under the moon-touched roof of Pillow's store, could hear the low murmur of men's voices coming through the partition to her shed bedroom. Mingling with the voices was the clink of money and the ripple of shuffled cards. A poker game was in progress in the store, a game that had begun before supper and continued. Sam

Pasmore, Blair, Art Ragland, and Tully Pillow were playing cards. The girl turned restlessly on her thin mattress and wished that morning would come.

There seemed no end to the game and there seemed to be no end to the circle of Arlie's thoughts. There was Silvertip, crippled, helpless, and in trouble. Somehow, in some manner, she must help Silvertip. And, too, there was the lashing scorn of the dark-eyed girl who had found Arlie at the J Pen cabin. Again and again Arlie reverted to one sentence that Lois Elder had spoken: "Chance Pagan was engaged to me . . ." It seemed to the girl on the bed that she could never forget those words.

And what had she done to Chance Pagan? Lois Elder had gone, had flung herself away from the cabin without giving Arlie a chance to explain, a chance to refute the charges that she made. Arlie had never met Lois Elder but she knew of her by reputation and had placed that dark-eyed, scornful girl, as the daughter of the Spear owner. Somehow, in some way, Arlie had to see Lois, explain to her, make her listen, reinstate Chance Pagan in the girl's graces. It was the least she could do. It was all she could do.

It was a bitter decision but Arlie made it. She would, regardless of consequences, slip away from the Basin in the morning. She would see Lois Elder and tell her the truth about her own presence in the J Pen cabin, then come what might, she would have done the right thing. She would have cleared Chance in the eyes of the girl he loved.

Having reached that decision Arlie felt easier. She

wept into her pillow for she knew that she was giving Chance to the other girl, and Arlie loved Chance. After a time Arlie relaxed, dozed, and finally slept.

She was awakened by the sound of voices rising beyond the partition. Pillow's voice and Art Ragland's and another that, momentarily, she could not place. Listening she heard the strange voice again and after an instant knew that it belonged to Cliff Nowlen.

"They're comin' here?" rasped Pillow. "You say they're comin' here, Cliff?"

"As sure as I'm a foot high," Cliff Nowlen answered Pillow's question. "Babe Wilmot brought me the news straight from the Spear."

"Melody an' all the rest of 'em, all the Spear crew?"

"Somebody in the Basin cut down Wayne Elder an' they're comin' to get the man. At first they thought it was Pagan, but they learned different an' now they're comin' here."

"Nobody has been out of the Basin." Pillow's voice was angry. "Nobody here shot Elder."

"Just stand out an' tell 'em that," Nowlen answered. "Do you think they'll wait to listen to you, Tully?"

Tully Pillow swore helplessly. Then his voice sobered and took up its harsh rasp again. "If they're comin' here we'll welcome 'em. When did you say they'd get here, Cliff?"

"I don't know," Nowlen answered. "Mebbe tonight, mebbe not until mornin', but they're comin' sure as snakes have rattles."

There was sudden decision in Pillow's voice. "We'll get fixed," he snapped. "If the Spear thinks they can ride in here an' do what they want, we'll learn 'em. We'll be waitin' for 'em when they come."

"That's the fight!" approved Nowlen. "Now yo're talkin'. That's why I come up here, so they wouldn't catch you by surprise."

"We'll fix 'em," promised Pillow. "Art, you go down along the east side an' wake up the boys. Blair, you take the west end an' Little Fork canyon. Get 'em all in here. Get 'em here an' hurry."

Arlie heard Ragland say: "Good!" and his boot-heels thump on the floor. Blair must also have gone out for she heard the front door slam. Ragland and Blair must be getting horses and riding to waken the Basin, she thought. There were fifteen men in the Basin, counting those in the store. Arlie wondered if all fifteen would respond to the summons. She imagined that they would, for Pillow had brought them all into the camp.

"Chance Pagan is loose," Nowlen spoke to Pillow again. "Melody went to arrest him an' he got away. Likely he headed for Silvertip's."

"Pagan, huh?" Pillow spoke as if he had no high opinion of Chance Pagan. "I don't care what happened to Pagan. Where's Wilmot an' Suel?"

"I left 'em at the ranch. I thought . . ."

"You thought you'd go back an' stay with 'em," Pillow snarled. "Well, you won't. You'll stay right here an' help. Yo're in this deal up to yore neck, same as the rest. You'll be here to welcome the Spear an' Melody when they come ridin' in."

"I'd ask nothin' better," said Nowlen. "Tully . . ."

"An' that makes me think," again Pillow interrupted.

201

"Silvertip! I been layin' off a long time to kill that old coot an' I'll do it now. As soon as I tell the boys what to do I'll go up there . . ."

Arlie heard no more. She swept the scanty coverings from her body and sprang from the bed. Tully Pillow was going to kill Silvertip. Arlie must warn him.

She dressed with feverish rapidity, flinging on her clothing. Carrying her shoes, she tiptoed away from the partition beyond which voices still rumbled, and carefully turned the door knob. The door usually squeaked. Arlie hoped and prayed that it would not squeak now and betray her.

Fractionally, an inch at a time, she opened the door. It responded kindly to the treatment, giving off but one tiny, high pitched sound. Still carrying her shoes she slipped across the kitchen and reached the back door. The back door was oiled, no need to treat it so gently as the other. Arlie fumbled with the bolt, drew it, and flung the back door open. Outside the moon was high and bright. Arlie, bare-footed, ran across a silver path. She reached the shadow of the knoll and fled up its slope toward the darkened cabin on the summit. Her breath came in gasps and the sharp gravel cut her feet. At the top of the knoll she paused, panting. She had got away and now she must alarm Silvertip.

Carefully she approached the cabin and almost at its walls she called, low-voiced: "Silvertip! Silvertip!"

Inside the cabin, sleeping on the bedding spread on the floor, Chance Pagan wakened to that call. In the bed Silvertip Upton moved his hand until the gun he held pointed to the lighted opening. "Arlie?" queried Silvertip. "Is it you, girl?"

"It's me, Silvertip." Arlie's voice was just at the door. "I've come to warn you . . ."

"Come in, girl," ordered Silvertip.

Chance, getting to his feet, kicked his bedding under the bunk. Arlie Pillow's shadow was black in the doorway and then was gone.

"Pillow!" said Arlie, her voice hurried and breathless. "He's coming to kill you."

There was silence for a moment and then Silvertip spoke slowly. "Now?"

"Right away. Cliff Nowlen came and said that there was a posse on the way to the Basin and Pillow said that he was coming to kill you."

"That," said Silvertip Upton, "is the best news I've heard. The very best."

"A posse coming here?" Chance Pagan spoke to the girl. "Is that what Nowlen said?"

"Chance?" There was a question and a caress in Arlie's voice.

"I'm Chance," assured the man. "What about the posse?"

"Nowlen said that there was one headed for the Basin. Oh, Chance . . ."

"They're coming after me," Chance said grimly. "I reckon I'll . . ."

"No!" The girl flung the word at him sharply. "That's not what they want. Nowlen said that they knew you didn't shoot Elder. That's why they're coming here. Pillow has sent Ragland and Blair to get the men together and when the posse rides in . . ."

"They blow the damn' fools off their saddles," finished Silvertip. "Serve 'em right, too. So they know that Chance didn't shoot Elder?"

"That's what Nowlen said."

"Listen," Chance spoke, quick and sharp, "we can't let them run into an ambush. We'll have to get word to the Spear . . ."

"I thought you was an outlaw." Was there a little chuckle in Silvertip's words? "I thought you was done with the Spear. What do you care what happens to 'em?"

"I've got friends . . ." began Chance hotly, and then stopped. Silvertip was right, what did he care for the Spear? What did he care . . . ? "I'm goin' to get word to 'em," said Chance Pagan slowly.

Silvertip laughed. "You never was an outlaw, kid," he said. "You never could be. Sure, you'll get word to 'em. You an' Arlie . . ."

"There's a lantern on the porch of the store," Arlie spoke in a tense whisper. "It's moving, coming this way!"

"Get that kid out of here, Chance," rasped Silvertip.

Chance was at the door. "It's too late," he answered. "They're at the bottom of the hill."

"Then get her in the stable. Get back with her."

"No. I won't go. Arlie, you get back in the barn. Hide there. When you can make a break, get away."

As he spoke Chance caught the girl's arm, the flesh firm and warm under his grasp. He pushed her back toward the further wall, groping along it for the door. The smell of horse and hay and leather came strongly into the room as Chance opened the door and pushed the girl through, the smell weakening again as he closed it.

Once more Silvertip spoke from the bed. "I couldn't go to Pillow so he's comin' here. Quiet now. Get out of the way an' let me handle this."

Gravel crunched softly and then there was quiet as the men who had stepped on the stones waited to see if the noise had been heard. On the bunk Silvertip snored gently. Chance, crouching against the wall over behind the table, held his breath and waited. This meant a lot to Silvertip. Chance was not going to spoil the play.

Again a faint noise on the gravel. There was a flash of light outside, a light that was hastily muffled as someone covered the lantern. Pillow and the men with him were walking into a trap. Chance could feel no compunction, no sympathy with those men. They had come to kill an old man in his sleep. If they walked into trouble that was no more than their due. Every nerve in Chance tingled. Now it was coming. Again on the bunk Silvertip snored his decoy.

Against the light background of the door, a body showed, a short, twisted body. Pillow was coming in to do his own killing.

Silvertip's voice, calm, triumphant, was clear in the cabin.

"Mighty nice of you, Pillow. I wondered how I'd get to you."

A shot placed a period to that utterance. The Colt that Silvertip had cradled, had nursed so long, spoke peremptorily. Hard upon the heels of that shot came the flash and roar of a shotgun, setting the cabin walls to reeling, the echoes dashing back and forth, seeking a place to escape.

One shot the shotgun belched and then no more, but the Colt spoke again and then again, harsh and deafening, and, punctuating the clamor of the Colt, a man screamed, high and shrill and terrible in agony.

Chance came up from his crouch behind the table. Leaping forward he reached the window and the gun in his hand smashed the little frames and the glass. There were men outside the cabin, men struck motionless by surprise. Chance fired at those men, hurriedly and without aim. The men scattered like quail. The lantern, dropped by one, fell on its base and miraculously stood upright, the screening cloth falling away. The lantern shed light and down the hill a man yelled:

"There's Pagan!"

That was Cliff Nowlen's voice. Chance fired again, not at the voice but at the lantern. This time he aimed. The glass chimney shattered and the lantern went out. Chance backed away from the window. Lead thudded into the cabin, whined in through the door. In the cabin something was stirring, flopping like a trout freshly caught and dropped into a creel.

"Silvertip?" asked Chance hoarsely.

The flopping stopped. Waiting, listening, Chance could almost hear his heart beat. Again there was a stir on the floor beside the door, a little rattle of kicking heels. Then silence again.

"An' that's for you, Pillow," said Silvertip calmly.

"Silvertip! Are you all right? Did he hit you?" Chance

was across the room and beside the bunk.

"I got him clean the first shot," said Silvertip with satisfaction. "I saw him take it an' gave him two more."

"Did he hit you?"

"I didn't feel a thing. Get him out of here, Chance. Arlie's in the stable an' he was her step-daddy. Can you drag him out?"

Chance bent down. His reaching hand struck cloth as he felt along the floor. There was a leg under the cloth and Chance caught it. He was sick, almost nauseated, but he dragged the bundle that had been Tully Pillow, to the door and pushed it through. A gun flashed redly down the hill and Chance jumped back from the door.

"They're watchin'," Chance said needlessly.

"What would you think?" asked Silvertip. "The moon's high an' they can see. After a while it'll set, an' when it does you an' Arlie can pull out."

"And leave you?"

"Why not?"

The door of the stable creaked as Arlie came into the room. She brushed past Chance Pagan. Silvertip felt her presence. Silvertip spoke. "I killed Pillow, girl."

Arlie made a little gasping sound, then her cheek was against Silvertip's and her voice, low but hard and tearless, came clear.

"I'm glad! Glad! He killed my mother. I'm glad that he is dead."

"Lights in the shacks," reported Chance. "The Basin's waking up."

No response to that statement and Chance came back toward the center of the room. Silvertip spoke again.

"You an' Arlie will have to pull out."

Chance found the girl beside him. Her body moved as she shook her head and her voice was steady. "No!"

"You pull out, Arlie," directed Chance. "My horse is in the shed and you can take him."

"No."

Down below the knoll men were calling to each other. A man cried: "Pillow! . . . Pillow!" and then broke off.

On the bed Silvertip chuckled. "Pillow ain't answerin' calls," he said.

"They're going to start up here in a minute," Chance announced. "I wonder . . ."

"Move me close to the window," Silvertip commanded. "You an' Arlie will have to watch the back. You'll have to stick until the moon sets."

Together Chance and the girl shifted the bunk and the heavy body on it. Chance kicked the door shut and found the bar. The door was heavy enough to stop lead, stout and made of oak planks. Silvertip, by lifting himself, could look out the window which commanded the front of the cabin.

Chance, with Silvertip in place, slipped away to the rear. In the stable he spoke low voiced to Farmer and then carefully peered over the pile of hay at the stable door. There was a movement on the slope below and Chance fired at that movement, dodging back after he had fired. His shoulder struck against a body and he spoke to the girl.

"You get inside, Arlie. They'll make a try this way pretty soon."

"I want to be with you," Arlie answered simply.

Chance put his hand on the girl's arm. "You'll be safer inside," he said. "Silvertip needs you. When the moon sets you can make a ride for it."

"Are you going?"

"I'll stay with Silvertip."

"Then I'll stay, too!"

Chance could not argue that. The girl was close, pressed against him. Her presence was singularly sweet, reassuring.

"Did you go to the J Pen?" Chance asked suddenly.

"Silvertip sent me. I saw you with some cattle in the canyon and when I told him he said for me to get you. I . . ."

"Wait," Chance cautioned. Again he peered out, over the pile of hay before the door. The slope below was lifeless but the moon had lowered until it was almost touching the rim of the Basin. Behind Chance Arlie spoke again.

"Lois Elder came while I was there. She accused me . . ." The voice hesitated, "She said that you . . ."

"I know what she said." Chance was grim. "I saw her and she said it all to me."

Silence for an instant while Chance inspected the slope. "Do you . . . did you love her, Chance?"

"I thought I did." Bitterly. "Arlie, did you come to the J Pen before that? Did you scrub the place and darn some socks for me and leave me a pie?"

"The cabin wasn't very clean," Arlie answered. "I didn't have time to do much. I . . ."

"Why waste yourself on a man like me?" Still the bitterness in Chance's voice. "Why, Arlie?"

"Because I . . . I must go in with Silvertip. He needs me."

The girl was gone. Chance looked out over the hay again. The edge of the moon touched the Basin rim. In five minutes more it would be dark.

And when darkness came what would happen? Chance knew. He knew that when the moon went down, all those men below would come up the hill.

But there would be a little time before they came, a few minutes of freedom. In those minutes a man could get away, a man could take Farmer and make a ride, fighting his way through if he had to. A man could . . . a man could stay with his friend and fight it out, but a woman could go. Chance pulled back from the pile of hay. His saddle was on Farmer, the cinch loose. Chance pulled the cinch tight and went into the cabin. Silvertip's head showed where he sat propped up, watching through the window. Arlie was close to Silvertip.

"The moon's setting," Chance announced. "You'll have to ride, Arlie."

"Not without you and Silvertip."

Silvertip chuckled. "You'll go without me," he stated. "You know I can't make it."

"You could get help," Chance argued against the finality in Arlie's voice. "If you could get to the Spear . . . You said once that you would do anything for me, Arlie. Will you go for help?"

The girl came close to him. Again Chance touched her, feeling her tremble under his hand. "Will you go, Arlie?" he repeated.

"I'll go," answered the girl. "I'll go, Chance."

Silvertip said nothing. Chance, his hand still on the girl, led her to the shed door. Inside the stable he helped her mount, untying Farmer and handing up the reins, putting her feet into the loops above the stirrups. He led Farmer to the door, Arlie bent low in the saddle. Nothing now remained of the moon but a thin edge. That edge disappeared, the moon-glow died, slowly, leaving darkness. Chance released the reins and stepped back.

"Good luck, girl," he said, and slapped Farmer on the hips sharply.

Farmer went through the pile of hay, scattering it. Farmer went down the slope pell-mell, at a long run. At the foot of the knoll a flame blossomed at the end of a gun. There was a little ring of fire about the knoll but the steady pound of Farmer's hoofs never faltered, only grew fainter as the distance lengthened.

Chance Pagan stepped away from the stable door. Back in the cabin he spoke to Silvertip. "She got clear."

"Good," said Silvertip, and then with curiosity in his tone, "Why didn't you go with her, Chance?"

"And leave you?" Chance spoke his astonishment.

Silvertip's mirthless chuckle came once more. "I reckon you couldn't at that," he said. "No. I reckon you couldn't go."

Chance went back into the stable once more, back to the open door, and crouching beside it, waited. Those men down below, those men that ringed the knoll, would be climbing the hill soon.

16

A T THE SPEAR, when the first gray streaks of morning came in the east, men untied their horses from the corral. They were fortified with coffee and food, for Lee Su had been busy. John Comstock, mounting, rode over to Tom Melody where he sat his horse.

"You think the NOW first?" he asked.

"Where else?" Melody answered. "That's where Babe went. He had a reason for goin'."

"I think so too," agreed Comstock.

The Spear round-up crew, a posse now, rode away from the corral, heading east toward the river and the NOW crossing. They did not talk as they rode, did not smoke, simply followed at the pace their leaders set. John Comstock rode beside Tom Melody, and back with the rest was Bill Fahrion. At the river crossing the horses drank, sucking thirstily at the water; then, with horses watered, they went on, deliberately, a little rope of horsemen.

The sun had not yet risen when they reached the Sudden. The NOW was lifeless as a dead man's face, and the door gaped like a dead man's open, gaping mouth. In front of that door John Comstock and Tom Melody dismounted, while Ben Godman and another circled the building toward the bunkhouse and the barn. Just at the threshold Melody, in the lead, stopped short. Comstock looking past the tall sheriff, saw what held his attention. There was a dragging, smeary trail across the boards, a trail that ended at a body. Beyond that body lay another. Tom Melody stepped through the door, and after him John Comstock.

Neither spoke as Melody bent down over Suel James. James was dead, shot hard and low, another bullet wound piercing his arms and head. Melody, looking up at Comstock, shook his head.

"He went crazy, I reckon," said Melody. Comstock nodded.

"Both Babe an' James," he said, low-voiced. "He must have gone crazy."

"Look around," directed Melody.

Comstock stepped away. His hard blue eyes searched the room and with swift strides he crossed it. From behind a chair placed in a corner, he lifted a rifle. "It's a .38-.55," he announced. "Tom, this is . . ."

"Babe's alive!" Melody's voice rasped against the silence of the room. "Get some liquor!"

Comstock put the rifle down and wheeled to obey. At the door curious faces appeared. Ben Godman, pushing through into the room reported: "Nobody at the bunkhouse or the barn. I . . . What's this?"

Comstock placed a bottle in Melody's hand. Melody carefully lifted Babe Wilmot's lolling head. He placed the uncorked bottle against the pallid lips and a thread of whisky trickled in. Again Melody applied the bottle and putting it aside, stroked the little man's thin throat. He waited then, waited for the whiskey to filter through into the little blood that was left Babe Wilmot. The minutes ticked past, each one an era. Again Melody applied the bottle. Again he stroked the thin throat, forcing the whisky down. Babe Wilmot opened his eyes. They were blank, lifeless, and then gradually a little recognition came into them.

"Where's Nowlen, Babe?" asked Tom Melody, bending close to get the reply. "Where's Cliff?"

Wilmot's white lips moved. Melody caught the word that was lost to the rest: "Gone."

"I know he's gone, but where?"

Babe Wilmot made an effort. Babe Wilmot paid his debts, all of them. Babe Wilmot had ridden to the NOW to pay Cliff Nowlen. He had paid him and been thanked with lead. Now he paid again.

"Nowlen . . . shot . . . Elder. . . . Stole sorrel . . . horse. . . . Shot . . . Suel . . . an' . . . me. . . . Gone . . ." The effort was too much. Babe Wilmot gasped.

"Gone where, Babe?"

"Basin . . ." murmured Babe Wilmot and his eyes closed.

Tom Melody reached for the whisky bottle, raised it, and then put it down again slowly. There was no more use for a stimulant.

Tom Melody rose wearily to his feet. "I reckon," he said slowly, "that we'll go to the Basin."

Back at the Spear, with the morning growing lighter, Lois Elder sat beside her father. From a chair nearby Carl Terril watched the girl, his eyes troubled. Lois had refused to rest, had resisted all efforts to make her relax. She sat, hard-eyed, her hand on Wayne Elder's arm. Wayne Elder slept. There was no need of this unrelaxing vigilance. Carl Terril got up from his chair.

"Lois, dear," he said, "can't you come now? Can't you drink a cup of coffee and lie down awhile? I'll stay here. I'll call you if Wayne wakes."

The girl shook her head. "I'll stay here," she answered.

Terril restlessly paced to the bedroom door. "It's so useless," he said, turning. "You're wearing yourself out. Wayne is all right. The doctor said so. You . . ." He stopped. A horse, hard-ridden, had pounded up to the Spear and stopped.

Lois, too, heard the sound. She got up from beside the bed and stood poised, waiting. Terril moved hastily into the living-room and faced the door which had burst open. Lois, with a quick glance at her father, followed Terril. Just inside, the door wide behind her, stood a girl, a disheveled figure, dress briar-torn, hair whipped by the wind, breast rising and falling from exertion. The girl turned her eyes from Carl Terril and looked at Lois. They were wide eyes, blue and filled with fright and with something else.

"Chance and Silvertip are in the cabin," panted the girl in the doorway. "The whole Basin is around them and they can't get away."

"What . . . ?" began Terril.

"It's Chance, I tell you." Arlie threw the words at Lois Elder. "He needs help. They'll kill him! They'll kill him and Silvertip."

"Chance Pagan?" asked Terril. "Where is he?"

Arlie did not answer the question. She was looking at Lois Elder, talking to her. "It wasn't Chance's fault that I was there," she said. "I'd come with a message from

Silvertip. Chance . . ."

Lois Elder, with a swift movement, came to Terril's side. Her hand sought and found Terril's shoulder and she leaned against him. Carl Terril's arm went around the girl beside him.

Arlie caught the possessiveness of that motion, the caress that was in the hand on Terril's shoulder, the sure closing of the arm. Arlie was weaving on her feet, trying to stand, trying to stay erect. She flung out an arm as if for support and gasped an exclamation: "Oh!"

Her legs would no longer hold her up. The room swam about her, the walls rocking, and then suddenly the walls were gone and there was only blackness. Arlie pitched forward, falling full length.

In an instant Lois and Terril were beside her. It was Terril who lifted the girl, turning her until she lay upon her back, but it was Lois who saw the deep red stain beneath Arlie's arm, and ripped the torn dress away. An angry red furrow stretched across the white, firm side, just along the ribs. Beneath that furrow the red stain spread and blood oozed from the cut. With swift, exploring fingers, Lois pressed the wound. It was not deep; the bullet had not penetrated, but plowed. Lois looked at Terril.

"You'll have to go," she said. "I'll look after her, but you must ride and find Tom Melody and our men. Tell them that Chance Pagan and Silvertip are in the Basin and that the Basin men mean to kill them! Hurry, Carl!"

Terril hesitated. "I don't know the country," he began. "I'm not sure that I can find Melody. And I don't think that I should leave you, Lois. You . . ."

Terril gazed anxiously at Lois.

"I can look after father and this girl." Lois Elder's eyes were steady. Already she had pressed the wound together, checking the flow of blood. "You can ride east to the river. You'll see where the men crossed. After that you can't miss the trail. Ride, Carl! If you love me, you will!"

Terril slipped his arms under Arlie and lifted her as he rose.

"Put her on the couch," directed Lois. "Hurry, Carl!"

Crossing the room Carl Terril deposited Arlie on the couch. Lois was beside him and when he had put down the girl he caught Lois' shoulders and kissed her, quick and hard on the lips.

"I'll find them," he promised, and turning, hastened out of the door. Lois bent down over Arlie, and then, straightening, hurried to her father's room. There was bandage there, and lint, and all the necessities. She returned carrying these things, placed them on a table and hurried to the kitchen. Lee Su was there pottering about the stove.

"You go to father, Lee," directed Lois. "Stay with him. I'll be busy!" As she gave the order she poured water into a basin.

Lee Su grunted and went to the door. "You got sick?" he questioned.

"No. You stay with father. I'll be close by."

Lee Su obeyed the command in her voice.

Returning to the girl on the couch, Lois cleaned the wound. It was raw and red and Lois bit her lips, forcing herself to the task. When she had washed Arlie's side she drew the edges of the furrow together, pressing them close and holding them in place with the bandage that she wound about the body. To do this Lois was compelled to lift Arlie and hold her against her shoulder so that her hands would be free.

She had barely lowered her patient and reached her feet when Arlie's blue eyes opened. There was a question in those eyes. Lois answered it.

"I've sent for the men," she said. "They will go to help Chance."

"You love him, don't you?" Arlie asked. "You love that man who was here?"

"Carl?"

"If that's his name."

Lois nodded. "You must rest," she said. "You were shot and . . ."

"That was when I rode away." Arlie's voice was dreamy, as though she recounted some past vision from her sleep. "We were in the cabin, Silvertip and Chance and I. Chance put me on his horse and made me ride. He wouldn't go. He stayed with Silvertip. I rode down the hill and I felt something against my side and heard the shots, but the horse kept running."

"Rest now," said Lois gently. "You are hurt. Chance will be all right now. They will reach him in time."

"Chance . . ." Still the dreamy quality in Arlie's voice. "He knew that he couldn't go, but he made me ride." Then the voice sharpening, "You sent help? You . . ."

"I sent help. Lie down now. I sent for help."

Arlie relaxed, letting her shoulders rest on the couch once more. The blue eyes were fixed on Lois.

"You're Lois Elder, aren't you. Chance is in love with you. You said that you were engaged. You said that Chance had kept me while you were away. Chance didn't keep me. I came with a message from Silvertip. Chance . . ."

Hot blood flooded Lois' smooth cheeks. "I know," she assured. "I was wrong. I . . ."

"But you don't love Chance," Arlie's voice went on. "You love that other man. I love Chance. I . . . I must go back to him! They will kill him. I must go back!" Arlie struggled up against Lois' restraining hands. The blue eyes were wide, filled with fright. Lois pushed against the heaving shoulders.

"Lie down," she commanded. "You must lie down. Chance . . ."

"Chance . . . !" echoed Arlie wildly.

"He will come here. Chance wants you to lie down."

The shoulders relaxed. Lois placed a hand behind Arlie's head, lowered the girl to the couch again. Arlie lay there, quietly staring up, her eyes still wild.

"You must lie still," Lois commanded, and then seeking a word that would enforce her command: "Chance wants you to lie still."

"Chance," said Arlie obediently, "I will be quiet."

Turning, Lois hurried to the bedroom where Elder lay. There was a soporific there, a medicine left by the doctor for Wayne Elder, should he waken. Carrying the glass, Lois returned.

"Drink this," she ordered, lifting Arlie's head. "Drink this, dear."

Obediently Arlie sipped the bitter dose. The blond

head was lowered to the couch pillow. Gradually, as the medicine took effect, the blue eyes dulled, losing their wild light. When they closed, Lois Elder let go the breath she had caught and held. She placed the glass carefully on the table and then returning to the couch stood looking at the other girl. So this was what it meant to love a man? This was what a man could mean. Life or death or trouble or grief, did not matter. This girl had crouched quietly in a cabin when death stalked outside, content to be with the man she loved. This girl had ridden past a ring of fire, had taken a wound and gone on because the man she loved had wished her to go. Lois Elder's mouth set firmly. She could do what this girl had done, would do it if danger threatened Carl. Love did things like this to a woman, made them suffer and brought them pain and the woman rose to it. Lois pulled a chair to her and sat down beside the couch.

Carl Terril's horse splashed across the river crossing, and on the long road that led to the Basin, John Comstock spoke to Tom Melody. "Almost there," said Comstock.

In the Basin, inside the walls of Silvertip's cabin, Chance Pagan looked with accusing eyes at the man on the bed. Silvertip lolled back, his shoulders against the end of the bunk. By lifting himself Silvertip could command the window. The bedding was a tangle at the lower end of the bunk, and around his body there was a bloody bandage, a blanket twisted and lumpy, just at the groin. Light was streaking the east and the cabin was a dim gray.

"You said he didn't hit you," accused Chance. "When did you get that?"

"I said I never felt a thing," refuted Silvertip weakly. "I didn't. I ain't been able to feel a thing below my hips for a week. Pillow gave me that. Him an' his shotgun."

"You knew you were hit." Still Chance was unforgiving. "You twisted that blanket on. Why didn't you tell me? You been bleeding."

"Why should I tell you?" Silvertip's voice was calm. "I'm dyin', anyhow. Does it make any difference whether I bleed to death or just die slow? It don't hurt. I can't feel it."

"I'm going to bandage it," said Chance.

"You can if you want." Utter apathy in Silvertip's voice. "It ain't goin' to make any difference either way."

Chance unknotted the blanket and repressed an exclamation at what he disclosed. Silvertip had been shot through the groin, more than one buckshot having bored in. Chance knew when he saw the wound that there was no chance for Silvertip. Still he worked, washing the wound clean and twisting on a clean towel as a combination bandage and tourniquet. The towel grew red even as he fastened it.

"You reckon Arlie got through?" Silvertip asked as Chance worked.

"I think so," Chance answered. "I heard the horse go on after they'd shot."

Silvertip grunted. "I hope the kid made it," he said. "What about Arlie, Chance?"

"Well," returned Chance, "what about her?"

"She's in love with you." Silvertip lifted himself

slightly and looked out the window. Lead thudded into the cabin, and from down the hill came the sound of a shot.

"You keep down," warned Chance. "Ever since we drove those fellows back, they've been trying to get you."

Again Silvertip grunted. "They ought to put a man with a rifle out in front," he criticized. "I've made plenty of targets for 'em."

Chance straightened from his work and wiped his forehead. He was sweating. "I reckon that will hold," he said.

"You just don't give a good damn, do you?" Silvertip spoke not of the wound that Chance had bandaged, but of Chance himself. "You don't care a hang what happens to you, do you?"

"Not much," Chance agreed.

"I reckon not. Last night when they rushed the place an' you went out the back door, I figured you felt that way. Why?"

"We drove 'em off." Chance did not answer Upton. His eyes brightened as he thought of that rush, stopped in its tracks. "They didn't know what to do with me flanking them and you holding down the front."

"But it was a fool thing to do. You could have done just as good from the door, but you stepped out. Why was that?"

Chance shrugged. "I don't know," he answered. "I went bad a while back, Silvertip. I bucked Fahrion and the Spear. I stole some calves from Wayne. I . . . well, what's the use?"

"Plenty of use. I went bad once. I've been bad ever since. Now I'm right here, right at the end of the road. I'll go out with lead in me; maybe throwin' some lead myself. Anyhow, I hope it's that way. But yo're young. You ain't gone bad."

"You might look at it that way, though," Chance argued.

"No," Silvertip shook his head, "there's two roads for men like you an' me, Chance. Just two sides to the fence. We can't straddle it. We go one way or the other. I went bad. There wasn't a reason, but I did. No sense in you doin' it. You got Arlie."

"Arlie?"

"Arlie. She loves you. She'd go to hell for you. Didn't you know that?"

Chance was silent, his eyes intent on Silvertip.

"A good woman," Upton resumed softly. "If I had had . . . well, never mind. But you got every reason to make it go. Think it over, kid. If you an' Arlie . . ."

"We'll go no place if I don't get out back," Chance interrupted. "They'll come up the hill and we'll go to hell." He moved away as he spoke, leaving Silvertip to watch the front.

In the stable, peering cautiously through a crack between the logs, Chance surveyed the hill. There were men down there. There was a man with a rifle over to the left and there were two rifles in Pillow's store. Chance wondered where Cliff Nowlen was.

Nowlen! Chance's mind filled with bitterness at the thought of the man. Nowlen! Nowlen had played his friend! Nowlen had picked up some of the J Pen stock and fed it, fed yearlings that didn't need feeding, just to make an impression on Chance. Nowlen had lent him horses, lent him the sorrel, still playing friend. Nowlen had taken that sorrel horse to ride when he shot Wayne Elder, and then had fled, leaving the horse at the J Pen. Cliff Nowlen. He wanted the vega, wanted the hay that would make the NOW the big ranch in the upper end of the Calico Hole. Chance and Silvertip had talked during the night, piecing things together, things that Chance knew, things that Silvertip had heard from Arlie. Cliff Nowlen was down there now, ramrodding the spread, occupying the position of the dead Pillow. Chance narrowed his eyes. He hoped, before this thing was over, that he'd have a shot at Cliff Nowlen.

And he hoped that he would have a chance at Sam Pasmore. Pasmore wanted Arlie. Silvertip had spoken of that. Chance should have killed Sam Pasmore that night in the cabin. As long as he lived he would regret that he hadn't killed Pasmore. As long as he lived! Not very long at that, likely. But if Pasmore were dead then Arlie would be safe . . .

Arlie! The whole thing hinged on Arlie. Arlie who had ridden out from the cabin, taking her risk for him, for Chance Pagan. Arlie! Arlie with the soft rounded arms and the level steady eyes. Arlie who had said so willingly: "I'll go, Chance." A woman like Arlie . . . The girl deserved better than Chance Pagan!

Down behind the rock the man with the rifle saw a movement and fired at it. Chance ducked back.

In Pillow's store Cliff Nowlen peered through a shattered window, watching the cabin on the hill. Sam Pasmore, crouched beside him, also watched the knoll. Art Ragland, hit in the rush up the knoll when Nowlen had tried to take the cabin, squatted by the door, a cloth about his head. Blair was up there on the knoll. In another hour, the flies would be buzzing over Blair. Buzzing over Pillow, too. Nowlen swore, low-voiced.

"Why don't we pull out of here?" Pasmore whined. "We'll never get 'em. They're forted up . . ."

"An' leave Pagan go?" Nowlen blazed at the man beside him. "I'll kill Chance Pagan. He spoiled it last night. He . . ."

"But Pillow's dead. You can run the Basin, Cliff."

"Shut up!" Nowlen snapped the order. He had to stay here, had to see this thing through. There were two dead men back at the NOW; there was Wayne Elder, shot from ambush. Cliff Nowlen had to stay, had to see it through. "Are some of the boys watchin' the hill?" he questioned.

"There's half a dozen," Pasmore answered. "Cliff, I . . ."

"Shut up!" Nowlen snapped again. "When the Spear rides in an' gets what's comin' to 'em we can go, an' not before. Why do you think I let Arlie go last night? I saw who it was. I knew she'd ride to the Spear. When she tells 'em Pagan's here they'll come aboilin'. That's why I stopped the boys shootin' at her!"

"But . . ."

" 'But' hell! When we clean the Spear, we own it, Sam. Own the Calico Hole. You can run the Basin an' me the country down below an' we'll clean up!"

Pasmore jerked his head toward Ragland. "What about him?" he asked.

"What about him?" Nowlen countered. "If you can't handle him, I can. He needn't think he can take over after Pillow. Silvertip done us a favor when he downed Pillow."

Pasmore wet his lips nervously and peered out once more. "Mebbe," he said, "but I think we're . . . ."

"I'll do the thinkin'. You watch the cabin!" Nowlen moved away. In the front of the store, beside Ragland, he crouched once more, peering out through a chink that Ragland had cleared of mud. "What's doin'?" he asked.

Ragland shook his head. "Nothin'," he answered. "Nowlen, where's Suel an' Babe? Why ain't they here?"

"I don't know. They're back at the ranch, I reckon. They . . ."

"There's somethin' damn funny about this. Suel never was one to hang back. He ought to be here. Babe brought you news of the posse. Why didn't he come with you? Where is that posse? You come ridin' in here sayin' that the Basin was to be cleaned out. I ain't seen the bunch yet. We go up the hill to get Silvertip an' Pillow gets his. When we make for the cabin again that damned Pagan jumps out. Everythin's gone wrong. You . . ."

"Look!" snapped Nowlen. "Look at the rim!"

There was a horseman on the rim, a little dark figure against the sky. Another rider appeared, and then another and another.

"That's them," breathed Cliff Nowlen. "That's the Spear!"

In Silvertip's stable Chance Pagan watched the rock and the store. Both were lifeless. Restlessly Chance stirred. Rising from his crouch he moved back, reached the wall, and went through the open door. Silvertip was on the bed, propped up, motionless, head turned toward the window.

"Anything in sight?" Chance asked.

There was no answer. Apparently the old man was staring intently toward the rim.

"What is it?" demanded Chance, going toward the bunk. "Is there something . . ." He stopped. He was beside Silvertip now. Upton did not turn his head. Chance, bending forward to see, caught sight of the old man's eyes. They were staring unwinkingly toward the rim, but there was no sight in them. Chance was alone in the cabin on the knoll.

For a long minute. Chance looked at Silvertip, then following that lifeless stare he glanced at the rim. Silvertip was gone. Silvertip . . . But there was a horseman on the rim, a horseman that was joined by another and another and still another, until there was a little clump of riders. Arlie had gone through then! Arlie had reached the Spear.

The clump of men dissolved, separated into units that formed a line. The line came down the slope, breaking over the rim, following the road down. The Basin was still, quiet with a deadly silence. Those men riding down . . . Chance had to warn them, stop them before they rode into the thing that waited for them. He stepped back from the window and Silvertip. Tom Melody's gun lay on the table. Chance picked it up. He went to the door, lifted the bar, and pushed the end of the bed back so that the door would swing clear. Opening the door a crack, he waited, watching the riders come on. They were growing in size, getting bigger as their horses came down the slope. He waited a minute. They were close enough now.

"So long, Silvertip," said Chance, and swung open the door.

Riding down the slope from the rim Tom Melody spoke to Comstock. "Mighty quiet down there. I wonder if . . ."

"Look!" commanded Comstock.

Tom Melody followed Comstock's pointing arm. Below them the Basin lay, unstirring save that at the door of the cabin on the knoll in its center, a man had appeared. The man raised his arm. Tom Melody and John Comstock could see the arm move, jumping up, once, twice, again.

"Shootin' . . ." Melody began.

Something kicked up gravel a hundred yards down the slope. Again the gravel bounced and a bullet richochetted, whining. Faint, but distinct enough, came the sounds of shots.

"Shootin' at us," said Comstock quietly. "Now what . . . ?"

At the cabin door the man moved, breaking into a run, a zig-zag, weaving movement down the hill. From Pillow's store, from cabins below, from a windfall to the left, guns spoke. Lead whined thinly. Above Tom Melody a bullet snaked flatly into the air. Tom Melody threw himself from his saddle; his horse, turning, ran up the slope. John Comstock was down, a gun in his hand, his shots searching into the windfall. The Spear riders, caught by surprise, but ready enough for action, were out of their saddles, seeking shelter. The trap had failed, had been sprung before the jaws were filled. Tom Melody reached Comstock where he crouched behind a rock beside the road.

"What . . . ?" began Tom Melody.

"That fellow at the cabin," said Comstock, "he shot to warn us an' then ran for the store. I didn't see him go down. I reckon he made it."

"Who do you think?" asked Melody.

"It was Chance." Comstock's voice was positive. "It must have been. But why . . ."

Lead whined from the rock. Tom Melody wiped his eyes, filled with rock dust.

"They laid for us, all right," he said. "I'm goin' to find another place. This rock is too blame little!"

At the side of Pillow's store, flat against the wall, Chance Pagan caught his breath. There was a red streak from wrist to elbow on his left arm. His hat was gone, dropped as he ran. There was a bullet hole in his shirt and one boot heel was lost, shot off or kicked off coming down the slope. His own gun was in its holster and Tom Melody's gun was in his hand. He would catch his breath and then . . . Why then he would go in.

17

FTER THAT first mad flurry the fight in the Basin settled down into a grim, long-drawn-out business. Tom Melody was an old hand and a wise head when it came to battle. John Comstock was cool, although this was his first experience. Ben Godman knew just what it was all about, and Bill Fahrion, the only hot-head who might have led a charge and upset the apple-cart, had his impetuous ardor restrained by a slug that burned through the skin of his thigh. Bill Fahrion was going to be uneasy in a saddle for some time, due to that lead burn. The only immediate danger to the men from the Spear, was in the windfall. There were a couple of men in the windfall that offered a sad handicap, and accordingly Godman and his partner, Cal Davis, the cook, set about cleaning out the trash.

Davis, a fighting man of no small ability, slid along toward the edge of the tangle of fallen trees. He was carrying his own .30-.30, recovered from John Comstock, and he had a pocketful of shells. Ben Godman crouched behind a boulder that was at least four feet wide, and mourned over the small size of the stone. It seemed to Ben Godman that he had never seen so small a rock. Nevertheless he was loath to quit it when Davis gained position.

Davis, over at the edge, found a man who had placed his confidence in a six-inch pine tree and gleefully put two slugs through the log. The trusting soul got up to leave and Ben, with his Colt, put a period to his departure. That left one or two men more, and, calling to Davis and Ben to work in, thus effectually bottling the windfall, Tom Melody and the rest of the posse began the slow business of working down the hill.

They progressed nicely, listening to the fight that still continued at the windfall as they worked down, and were for the most part within long pistol range of the Basin cabins and the store, when there was a fresh arrival at the rim. Carl Terril pulled up at the edge, surveyed the scene below, and then coolly threaded his horse through the broken rock of the slope, coming at a sharp trot, as fast a speed as the slope would safely permit. Apparently Terril had less confidence in his horse than in his luck, and would not trust his neck to a run.

Melody called to Terril, directing him, and with lead kicking up dirt and rocks close by, the young man swung his horse and rode toward the call. Reaching Melody, Terril dismounted and let the horse go, which the animal promptly did, as if glad to get away.

"Kind of took yore time comin' down," chided Melody when Terril was safe beside him. "What you doin' here anyhow?"

"A girl came to the ranch after you had left," Terril answered. "She was wounded. She told Lois and me that Chance Pagan and a man called Silvertip were in a cabin here in the Basin, and needed help. I followed after you, missed you at the NOW ranch and took your trail and came on here."

Melody grunted. "That'd be Arlie," he said. "She hurt bad?"

"Not badly," assured Terril. "You seem to have a fight on your hands."

"An all-day business," growled Melody. "They're in those shacks an' the store. If we could get to the store we might make a little change in it, but gettin' to the store will be somethin'."

"What about Pagan?"

Again Melody grunted. "I reckon he saved our bacon," he stated. "We came in here not particularly watchin' an' if he hadn't stepped out an' fired a warnin' shot or two, we'd of got our needin's."

"What happened to him?"

"He made a run for the store. Don't know whether he made it or not."

Carl Terril looked at the store building, at the peeled logs that formed its sides and front. His face was expressionless. "Well," he said casually. "I'm here. I might as well stay." With that comment he produced a blue steel gun from under his arm, broke the top and looked at the cylinder. Then, settling his hat firmly, young Mr. Terril left the shelter of Tom Melody's rock and made a run for a pine, thick and stalwart, some twenty yards away. He was behind the pine, safe and sheltered, before a rifleman in the store sent a slug smacking through the air he had occupied.

"Huh!" Melody grunted grimly. "So that's the way they do it in Texas, is it?" With that comment he peered over his rock and devoted himself to his rifle sights. Over to Melody's left John Comstock fired twice with the .38-.45 he had brought from the NOW, waited a moment, and then fired again.

"Get him, John?" shouted Melody.

Comstock, without turning his head, answered. "In that little cabin. I think so."

Melody turned swiftly from Comstock. There was a fresh burst of firing from the store. Carl Terril was not behind the tree he had occupied. He had gone on. Melody swore. "He'll get himself killed!" he growled. Up on the slope Ben Godman yelled, in triumph. The firing from the windfall was done.

At the side of Pillow's store Chance Pagan crouched motionless, Tom Melody's old Colt tightly gripped in his hand. Having recovered his breath, Chance wormed his way along the wall to the end of the store. There, rising up, preparatory to making a run for the back door, he met a hot fire from the rifleman behind the rock. Splinters flew from the logs at the corner and Chance backed away. The gunman had missed Chance as he came down the slope, but was now in a position to command the corner. Chance could hear the men in the store as they moved about, could even hear their voices, but could not distinguish the words they spoke. Now and again the log walls reverberated from the gunfire within. Chance swore at himself. He had not, after all, bettered his position when he ran from the cabin. Here he was, the store wall against him, solid logs at his side, and he could not get to the door. There was a window further along the wall. The snout of a gun protruded from the opening and a bullet, fired along the logs, ripped out a splinter and glanced past. Chance snapped a shot at the window and the gun was hastily withdrawn. Those men inside knew that he was against the wall. It would be only a few minutes before chinking was removed and the wall would be untenable. And then what?

The man behind the rock was yelling to the occupants of the store, trying to make himself heard. The men inside could not, evidently, hear him, but Chance could, plainly enough. "He's against the wall! He's against the wall, Sam."

Chance scowled. That fellow certainly did a lot of talking. Once more he dropped flat and worked his way along. If he could deal with the man behind the rock . . . There was a fresh burst of firing from the store. Chance reached the end of the logs and peered around. No slug welcomed him. From the big rock a man fired twice, not at Chance, and then came suddenly into view. He was leveling his rifle around the edge of his fort when Chance used the next to the last cartridge in Melody's Colt. The rifle clattered free and the man at the rock sat down and then leaned back against the stone as though to rest. Chance came around his log corner. He was at the back of the store. Over by the rock the gunman reached for his lost weapon and then gave it up. There was a vote of thanks coming from Chance Pagan to whoever had smoked that fellow out. Chance was at the kitchen door, the door where Arlie had so often stood, looking up to Silvertip's cabin. Instinctively Chance glanced toward the knoll. Silvertip was still up there, looking out of the window. Chance pushed on the door, thrust his shoulder against it. The door was barred but a window beyond it promised entrance. Well, here he went!

The glass and the little square frame that held it offered no real obstacle. Chance shattered them. He went in through the window, head first, and fell to the floor. Instinctively, as he struck the floor, he rolled, expecting lead to strike him. It did not come. Chance sat up and gathered his legs under him.

Before he could reach his feet Sam Pasmore appeared in the store door. Pasmore was stained with powder, his face twisted with fear and hate, his eyes little red-rimmed holes. Pasmore had his gun leveled. The gun belched and Chance found that the hammer of the Colt he held was under his thumb. He let the thumb relax and Pasmore was suddenly gone from the door. The hammer clicked on an empty as Chance pulled trigger again. He dropped the gun and reaching back, brought his own weapon from the spring clip holster.

When he tried to get up he was clumsy. One leg bothered him, seemed unwilling to function. Chance glanced in disgust at that leg. There was blood on the blue denim of the Levi's. He had not known that he was hit, had not felt it.

The table aided him in gaining his feet, and holding to it he looked at the door. Pasmore had been there. He wondered . . .

A staggering, lurching step and he caught the door jamb. The store lay before him. A man, head tied with a rag, was at the door. Sam Pasmore lay just before him, his eyes still red and alive as glowing coals. The man with the white rag around his head turned and saw Chance. His mouth made a round smoke-grimed O of wonder. The man with the rag brought up a rifle, clumsily, the barrel knocking against the wall as he raised it. Chance fired at the man with the white rag, saw the rifle come level, and fired again. Chance clung to the door jamb. Both legs had gone bad now. The rifleman laid himself down. He did not fall, he simply lay down, like a man going to bed. The store was empty. Chance took a step and both legs gave way. He struck the floor. It seemed to him that someone had painted the store red. It was all red and hazy. Cliff Nowlen should have been in the store. Through the red haze Chance searched for Nowlen. He had to find him at all costs.

A sound came to his dulling ears, a sound of someone moving behind the counter. Chance waited, fighting to see through the crimson haze.

The sound was repeated. Cliff Nowlen's head showed above the counter. His head and face were red as the walls behind. Chance tried to get his gun up. It weighed tons. An awfully heavy gun. Nowlen was standing up, swaying there behind the counter, swaying like a target in the shooting gallery of the Deadwood Fair. If you hit a duck you got a cigar. If you hit a duck . . . Nowlen wasn't there any longer, Why, he had knocked down the duck! He had a cigar coming. He had a cigar for Silvertip. He had . . . Chance did not hear the rest of the window go out as a man came through it.

Carl Terril, leaving Melody for the pine tree, the pine tree for a fold of ground, the fold for a clump of bear grass that would not have stopped a twenty-two short, and the bear grass for a good sized boulder, reached a vantage point. He could see the back of the store, a side view. Beyond the store there was a boulder and a man crouched there. Terril sighted carefully, the long barrel of his Smith & Wesson .38-.40 motionless as he peered along it. The gun bounced and the man at the rock dodged suddenly out of sight. Terril waited. To right and left guns spoke, here a short gun, a Colt, or a Smith & Wesson, roaring anger, a rifle answering with the unmistakable whip-like snarl of the long-barreled gun. Terril held his peace. Twice he lifted himself, deliberately exposing a part of his body to the man he had missed. He did not draw fire. That was strange. Again Terril raised. Now a gun spoke but there was no slug to strike Terril's exposed shoulder and side, or the rock that shielded him. He dropped down as the gun crashed and waited again, waited and then raised up. Fire came. Terril bunched his muscles, firmed his feet under him, and swiftly ran for the back of the store.

When he reached it he saw that the window beside the door was smashed. He crouched beneath that window, scanning to right and left, watchful, alert. It was beyond reason that the rear of the store should be left unguarded. Beyond reason, but reason does not always command. Terril straightened, cautiously. Guns thudded inside the store, a fusillade of shots, one on the heels of the other. What had seemed forever to Chance Pagan, was to the listening Terril a roll of gunfire and then quiet. Still cautious, cool but impetuous too, Terril raised up and peered through the window. He saw an empty room. Carl Terril caught the broken edges of the window frame, swung himself up, and went in.

Cat-like he gained his feet, crouching, poised, eyes narrow, face in the mask of a fighting man, gun ready.

Then, carefully, he advanced to the open door across the room. Reaching it he stopped. There was a man on the floor beside the door, a man that lay on his back and did not stir. Over beside the door a man lay comfortably on his side, a rifle beside him. That man lived; his eyes watched Terril. Across the counter, body half hidden, was another man, inert and motionless; and in the center of the long room a fourth man sat, swaying back and forth, a gun held in his two hands and facing the man across the counter. As Terril advanced a step the swaying increased, the man overbalanced, and his shoulders struck the floor. Stepping past, Terril could see that blood streamed down into that man's eyes from a gash across his forehead.

Terril reached the door. He unbarred it, putting the bar aside, then he flung the door wide, jumped back and shouted:

"Melody! Melody!"

Quiet followed that shout. The guns had stopped. There was no sound in the Basin. Then came Tom Melody's answering call.

"Yeah?"

"It's Terril. I'm in the store. They're all done here!"

The silence was incredible. Somewhere, out in front, a man broke the quiet. "I'll be damned," he said, low-voiced.

Tom Melody called directions. "Hold down the store. We're comin'. John . . . Ben . . . !"

From a cabin protruded a white rag tied to the end of a gun barrel, flapping back and forth as its holder waved the gun. Melody saw that flag of surrender.

Others saw it.

Tom Melody answered. "If yo're done, come out with yore hands up, and what's more, *keep* 'em up."

The white rag was withdrawn. A man came from the cabin, his hands high. Another followed him, and another. Three hundred yards from the store, from the rear of a cabin, a rider appeared, bent low over his horse's neck, the horse full out and running. A rifle snapped but the horse went on, untouched. Men got up from behind rocks, from behind fallen trees. There were four of these and they held their arms above their heads. Tom Melody pushed his gaunt old body into the air. John Comstock stood up; Ben Godman, fat and globular, swaggered down the slope, and Cal Davis, carrying his rifle, emerged like a turtle from its shell, crawling out from behind a pile of posts. The Basin was done. The thing was finished.

There remained the cleaning up of the mess. Spear men searched throughout the rocks, through cabins from which fire had come. They found but little. There was a wounded man behind the store, a man who leaned against a big rock and submitted to whatever came. Art Ragland had been hit, shot hard. There were two bodies beside Silvertip's cabin. Pillow, twisted in death as in life, and the impassive Blair, still impassive. From the windfall up the slope Ben Godman, and another, retrieved a man. There had been other fighters in the windfall but they had slipped away. So, too, with others of the men that Pillow had gathered around him. Seeing how the fight was going, and with no stomach for it, they had pulled out, slid away to outlying cabins, there to get horses and leave as soon as they could make a break.

The bodies were carried to the store and placed side by side. Blair and Pillow, Cliff Nowlen and Sam Pasmore, an unnamed outlaw from the windfall. Separated by a little space from these were three others: Silvertip Upton, gray beard across his chest, and two more. The Spear had not come through unscathed. There were two riders, two of that breed who sold their loyalty, their labor, and their lives for thirty dollars a month and found, who would not again answer Cal Davis' call to "chuck!" These were placed beside Silvertip.

Cal Davis ran the hospital. He doctored outlaw and friend alike, treating them equally. Cal Davis had found a bottle of turpentine and a supply of rags, some clean and some not, and he was happy.

And Chance Pagan? Chance had a furrow across his forehead and another along his arm. Chance had a knee-cap nicked, and a hole in his thigh, and a smashed shoulder blade where a slug had gone through. Cal Davis chewed tobacco industriously and used a considerable amount from the turpentine bottle as he worked over Chance. Chance, returning to a world no longer red, bore the sting of the turpentine grimly and waited for Tom Melody to come.

When Melody arrived he did not go at once to Chance. Melody was a busy man. He had dispatched a man to the Spear. That man was to change horses and go on to Cassidy, there to wire for Doctor Grayson and to send a wagon to the NOW for the bodies of Suel James and Babe Wilmot. Other men, under Melody's orders, were searching the Basin, riding it out, a compact little group that stopped at empty cabins and then went on, finding and combing the hidden draws and canyons that ran into the Basin. When Tom Melody came into Pillow's store he looked at the sullen group of prisoners, watched by Fahrion and Comstock; he stopped before the dead men, lying so serenely beside the wall, and going further confronted Carl Terril. Terril was untouched, cool as always, and immaculate as though he had just stepped from a barbershop.

Tom Melody eyed Terril up and down and spoke his judgment.

"Well," said Melody, "I reckon you'll do." Under that praise Terril flushed.

Ben Godman, coming through the kitchen, stopped the sheriff as he moved on.

"There's six big horses in the barn," said Godman, "an' a couple of wagons that we can hook together. You goin' to take these fellows into town?"

"We got to," Melody answered. "We can take 'em to the Spear tonight. Get the teams hooked up, Ben, an' see if there is any loose stock. I don't want to leave any horses here." Godman nodded and went back through the kitchen, Melody following him.

The kitchen was the hospital. Tom Melody paid no attention to Cal Davis who came toward him as he entered, but walked to the spot where Chance Pagan lay upon hastily gathered bedding. He looked down at Chance, and Chance, pain burning through him returned that gaze.

"Yeah," drawled Melody as though answering some

question that he had asked himself.

Chance held his lips tight-pressed. Tom Melody touched the bandage about his own head, the bandage that made his hat sit so oddly, and nodding as though he was assured of something, turned away.

When he had harnessed the Clydesdales, Pillow's pride, and hooked them to the coupled wagons, Ben Godman brought the horses to the door. The prisoners were herded out and made to climb into the vehicle. The bodies of the two Spear men were carried out, each wrapped in a blanket, and placed in a wagon box. In the bottom of the lead wagon, bedding was piled upon straw, and carefully the Spear riders carried out the wounded.

Tom Melody stood beside the body of Silvertip in the store and debated a subject with himself. Finally he shook his head. "We'll leave him here," he said to Comstock who stood beside him. "See if you can find a spade or two, John."

Leaving Comstock, Melody went to the door. "Ben," he called to Godman on the wagon seat, "you pull along to the Spear. We'll catch up when we're done here. Terril, you an' Cal an' . . . I reckon you can ride a wagon, Bill . . . you go 'long. Keep an eye on those fellows, Ben—we'll catch you on the road."

With that he turned back into the store, and gathering the lines, Ben clucked to his teams.

18

THE RIDE to the Spear was dull agony to Chance Pagan. He lay in the wagon bed, bounced by rocks under the wheels, twisted and torn by the motion of the wagon until only pain remained with him. He was conscious when men lifted him out of the wagon-bed and carried him into the house, and he caught a flash of Lois Elder's face, white and big-eyed. The whole thing, trip, movement, pain, combined to make a terrible nightmare.

Sometime, Chance did not know when, sure, deft hands worked over him. He heard a kindly but unfamiliar voice growl: "Scapula shattered. Have to get the splinters out of there," and then there was a searing, grinding pain in his shoulder and he heard no more.

When he wakened he heard the voice again and saw a bearded face topped with a pair of gleaming eyeglasses. "I guess we'll put you back to sleep, young fellow," announced the face, and there was a sharp stab in Chance's arm. After that the pain lessened and he went to sleep.

When he wakened again Tom Melody was sitting beside the bed. Melody's face was long and melancholy and the stub of a cigarette smouldered in his mustache. Chance said, "Tom," and could hardly hear his own voice.

Tom Melody turned quickly. "You awake?" asked Melody. "I'll get Doc to put you back to sleep."

"No," Chance's voice was scarcely audible, even to himself.

Tom Melody grunted. "I got strict orders," he said. "I got to call the Doc."

"No. Arlie?"

"Oh," Melody grinned faintly, "wonderin' about yore girl, are you? She's all right. Wanted to come in an' set beside you, an' Doc said 'No.' She's got to stay in bed today. You . . . Hello, Doc."

The bearded face that Chance remembered was stern. "I told you to call me," said the face, gruffly. "Having some pain, young fellow?"

Chance did not answer. He was watching two hairy hands holding a glass cylinder that ended in a needle. The hands disappeared and again there was the prick in his arm. Things were very pleasant for Chance then, a sort of mysterious calm covering him. He was conscious of his body, of the bed, of Tom Melody, and of the bearded face, but they seemed very unreal. It seemed as though he, Chance Pagan, were sitting off somewhere, looking down from an immense distance at Melody and the bearded face. The face said: "I guess that will hold you."

The third time Chance came back Arlie Pillow was sitting beside him, holding his hand. Arlie was looking off into distance and Chance moved his fingers before she turned. Her eyes found Chance's eyes and held them. Then the girl moved from her chair, dropping beside the bed.

"Chance!" she exclaimed, and that was all. Her hand was warm and soft, yet strangely strong about Chance's fingers. Chance let it go at that. He said nothing, did not try to move. He was content to be still, Arlie's hand wrapped about his own.

Gradually the effects of the morphine cleared. A steady pound, pound, pound, was in his shoulder. The pain seemed to come like the water from a windmill, rising and falling with the pump rod. Still it wasn't so bad. Chance closed his eyes. When the pain rose he could feel Arlie's hand, and when it lessened the hand was still there. Lois Elder and Doctor Grayson, coming into the room, found the two, the girl kneeling beside the bed, her head on the coverlet and her hand wrapped about Chance's fingers, and Chance quiet and with his eyes closed.

Grayson came over and Chance opened his eyes. He could see the bearded face that had become familiar, and behind that face Lois Elder, wide-eyed and wan. Chance tried to smile at Lois. Arlie's fingers tightened their grip and he did smile.

"So," said Grayson. "How do you feel now?"

Chance did not answer and Grayson, moving briskly, shifted the covers over Chance. Arlie had released his hand and risen. "You've a smashed shoulder blade," Grayson announced professionally. "That's the worst thing right now, I suspect. Of course later, that knee may give you some trouble—the patella was nicked— and you will probably know that you were hit in the thigh and grazed across the forehead, but right now that shoulder blade is the worst. I think . . ." Grayson broke off. His thick fingers held Chance's wrist and his lips moved as he counted. He said "Hmmmm," with some concern in his voice, and releasing the wrist turned and spoke to Lois. Chance did not hear what he said, but Lois hurried away. Things were beginning to fog up again.

After that it was a conglomeration. Men shot at Chance and he shot back. He shot Sam Pasmore, shot him again and again and Pasmore wouldn't fall out of the way. Arlie was back of Pasmore and she was in danger. Sometimes it was not Pasmore that blocked him from Arlie, but Cliff Nowlen. Silvertip was there, too. Silvertip tried to help him but couldn't get up. Silvertip had pneumonia and had to be nursed. Sometimes there was a bunch of bawling cows and a little bunch of calves with them. He was riding Farmer, cutting the cows back through a brush fence. Farmer wouldn't turn the cows. He pitched and threw Arlie, who strangely enough was riding him. And there were men shooting at Arlie and it was night and of course Farmer wouldn't turn the cows at night; he couldn't see them. A very pretty delirium with now and then a moment when he knew that Arlie was beside him, holding his hand. Dr. Grayson did not go back to Fort Logan at once. He stayed at the Spear during that week, sleeping in his clothes and getting up during the night to pad in and look at Chance Pagan and at the girl who would not leave Chance.

But delirium cannot last forever and fever burns itself out when it finds a body too healthy to succumb. There came a night when the fever was gone and Grayson slept for eight full hours. In the morning Chance opened his eyes and they were no longer wild and blazing. Arlie was with him, holding his hand. It seemed as though she would never let go. On that day Chance ate a little, soup and some juice strained from a can of tomatoes. By nightfall he was definitely on the mend and the next morning Grayson packed his bag and said gruffly that he had a practice in Fort Logan and that they could send for him if they needed him.

But another week went by before Tom Melody was admitted to see Chance. Melody came in, shook his head at Lois Elder and at Arlie, and ordered them out. "I want to talk to Chance," said Melody. "We don't need any women."

The girls went out together and closing the door stopped outside and listened. During that week Arlie and Lois Elder had become very close friends.

"Well," said Tom Melody looking at Chance, "they tell me you been askin' questions."

Chance moved his bandaged head. He had been asking questions.

"Yeah," Melody continued, "they stand this way: as far as I'm concerned there ain't a thing against you. You got away from me an' hit me on the head an' I reckon you knocked some sense into my thick skull. It was Cliff that shot Wayne. He taken that sorrel horse he'd loaned you, an' rode over to where you'd penned them calves. That was the only place you was out of line much, them calves."

Chance made no movement and Melody continued. "Wayne is gettin' along all right. He's got to stay in bed a while longer but he's frettin' because he ain't up an' around. He said to tell you that as far as he was concerned you could forget it. After all, if Bill Fahrion hadn't been so dang' jealous, you'd never of took them calves. Bill has been wantin' to see you. I reckon Bill has got some crawlin' to do."

"Tell him it's all right," said Chance weakly. "I don't . . ."

"Yeah," Melody growled his interruption. "I'll tell him. You shut up an' let me talk. Them dang' women said I wasn't to let you say a word. You want to know how things come out, I reckon."

Chance answered that with his eyes and Melody resumed. "After you'd got in the store it was all right," he said. "You remember some of that, maybe. Cliff was dead an' so was Sam Pasmore. Cliff had went haywire an' shot Babe Wilmot an' Suel James over at the ranch. They knew what he'd done an' he was afraid they'd talk, I reckon. He didn't kill Babe. Babe talked a little after we'd got there. That sent us to the Basin. Art Ragland told us that Nowlen had come in there an' told Pillow that a posse was comin' to clean him out. Pillow went up to start on Silvertip an' got his needin's. Then Cliff an' Ragland taken charge. You kind of saved our bacon, Chance, when you stepped out of that cabin an' shot. We'd of ridden in there an' had some trouble. Yeah . . ."

Melody let the word trail off, his eyes staring moodily at the wall. After a moment he turned to Chance again. "We cleaned up what you'd started," he said. "Some of 'em got away, but we got four in jail an' Art Ragland is in a hospital at Logan. I reckon he's goin' to get well. Wasn't much the matter with him except that you'd hit him in the belly. How in hell can a man live when he's been shot through the belly?"

Chance did not answer that question. He asked another. "Silvertip?" he whispered.

"We buried him," Melody said gruffly. "Up close to his cabin where he can watch the Basin. Silvertip . . . I reckon Silvertip was all right, Chance. He got what he wanted."

Remembering the blue eyes that had stared out at the Basin rim Chance could not but believe that Melody was right. Silvertip had got what he wanted.

"A funny thing," Melody resumed after the pause, "fire broke out up there while we was buryin' them that got killed. It broke out in Pillow's store an' seemed like it spread. There ain't a shack standin' in the Basin!"

Remembering how those shacks had been scattered, remembering the distances between them, Chance knew just how that fire had spread. He could almost see the Spear riders, hard-faced, determined, piling kindling in the center of those shacks, could almost see the flaming matches that had started the fires. He smiled faintly.

"Yeah," drawled Melody again. "There ain't a one left. Funny how fire will run."

Lois appeared at the door. "You have stayed long enough," she announced.

Melody got up. "I got to go," he said. "They've run me off. Don't you worry, Chance. Yo're all right now. Yo're clear with me, an' yo're clear with Elder. Elder's got a proposition to make you sometime. There's a fellow here wants to buy the Spear an' yore vega with it. Fellow named Carl Terril. He's considerable man, too. Come up to find us when Arlie reached the Spear, an' he taken hold like he knew what it was all about. He got to the back of the store after you'd gone in an' I reckon he wasn't five minutes behind you. You'll like Terril." So prophesying, Tom Melody stalked out of the room.

On another day Chance had other visitors. Lois had been in and out of the room countless times, but this was different. With her came a tall, straight youngster who stood with her beside Chance's bed. Lois was flushed, but the man with her, his hand on Lois' arm, was calm and steady.

"This is Carl Terril, Chance," Lois said. "He . . . I've been wanting to bring him to see you."

"I've been wanting to come," said Terril. "I happened to get into Pillow's store after you had gone in. I've wanted to meet the man that did that job."

"You go now, Carl," Lois looked up at the man beside her and Chance could read her eyes, "I want to talk to Chance."

Terril smiled, nodded, and reaching down, took Chance's hand in a quick, strong grip. "I'll talk to you later on," he said. "I've some business that might interest you." With that he turned, smiled at Lois, and went out, leaving the two together.

Lois was flushed and tremulous. She stood beside the bed trying to find the words that she wanted to say, and not finding them. Chance helped her.

"You love him, don't you?" asked Chance.

Lois nodded.

"He looks like a good one." Chance spoke more strongly then he had before. "It's all right, Lois. You and I were kids. We were together a lot and we thought . . . well, you learned different, didn't you?"

Again Lois nodded. "I . . ." she began, "I . . . Chance, I didn't mean what I said to you or to Arlie. I don't know why I acted as I did. I've been . . . I've accused myself ever since. The way I talked . . ."

"Let it go, Lois," directed Chance. "There's nothing between you and me but good wishes. You know that, don't you?"

"But I . . . There was a while that I wanted you to die, Chance. I blamed you . . ."

"I was to be blamed," Chance's voice was quiet. "I went bad, Lois."

"But you came back. You straightened it all out. If it hadn't been for you . . ."

"If it hadn't been for me all this wouldn't have happened. I've brought all this trouble."

Lois Elder looked Chance squarely in the eyes. "That is not true," she refuted. "We've found out that Nowlen planned to take over the whole Calico Hole. Nowlen was to market the cattle they stole and Pillow and his men were to live in the Basin and do the stealing. Nowlen wanted to kill father. He almost succeeded. He wanted to get your hayland. It didn't matter to him how he got it. The whole thing was to be placed on you. Tom Melody knows all about it. Ragland told him. If it hadn't been for you, Nowlen and Pillow would have wiped out the Spear. You can't blame yourself for what happened, Chance. You must not blame yourself.

Father feels just as I do, and so do all the rest."

The morose glow of Chance Pagan's eyes lighted, then the eyes darkened again. "Still I'm to blame," he repeated. "You can't get around that."

"You're not to blame," Lois insisted. "You're not to blame at all. You talk as though you'd planned all this trouble. You didn't plan it. You stopped it. You were just human, Chance; if you've done wrong, you have paid for it in full. Can't you realize that?"

Chance stared moodily ahead.

"It's so! You know it's so. You blame yourself for things that you didn't do. You must not do that."

There was silence for a moment and the man and girl looked at each other.

Slowly the strained, hard look left Chance's face. The girl leaned forward. "I . . ." she began, "If it weren't for Carl . . . I would . . ."

The hand on Chance's tightened. Lois bent further. Swiftly her lips touched Chance's cheek, and then she was gone.

Chance lay quiet, thinking. He had accused himself, had laid all the trouble at his own door. Perhaps he was wrong. Perhaps Lois was right. Perhaps a man is not to blame for all he does. Perhaps a man can go to the Badlands and come back. Silvertip had said so. Silvertip had said that he, Chance Pagan, was no outlaw. Silvertip had said that with a woman like Arlie . . .

Swift steps sounded outside the door. It opened and Arlie stood there, lithe, blue-eyed, breathing quickly. For an instant she was framed in the doorway, and then she was kneeling beside the bed, her hand warm and soft and trusting in Chance's hand.

"Chance . . . Chance . . ."

"Arlie! Arlie, girl . . ."

The room was silent.

19

IN OCTOBER the Calico Hole takes on its gaudy fall dress. Calico Mesa is red and yellow and green where the cedars show through the scrub oak. The brown winter grass, the heads almost white when the sun shines, forms a frame for the beauties of the mesa.

With the sun low to the west Chance Pagan and Arlie, his wife, sat their horses on a mesa bench and looked down. The Big Muddy, banks still touched with green, wound away from them to the north. To the north was the Spear, beyond eyesight, but there. The Spear was not the Spear of old. There was a Terril & Blake foreman at the Spear now, a brisk old man that knew steers. In Chance Pagan's pocket was a letter from Wayne Elder, a letter that bore an Arizona postmark. Elder, so the letter informed, had finally located a place, a place that both he and Ben Godman liked. "It's browse range," Elder had written, "but Ben an' me think it will raise cows." The letter crackled reassuringly as Chance moved.

For now, the J Pen was home enough, a place for Chance and Arlie really to get acquainted with each other. But later, when the J Pen became a line camp once again, they would move on. Where? Chance grinned at the thought. There was more of that good browse range in Arizona. Twenty thousand acres of it that lay against the range purchased by Wayne Elder, belonged to Chance Pagan now. In another month there would be a new brand in the Arizona brand books: J Pen.

Still further north, beyond the Spear, lay Cassidy, a little collection of houses and stores with a railroad that crawled through it from east to west. Tom Melody was in Cassidy. Probably at that moment he sat in his office, feet propped on a chair, twisting a thin cigarette with gnarled old hands. Tom Melody and Cassidy were inseparable.

The thought of Cassidy brought other recollections. In Cassidy Lois Elder, Lois Elder no longer, flushed and tremulous, had kissed both Chance and Arlie before she boarded the train with Carl Terril. Terril's grip on Chance's hand had been strong and his voice hearty as he spoke. "When you're ready, Pagan, let me know. I've a place in mind . . ."

The conductor had called "All aboard!" then, and Terril's voice had changed. There was tenderness in it, and humor, too.

"Come on, Mrs. Terril. The train won't wait."

Chance had not written to Carl Terril yet, but he would write. A man cannot afford to lose touch with a friend like Carl Terril.

Beneath Chance the big bay Farmer stirred restlessly. Farmer was plenty of horse these days. He got but little riding and he was fat. Still, he did not buck. Farmer had not bucked a jump since that night, months ago, when he had gone outlaw in the J Pen corral.

The J Pen! It was down there too, the vega primly fenced squares. Terril & Blake steers would eat the stacked hay from the J Pen now. Chance looked down at it.

"I am glad that we went to the Basin, Chance," Arlie spoke low voiced beside her husband. "I didn't want to go, but now I'm glad."

"Yes," said Chance. Farmer's shoulder touched the shoulder of Arlie's horse and Chance's hand went out and settled on Arlie's where it rested on her saddle cantle.

"I . . . I was afraid to go," Arlie continued, talking almost to herself, it seemed. "But now . . . Silvertip can watch the Basin, Chance. He can see it all from where he is, can't he?"

Arlie turned to Chance.

"He can see it, dear," Chance assured. "He can watch it."

To both of them, sitting there, Silvertip still lived. He would always live, strong and gentle and real in their minds.

"Yes," said Chance once more, "Silvertip can watch the Basin."

Farmer lifted a foot, brushing away a late fly. A wind rustled through the scrub oak along the bench. The sun dropped down, out of sight, touching only the tops of the mesa and gilding it, painting the top of the Badlands, the Badlands that lay behind Chance Pagan and his wife.

Arlie turned her hand and her fingers wrapped around Chance's fingers, strong and warm and true. Farmer held his shoulder close against the shoulder of the little brown horse, and Arlie Pagan leaned toward her husband.

Center Point Publishing
600 Brooks Road • PO Box 1
Thorndike ME 04986-0001 USA

(207) 568-3717

**US & Canada:
1 800 929-9108**